PENGUIN CRIME FICTION

THE CONDUCT OF MAJOR MAXIM

Gavin Lyall flew in the RAF for two very "educational" years before taking his degree at Cambridge. He subsequently became a professional journalist and directed news films for the BBC before beginning a "flying thriller," *The Wrong Side of the Sky*, which was published in 1961. In 1965, Mr. Lyall won the British Crime Writers Association's highest award for *Midnight Plus One*, the first of his two Silver Daggers from the BCWA. This is his second Major Maxim novel, following *The Secret Servant*. When not otherwise engaged in researching his novels, Mr. Lyall lives in London.

D0630442

The Conduct of Major Maxim

Gavin Lyall

PENGUIN BOOKS

PENGUIN BOOKS

Viking Penguin Inc., 40 West 23rd Street,
New York, New York 10010, U.S.A.
Penguin Books Ltd, Harmondsworth,
Middlesex, England
Penguin Books Australia Ltd, Ringwood,
Victoria, Australia
Penguin Books Canada Limited, 2801 John Street,
Markham, Ontario, Canada L3R 1B4
Penguin Books (N.Z.) Ltd, 182–190 Wairau Road,
Auckland 10, New Zealand

First published in Great Britain by Hodder and Stoughton Ltd 1982
First published in the United States of America by
Viking Penguin Inc. 1983
Published in Penguin Books 1986

Copyright © Gavin Lyall, 1982
All rights reserved

Printed in the United States of America by
Offset Paperback Mfrs., Inc., Dallas, Pennsylvania
Set in Bembo

Except in the United States of America,
this book is sold subject to the condition
that it shall not, by way of trade or otherwise,
be lent, re-sold, hired out, or otherwise circulated
without the publisher's prior consent in any form of
binding or cover other than that in which it is
published and without a similar condition
including this condition being imposed
on the subsequent purchaser

Dawn is an army's time, not a soldier's. The traditional time for a surprise attack and the equally traditional stand-to in order to meet it. The moment when chirruping bugles and the echoing clatter of barrack-block doors end the short privacy of sleep and gather the component parts to make an army again. A soldier's time is the night, when even unhappiness can be a luxury because it doesn't have to be shared.

Chapter 1

High over London, a single aircraft trail was just beginning to glow like a hot wire against the steel-blue sky, picking up the sunlight that was still below the horizon to the ground. A lone cyclist in a track suit rushed down Kingsway at a speed impossible at any other time of day. An electric milk float whined around Aldwych and a baker's van was delivering French loaves, carried like big bundles of orange firewood, to the Waldorf Hotel. But most of the city was still asleep, its streets empty and at peace.

High up in Bush House, two men and a girl sat reading the newsflashes on a television screen, calling up fresh ones by tapping instructions on a computer keyboard. The shimmering green printout made the news seem unreal, like stock market prices, and they longed to hear the original broadcasts that the BBC monitors at Caversham Park had picked out of the air. Six hundred miles away, where it was already full day, an army was out in the streets of East Berlin.

The girl asked: "Why do they always use tanks?" She spoke German with the stiff Hanseatic accent.

"Just a reminder." The older of the two men wore a shabby but once-expensive leather jacket and had a neat dark beard.

"But they aren't even practical," the girl persisted. "You can't send a tank into a building. They could do it all just with their soldiers. This way, tomorrow there'll be pictures of tanks in the Unter den Linden all over the world. It's become a cliché of Russian occupation, and it's so unsubtle."

"Ivan isn't always trying to be subtle." His voice was unmistakably Bavarian and he didn't do much actual broadcasting himself. Mostly he built up analyses for the Political Unit and the weekly 'Aspekte' round-up of East German affairs. "They don't mind people seeing a bit of armour plate every generation or so. I wonder if they'll call it an attempted *Faschisischter Putsch* like they did in 1953."

"A railway strike?" The girl stared at him, disbelieving.

"The Red Army takes railways seriously. No railways, then no petrol, no food, no bullets."

The second man was making quick notes. An announcer-translator, he would be reading the first of the BBC's German Language Service newscasts in three-quarters of an hour. He wasn't allowed to write it himself, just translate what the Central Newsroom sent up, and perhaps add a few non-controversial details – if he had them. He wasn't quite thirty and dressed neatly, by BBC standards.

"Heinz Manger?" he said suddenly. "As the new General Secretary? They can't be serious. I'd heard he'd got cancer."

"A caretaker, perhaps," the analyst said. "While they catch their breath and work out a real successor. If he's really dying, so much the easier when it comes to make a change." He leant forward as the story rippled across the screen. "Dear God, they've had a real harvest."

In all, six names had been dropped from the ten-man Secretariat, including the old General Secretary, Spiesshofer. All the others had some connection with railways or the cities where the strikes had been most complete. Only four men had been raised from the Politbureau to fill the empty seats. The A-T man started searching desperately for the office copy of *Who's Who In Eastern Europe*.

"Gustav Eismark," the girl read. "Do we know him?"

The analyst nodded thoughtfully. "Odd one, that. You might even say he's a bit of a liberal – in their terms. He was in shipping; he represented Rostock at one time."

"Are you sure of that?" the A-T man called, still unable to find the *Who's Who*.

"Oh yes. He went to Moscow after the war, then helped rebuild the Rostock shipyards. Then he dropped out of sight for a while." He tried to recall why but couldn't. "Then he started a comeback after the '62 economic shakeup."

"Who's in his tail?" the girl asked. No Communist politician – perhaps no politician anywhere – gets far without a 'tail' of well-placed friends and relatives, they pushing him ever upwards and automatically being pulled up after him.

"I don't know, except that his son's something in State Security. It's nice to have that in the family." A friendly link with the SSD was as vital as a Party card. "And the younger scientists and engineers like him, he talks their language. Probably he's been put up there to keep them happy . . . Ivan knows you can't do it all with tanks; you need the sugar-bread as well as the whip. And he's younger than most of them . . . it'll be interesting to see what happens at the Party Congress, probably not this year, but . . ." He was already working on his 'think-piece' for later in the week.

"I can't use speculation!" snapped the A–T man, angry at the mess in the office.

The teletype rattled and the analyst and the girl walked across to read what the authorised version was to be.

Russian tanks and troops moved early this morning to break the strike that has paralysed the East German railway system for the past two days. Our correspondent in Berlin reports that there has been some shooting, and casualties are . . .

"I still don't see why they use tanks," the girl said stubbornly.

"It was his sister," the analyst suddenly remembered. "It was something to do with his sister . . ."

"And why does it always have to be at dawn?"

"Just an old army custom."

At a quarter past five the sun was a lemon disc hanging low in the faint mist over the dale. On the far side, the gentle hills were a sequence of flat shapes fading paler and paler into the distance. It was just like the Chinese watercolour her grandmother kept in the hall at Herzgerode.

Last night, the weather forecast had been thundery showers; it was pleasant when they got the bad news wrong as well.

At that time of day, she was the only thing alive, before the birds, before the roaring aeroplanes. She was the only thing that moved, even if every movement hurt in some way. She loved the loneliness of the dawn; the one thing better was sleep, and she longed for sleep from the moment she woke, but lying there pretending to sleep was the worst of all. Then her body, so difficult to make move, moved by itself in little twitches and jerks, as if it were trying to escape from her. So she had to get up and shuffle through to the little music room, struggling for control of the body that seemed to hate her as much as she hated it. Now she even bathed in the dark so as not to see who she was.

She swallowed one of the yellow tablets that made her dizzy and sent a buzzing in her ears, then two Disprin, turned on the radio and carefully filled the electric kettle. She listened vaguely to a review of new classical records, wondering with a flash of real bitterness *why* they let that Italian moron loose on Debussy, and mixed a mug of black tea flavoured with lemon juice from a plastic squeezer. There was a real lemon in the cupboard but it was too early for her to trust her hands with a knife. She put the rest of the hot water into a plastic bowl and cooled it from the tap until she could sit there soaking her hand in it.

Who was coming today? Thursday – that meant the younger Allison girl and after her the one who had cancelled on Tuesday because she had to go to the dentist in Pateley Bridge. Gillian something. That one could be good, if she kept at it. She at least had the advantage of parents who were totally ignorant of music, even the piano. When parents became convinced they had bred a genius, they were already halfway to turning the poor child into a nervous ruin.

Eismark, the radio said. Gustav Eismark. Or had it? She stood up suddenly and the first little twist of vertigo hit her and she clutched back at the table, spilling the bowl across the linoleum. But that was why it was plastic; any other she would have broken a hundred times over.

Had it said Eismark? Of course, now with the growing day, reception was getting patchy. She didn't know why; how did radio waves (whatever *they* were) know the difference between light and dark? She left the bowl and water and sat down to listen very carefully to the crackling, wavery voice.

When the news bulletin had finished, she went back and refilled the kettle, picked up the bowl, and started to soak her hand again. She felt frightened but not sure why; perhaps it was just being reminded of the wide uncaring world beyond the dale. Should she try and speak with Leni? She didn't even know if Leni was still alive; she had been meaning to get in touch for so long, and always putting it off. But maybe this time . . .

The water cooled. She stood up and walked carefully to the old upright piano by the window. Some of the feeling had come back into her hand, along with the tingling, but never the old flexibility and certainty. She stared at the flat muscles, waggling her fingers and willing them to belong to a 25-year-old girl again, and promising herself one – only one – glass of brandy before the first pupil arrived, and then only after she had done her own practice.

What had she set them to learn for this time? It would have been something from *Kinderszenen*; nowadays it almost always was. You came back to Schumann as you came back to the scenes of your own childhood that were like unbreakable toys, always bright and unchipped when the rest of your life had worn vague in the memory.

She sat down, and instead of the scales, her hands fumbled into the gentle nursery notes of *Träumerei*. The first aeroplane of the day rushed past up the valley, ripping up the dreaming and the loneliness with its crackling thunder.

Chapter 2

With a proper sense of His responsibilities, God had provided a vivid blue-and-white sky that quite obviously wasn't going to leak a single drop of rain on the crisp rows of Volvos, BMWs and Rovers parked around the playing-field in the valley. After all, as the vicar had argued in his prayers the previous Sunday, if the fête went well they should not only be able to pay off the final cost of re-roofing the vicarage, but have something left over to relieve famine in East Africa. It was the best bargain he had been able to offer God in months.

Harry Maxim knew nothing about the vicarage roof and not much more about starvation in East Africa, but he was reasonably familiar with the ceremony of the English county turning out in its best weekend clothes to buy cucumber sandwiches for a Good Cause. He drifted down the avenues of gossip between the stalls and marquees, a slim man in his middle thirties with shortish fair hair and a concave face that had hard lines running down around the hopeful smile that he had decided was the proper expression for the occasion.

To the experienced military eye – and there are usually plenty of those, both male and female, at a Kent village fête – he didn't look particularly like an Army major, but nor did he not look like one. If they thought about it at all, they just concluded that, with his loose-cut olive blazer, he couldn't belong to one of the Very Best regiments and wondered who had invited him. It didn't occur to them – and why should it? – that if you sometimes have to wear a shoulder holster, loose jackets are very useful.

However, that afternoon Maxim was quite unarmed. He bought himself a cup of tea and miniature sausage roll, then thumbed through a stack of old 78 records, hoping for a black Brunswick label that could be an early Duke Ellington. He had

12

just given up hope when the loudspeaker said something jovial about seeing the future defence of the country was in good hands and there was a volley of shots from the cricket pavilion. Maxim joined the tide as it flowed that way.

Two sections of Cadet Force schoolboys with long hair straggling from under their berets were attacking the pavilion across the cricket field; the actual wicket was roped off so that the attack had to split unrealistically around it. They moved in the classic pairs, one firing while the other lumbered forward in a zigzag run – at least when they remembered the boy sergeant's constant exhortation to: "Keep one foot on the ground!" He was aged about sixteen, with a dark angry face and a uniform that fitted.

Then somebody tried to throw a smoke candle while lying down, and sent it wild. Orange smoke billowed up from the bald but still sacred turf of the roped-off wicket and a unanimous gasp of horror came from all round the field. The battle stopped dead.

The boy sergeant stepped over the rope, kicked the candle clear and stepped back looking angrier than ever. "You stupid cunts," he raged in a penetrating undertone, "just lying there like stuffed pricks . . ."

"*Roger,*" said a lady in a wide hat just in front of Maxim, "did that boy say what I *thought* he said?"

"Probably didn't know what it meant," grunted Roger, who had cropped grey hair and a deep tan. Then he caught Maxim's glance and smiled. "But he'll need to get his biology sorted out before he's much older."

"*Roger,*" Mrs Roger said.

The attack began again. The light machine-gun section waved a rattle from the flank, the pavilion fell to a frontal assault and two prisoners were roughed up with obvious sincerity. The loudspeaker congratulated the professionalism of the 'young warriors', the crowd clapped and wandered away, and the boy sergeant went on looking angry as he herded the platoon across to a Land-Rover parked at the corner of the field.

There, an adult sergeant in a Paratroop beret took over and

insisted on all the rifles being properly cleaned and all the unfired blanks handed in, including the ones that had been 'forgotten' so that they could be experimentally toasted on a kitchen stove.

Maxim hung back until the last cadet had scurried off to the tea tent, then the sergeant swung round with a sharp salute and a broad grin.

"Good afternoon, sir. Glad you could make it." He clinked the brass cartridges and shook his head, still grinning. "They think you were born yesterday. They never think you might have been a cadet yourself."

They shook hands. "Jim, I didn't expect to find you cradle-snatching."

"Just part-time. I'm working for my father-in-law. He's got the garage over on the main road." Jim Caswell nodded at the steep green slope behind the church.

"Good job?"

"It could be. Mostly desk work, but . . ." He was a solid-chested man, a little shorter and younger than Maxim, but with the ageless middle-aged look that long-serving sergeants acquire. Caswell would be serving still but for a permanently stiff left arm that came from driving a Land-Rover over a Claymore mine while 'advising' on anti-guerilla tactics in Abu Dhabi. The Army would have kept him on – but no longer with a Paratroop cap-badge.

"You seem to be getting across the language all right," Maxim commented.

Caswell chuckled and rubbed his moustache – a straight bar of dark hair – with his right wrist. His left hand wouldn't reach that far. "That lad spent a week out in Germany with the Woofers; spent twenty quid of his own money and his folks don't have that much at all. He's all right. I think we could get him." Maxim had guessed that the boy had picked up his style from real soldiers, but not that Caswell would be taking the cadets so seriously – or still calling the Army 'we'.

Alone in the corner of the field, they leant against the warm metal of the Land-Rover. Caswell half-offered a packet of cigarettes. "You've still given up, have you?"

"I still dream about it."

14

"I've heard that. Funny." He took one himself and lit it deftly, but all one-handed. "Your boy, young Chris, he's getting on okay?"

"Yes. He stays with my parents down in Littlehampton, he goes to school there. It would be impossible, just me and him in London . . ."

"Oh yes. Nice lad."

"I think so."

The small talk petered out and Maxim braced himself for whatever the afternoon was really to be about.

"Did you know a Corporal Blagg, Ron Blagg?" Caswell asked carefully. "He did a tour in Sass. I had him in Armagh. He was good with machinery, and pistols. Bit of a boxer, too, or had been."

Maxim and Caswell themselves had met on tours in the Special Air Service. But Blagg? . . . You didn't forget people you'd worked with in the SAS, but it was scattered all over the world in handfuls. "Didn't know him."

"He's got a bit of a problem."

"Yes?"

"He came to me because he couldn't think of anybody else he could really trust."

"Yes?" Maxim said again, feeling a chill in the warm day.

"I thought you might . . . like being where you are, you could give him some sort of advice . . ."

"Jim, where I am these days is Number 10 Downing Street. It isn't the carefree life of Britain's Modern Army any more: I can't take a piss now without worrying if it'll cause Questions in the House."

Caswell nodded sympathetically. "Like, I don't know what you do there . . ." then waited for Maxim to tell him while Maxim waited for him to realise he wasn't going to be told anything more.

Eventually, Caswell went on: "I just think you ought to know what this lad says, or somebody up there should know . . ."

"Jim, is this chap of yours in trouble? – Army trouble?"

Caswell clutched his cigarette by his forefinger over his clenched hand, the way he always did, and let a smoke cloud drift towards the babbling tea-tents. "That sort of thing."

"He's on the trot," Maxim guessed. "Oh *Christ*, Jim, you can get a district court for that, aiding a deserter . . . no, I suppose not you, not now."

"It's a criminal offence for civilians, too."

"Good. I wouldn't like to think it was only me going to suffer. Has he been gone twenty-one days?"

"No. Not yet."

There was an unofficial unadmitted rule that if you came back inside three weeks you weren't jumped on so hard. After that time, the prosecution might argue that you'd crossed the great divide between being absent without leave, or just a little late, and true desertion, planning to stay away for good.

Even so, the Special Investigation Branch of the Military Police would have been told, and local coppers asked to snoop into your favourite pubs and knock on your mum's door at odd hours . . . It was a slow, sad business, a crime without a victim, but inarguably it had to remain a crime. And it could leave an indelible stain on a soldier's career.

"Why hasn't he gone back?"

"He doesn't really know his own officers. He'd only been back with the battalion a couple of months, after three years with Sass. You know how things can change."

"Where is his battalion?"

"Soltau."

"*Germany*? He came back from Rhine Army? He'll have a rough time explaining how he just lost his way back from the *Bierkeller*."

Caswell smiled wearily, as if he'd heard that many times already, or even said it himself. "Yes. He wants to go back."

"Has he got woman trouble?" That was usually the reason.

"No. Not exactly that . . . he'll tell you."

"Jim, all I can do is try and persuade him to go back, then tell the MPs where he is if he doesn't."

"I'd like you to hear what he says."

"You aren't doing this just because he was a good man in Armagh, are you?"

"He didn't save my life or any bullshit like that. No – he's just career. A real committed soldier."

"He sounds like it," Maxim said sourly. But even now, you still got a few, the odd ones who came into the Army on an unwritten contract that would turn the devil cool with envy. They usually had no homes to go back to, they wrote no wills and made no allotments of pay, they rarely married and always made a horrible complicated cock-up of it if they did. They simply did everything the Army asked of them, and expected it to be everything in return: a job, home, family, friends, and maybe six feet of regimental ground at the end of the day. They had one other clause in the contract: they never deserted. They had nowhere else to go.

In Downing Street you counted the corners and priced self-interest down to six decimal places. You forgot about people like Ron Blagg.

"All right," Maxim said. "Lead me to him." It was odd how bright the day had seemed a few minutes ago.

"Tell me something about yourself," Maxim suggested, trying to start in low gear. But Blagg immediately looked even more suspicious.

"You came in as a boy soldier, didn't you?" prompted Caswell.

"Ye-es," Blagg said reluctantly. "I joined when I was just sixteen, like."

They were standing, not sitting since there was only one chair, around the work-bench in the armoury of the village drill hall, watching Caswell sort out the afternoon's weapons. It was a tiny cell-like room with a high barred window on the back wall, and it smelled of eighty years of gun oil, dust and old leather. The only light was a shaded lamp on the bench that made Blagg's face look hollow and spooky with its upward reflections.

When it wasn't looking spooky, his face was all sticking-out bits: big ears, a jutting jaw and lower lip, heavy brows. His pale hair was cut shorter than it needed to be and he wore a uniform of faded jeans, a denim shirt and training shoes. He was only twenty-five but had spent the last nine years in the Army, which had done something to wear down a jerky South London accent.

17

"What made you choose the Army?" Maxim asked.

Blagg started an 'I dunno' shrug, then smiled quickly and slyly. "Well, you know I'm a bit of a bastard, sir. Fact is, I'm exactly one hundred per cent of a bastard. The real thing. My mother, bless her whoever she is, she dumped me on the Council when I was eighteen months. They unloaded me the moment I was sixteen."

"Did you want to stay?" Caswell asked dryly, his stubby fingers working with the precision of a pianist's as he stripped the bolt out of a rifle.

"Did I buggery," Blagg muttered.

"And you've worn the same cap badge right through?" Maxim asked.

"Yes," Blagg said aggressively, knowing the question behind the question. "Yes, all the way, except for my time with Sass."

So he hadn't been a troublemaker, shunted from regiment to regiment by commanders who didn't want to be caught holding him when the music stopped.

"I *like* the buggering Army," he added gloomily.

"But it's there and you're here," Maxim said.

After a pause, Blagg said: "Yes," then again: "Yes."

"Major Maxim can't do anything for you without you telling him the whole story," Caswell said. "And I don't think he'll be making any promises then. But he'll listen."

Blagg chewed a speck of dirt out from underneath a fingernail. "Yes. Well . . . I'm with the Battalion at Soltau, I've been back with them just over two months; I had some leave and there was this course I went on . . . Then I met this woman, Mrs Howard. I'd met her first in Armagh, that was over a year ago. I don't think it was her real name, you know? She didn't have a wedding ring. Captain Fairbrother, he brought her along. You'd know him, sir?"

Maxim nodded, vaguely recalling a thin, elegant Guards officer who had been at SAS's London end.

"Well, he took me to meet her. He said she was from Intelligence, I mean The Firm, not Int Corps. I wouldn't say she was English, she had a sort of accent. Could have been German, like. She was going to meet this bloke from across the border, a Mick, and she was going to have some money for him. Quite a bit. She wanted somebody to go along and make sure everything was really kosher."

"Why you particularly?"

"Captain Fairbrother said it was because I could use a pistol. It's on my records."

"You went in plain clothes?"

"Yes, sir."

"Did you have any back-up?"

"No." Blagg's face was blank and calm. "The Captain thought it would be best with just a man and a woman. It was real Provo country, that. Three or four strange men, they'd have stuck out like a spare prick at a wedding."

Blagg had guts, if not much sense of self-preservation, walking single-handed into a set-up like that, without any of the real spook-craft 'Mrs Howard' would have been taught. Usually in such a job you had four well-armed mates never more than a hundred yards away.

Maxim asked Caswell: "Did you ever meet this Mrs Howard?"

"No. Never heard of her until just now. We just got the word from Command that Captain Fairbrother wanted Ron for a week or so and off he went. He didn't tell us anything when he came back." That last was a small but perhaps helpful compliment.

"And the job went off as planned?"

"The Mick didn't turn up the first time. She said she'd have it set up again and we went back three nights later and it was all right. That was all."

So Blagg had actually gone in *twice*. When the first time could easily have been a rehearsal, for the other side to see how many men came along, and then three days to rig an ambush.

Blagg must have guessed what Maxim was thinking. "She said it was important, sir. And Captain Fairbrother."

Caswell glanced at Maxim with a lift of his eyebrows and a small humourless smile, then went back to the rifles.

"I see. And d'you mean she turned up again – in Germany?"

"That's right. At Soltau."

Chapter 3

It began quite simply: a message delivered to the barracks asking if he could ring Mrs Howard for a chat about old times. For a moment the name meant nothing – far more memorable things had happened during his time in Armagh – but then he remembered and was puzzled. There had been nothing personal in their brief meetings; she had been a trained professional, saying almost nothing during the drives down towards the border but chatting and smiling happily while they waited in a café. Mostly they had talked about films, he recalled; she looked at very little television and he hadn't read any of the books she mentioned.

Well, it was only a phone call . . . He got a German woman answering and asked distinctly for: "*Frau Howard, bitte.*" There was a pause, and the voice said: "*Ja, Mrs Howard,*" which convinced him that 'Mrs Howard' was just a code-name, not even a fake identity.

She came on a few seconds later. "Mr Blagg? How are you? Very good of you to call so soon. Can we meet, perhaps? Are you free now?"

A little dazed, he found himself committed to meeting her in an hour's time at a café near the station. He could just visualise it: a family place where British soldiers hardly ever went – which was probably why she had chosen it. He was still puzzled, but not yet apprehensive.

He wasn't even sure he'd recognise her, but of course he did. Even so, she looked different from the time in Armagh. There she'd been almost middle-aged and stolid, red-cheeked and fluffy fair hair. Now her hair was scraped back in a sort of bun, giving her a leaner look; her clothes were more expensive, though she still had a full and somehow loose figure inside them.

She could easily be German; she certainly sounded like it when ordering him a beer. For five minutes they talked about films and how was he fitting in with the Battalion again, then she said simply: "We would like you to do another job, just like last time."

By then, he'd been half expecting that, but still didn't know what to say.

She went on: "We are sorry there is so little time now. But we did not know how this job would go, when I came to Germany."

"When is it, then?"

"Friday – tomorrow – if you can. If not, perhaps we can make it for Saturday."

That was no problem. The training programme was on schedule – the Battalion hadn't been turned inside out by a Northern Ireland tour for the past two years – and he could be free from about five o'clock. But –

"Good," Mrs Howard said. "Can you bring a bag, a suitcase, some clothes? And some identification, not the Army. Do you have a passport?"

Most soldiers didn't bother to get passports until they married and thought of family holidays in Spain. But the SAS had insisted on Blagg having one – occupation given as 'Government official' – in case it needed to shoot him off incognito to somewhere to hell and gone, just as it insisted on keeping him immunised against so many unlikely diseases that his left arm was usually as rigid as Jim Caswell's.

"I'm all right," he said, "but –"

"We may have to stay at a hotel, a motel. That will be no problem? Good. Now – would you like to call Captain Fairbrother? Just to check that I am telling the truth? I will understand – I want you to be sure, quite sure. I can give you a London number, but can you please do it on a secure line? You understand that, I know."

He thought of the usual queue of soldiers outside the single telephone box inside the barrack gate, jingling 5 DM coins and looking at their watches every few seconds. A secure line? He *could* ask the company commander, but he could also imagine the answer. He chuckled. Being SAS trained gave you a glimpse behind secret doors that some officers didn't even know existed. And those two evenings out along the border had convinced him of her background.

"It's okay," he reassured her. "No problem. But I don't have a gun."

"I will bring one. A pistol or a revolver?"

"A revolver, if it's not too big."

"Of course." She smiled. Her teeth were large and rather wide-spaced, but very white. How old was she? Growing up without a mother or aunts, he was bad at guessing older women's ages. She could be forty or fifty, almost anything. She was just a different generation.

"I will be here, outside the station, at six tomorrow. In a blue Volkswagen Polo. Okay?"

When she'd gone, he stayed sipping his beer and wondering. He wished he could check with somebody. Captain Fairbrother, even Jim Caswell. But if it was no more a problem than the last time, he'd have forgotten all about it in a month. And this wasn't Provo country.

They drove south-west, roughly paralleling the East-West border, not getting significantly close to it. They were heading, she said, for Bad Schwarzendorn, a little spa town just into the hills beyond Paderborn. A strange little place; it had one of these great walls of blackthorn twigs fitted onto a wooden framework at least ten metres high. Pumps pushed the spa water up so that it trickled down the twigs and partly evaporated, making the water even thicker in minerals, before it was fed into the town baths. The twigs turned to rigid fossils, and you could sit in the downwind side of the great wall and breathe the cool damp air blowing out of it. That was supposed to do you good, too. The Germans were still great believers in spa cures. Half, more than half, the patients were paid for by health insurance schemes, and most of the local guest houses had contracts with one company or another. You bathed, you walked the neatly laid out paths in the pine woods, you breathed the salty air – then sat down to a huge *Fleischschnitte mit Bratkartoffeln*. She grinned, rocking her head from side to side. There was nothing the Germans would rather spend money on than alternately wrecking and repairing their health.

Just before it got dark, he had her stop the car on a lonely stretch of road and fired the gun out of the window at a tall flower sticking up in a field about ten yards away. The third shot exploded the head in a flutter of purple petals. The revolver was about what he'd expected: a Spanish near-copy of a .38 Colt, with a heavy trigger pull. He reloaded and they drove on.

"I could not get a holster," she said. "Did you want one?"

"No. They're like clothes: no use if you don't choose them yourself. Pocket's best, otherwise . . . How're we going to play this?"

She lit a cigarette and thought for a moment. "We will be apart. He does not expect you, but he is suspicious. He is about sixty years, small, fat, with chins. A big nose, the gold half-glasses, not much hair and he will dress like a businessman. Also he will have with him a newspaper."

"Just him by himself?"

She went straight on past the question. "There is a big café that is part of the Park Hotel, some of it inside, some outside. I will sit down there at ten, outside if it is warm enough, if there are others. He will come past, make sure that I see him, then I follow him. I think he will be alone; I do not know who he could get to come with him, but . . . that is what I want you to worry about. To watch me, not him. The man himself does not worry me."

Perhaps he should have asked why, then, but instead he picked on a more obvious problem. "He could take you to a car."

"I will not get in."

"D'you think he'll be there before you?"

She flashed him a quick smile of professional camaraderie. "I think so. So if you can go in first, you see him, then come out and . . ." politely she left the details of his work to him.

"It's a payoff job?"

"We will both have newspapers. But he may need time to read mine." From that, Blagg assumed she would have a wad

23

of money in the folds of her paper. Almost exactly the way it had been on the border. The other border.

She said suddenly, but mostly to herself: "He may not be ready to trust me . . ."

"If he's come across the border –"

"No, no, no. He is not from there."

Then she shut up for the rest of the drive.

Bad Schwarzendorn was small, elderly, rich, very clean, very quiet. Mrs Howard gave him an idea of the place by driving slowly around the flat unfenced park that was the core of the whole town. Almost half a mile square, the trim grass was criss-crossed with wide paths and avenues of lime trees, brightly lit by modernistic street lamps. And running diagonally across the middle was the huge blackthorn hedge, foursquare and utterly meaningless. Just a wall half a kilometre long, running dead straight from nowhere to nowhere and reaching way up beyond the lamplight.

It might cure anything you could name, Blagg thought, but who in hell could have thought of building it in the first place?

They parked just out of sight of the hotel, and he walked on ahead. It was only half past nine on a mild early summer evening, but already most of the residents were in bed or immobilised by *Fleischschnitte*. A few elderly couples doddered like moths around the blaze of light that was the café and a few more sat solidly at the tables, but it was a small crowd and Blagg felt obvious, apart from being generations too young. He went in through the hotel itself and came into the café from the back.

The man he was looking for was immediately obvious, crouched at a back table beside a large potted plant, complete with a folded newspaper, gold glasses and a bad case of nerves. He looked so obvious that Blagg spent the next twenty minutes covertly watching for a second man, but couldn't identify one. At ten to ten he walked out towards the park and kept strolling around – a moving man is less suspicious than one standing still – then bought an ice cream from a stall. A strolling, eating man is positively innocent.

He saw Mrs Howard go in; five minutes later, the fat man

came out, walking awkwardly because he wasn't sure at what pace to go. Mrs Howard followed, moving easily, glancing naturally up to check the weather, then down at her wrist-watch. They went on past the ornamental fountain and the rows of plastic chairs in front of the bandstand and on down the far side of the wall.

The path was well lit and as straight as the wall. Blagg gave Mrs Howard fifty yards, then followed on the grass, keeping the row of lime trees between himself and the fat man. It couldn't have worked if the *Bürger* of seventy years before hadn't planted with eyes like rulers; as it was, he could make each tree overlap the next to give himself a reasonable amount of cover. And any second man could be no closer.

They moved like that for nearly a quarter of a mile, passing nobody and in silence enough for him to hear the clicking of Mrs Howard's high heels. The cold moist air drifted out of the wall at him, an unnatural feeling on that gentle evening.

Then, leaning in for a snatched glance at the fat man, he saw it and wished to hell he'd seen it on their drive around the park. Halfway along the wall a tunnel led through it from side to side, framed by a heavy wooden arch. If anybody was waiting, it had to be there.

He dropped the last oozy remains of the ice cream and hurried forward, abandoning caution (a running man is always suspicious). He had gained only fifteen yards when he heard Mrs Howard's footsteps hesitate and knew the fat man had turned into the tunnel. But then she walked calmly on. He moved cautiously again – the man was probably looking back from the archway – and took out the gun. She stopped again, he heard a mutter of voices, and then her steps faded in the archway.

He had made only a few more yards when a small pistol went *smack*, echoing out of the tunnel. He ran. Another gun fired, then the small one again, and Mrs Howard staggered back out of the archway and sat down heavily, losing her newspaper but keeping the gun. The fat man wobbled out after her and both shot each other from a few feet apart.

Blagg snapped his wrist against a tree-trunk for steadiness and started shooting from thirty yards' range. The third shot hit the fat man's head and pieces burst off it, like flower petals. The body flopped and tumbled into the trough of water that drained from the wall. Mrs Howard wriggled and moaned a little and lay still.

Suddenly it was all very different from the two evenings in Armagh, and Blagg began to feel very lonely.

"I didn't know she'd got a gun," he finished. "I mean – that was why *I* was there. She should have let *me* decide." He sounded professionally affronted.

"You're sure they were both dead?" Maxim asked.

"Yes. I know."

"Why didn't you go to your own platoon commander?"

Blagg gave him a brief and almost sneering look, then shrugged. "He wouldn't have understood, like. He's a nice boy, but . . ."

"Your company commander, then?"

"Yes, but . . . I mean, I haven't been back there long and none of them was ever in Sass . . ."

Certainly some things the SAS did routinely would surprise a normal regimental officer. Or, as the regimental officer might put it, *nothing* the SAS did would *ever* surprise him. Caswell had finished the rifles and half leant, half sat on the bench, a new cigarette smouldering in his fist. He watched Blagg and nodded occasionally.

"Did you jump off right away?" Maxim asked.

"Well, I sort of . . . First I just took the car. Got the keys out of her bag. I mean, nobody would know about the car."

"You didn't have to stop and fill it up?"

"No, sir. But there was a five-litre can in the boot; I put that in, just for safety, like. I just drove around, thinking. In the morning I got on a train at Dortmund for Ostend and got on a ferry."

"What were you using for money?"

"Well, I had a bit, of course . . ." Blagg looked at the floor.

It was perfectly clear what he'd used for money. In a way, Maxim was pleased that he'd been cool-headed enough to think of it. Still . . .

"How much was there?"

Blagg cleared his throat. "3,750 Deutschmarks. I don't know why it was that, seems a funny sort of amount, really . . ."

Maxim guessed it was the result of bargaining: the German had wanted 5,000, Mrs Howard had offered half . . .

Caswell had been doing a little currency conversion in his head and was looking slightly shocked. He obviously hadn't heard any figure mentioned before.

"Well, don't chuck it around," Maxim said. "A lot more people'll believe you if you hand in a big wad of ready cash. And what happened to the gun?"

"In the river."

"And her luggage?"

"Same place. I went through it – it was only a bag – and she didn't have anything special, like passports or things. Just ordinary."

"You've been back here over a week . . ."

"It took me a bit of time to find out where Sergeant Caswell was, sir. I mean, I couldn't just ring up and ask, could I?"

"Did you try and get hold of Captain Fairbrother or anybody else in the Army?"

"No, just Jim here, sir."

"Does anybody else in this country know you're back?"

Blagg frowned at his fingernails.

"Come along, lad." Caswell's voice was sharp but quiet. "Major Maxim may be able to do something, but God Himself won't be able to help you if you don't tell the whole story."

The theology of that wasn't too sound, Maxim thought, but it seemed to work. Blagg muttered: "Couple've people I know, Rotherhithe way. You want to know what they'd tell the pig-feet if they come asking around?"

"You needn't bother."

"All I want, sir, really – is if you can get Captain Fairbrother to say I really was working for The Firm. Or them themselves. If they'd just tell Battalion that, it would be all right." Blagg sounded frighteningly earnest, as if life – and death – was just that simple.

"I'll do what I can." Maxim glanced at Caswell: any further

questions? Caswell gave the smallest shake of his head, ground out the cigarette in a tin-lid and began picking up the rifles.

Blagg reached. "Here, Sarge, let me –"

"I'm not a bleeding cripple!"

Blagg snapped into a fighting crouch and immediately Caswell was ready for him, a rifle held across his chest like a quarter-staff. The oil-dusty air shimmered with pent-up violence.

"It's a great day for the Army," Maxim said pleasantly, "when the sergeants insist on doing all the work."

The tension died like a match flame. Caswell straightened up, nodding angrily at his own obtuseness. Blagg wasn't offering to help because of any stiff arm; the lad wasn't that sensitive. It was just that although he'd run away from the Army, he wanted to prove he was still a soldier, even by something as simple as putting rifles in racks.

Caswell stroked his moustache with an oily forefinger. "Behind the door there. Don't drop more than half of them."

Blagg picked up four of the gutted weapons. "You're sure they aren't loaded, Sarge?"

The rack looked as if it had been built for the long Lee-Metfords of the South African War. Blagg fitted the rifles in, ran a chain through the trigger guards and padlocked it. The bolt actions went in a small safe bricked into the outside wall. They were ridiculous precautions for guns that couldn't any longer fire live ammunition, but airliners have been hijacked with toy pistols. Terrorism didn't take sunny Saturday afternoons off.

"You left the car in Dortmund," Maxim said. "Do you remember the number?"

Even better, Blagg seemed to have written it down. Maxim sighed. "Anything else that might interest the police if they pick you up?"

Silently, Blagg showed him the paper. The car number was worked somehow – Maxim couldn't see how – into an innocent-looking sum of minor expenses. Almost the first thing taught in the SAS is to memorise map references, so that no piece of paper will betray your base or objective.

28

"Sorry," Maxim said. "How about the phone number she gave you in Soltau?"

That wasn't part of the sum; Blagg looked annoyed with himself.

"Never mind, you weren't to know. How do I get hold of you?"

Blagg glanced at Caswell, who said: "I'll know how."

Maxim was about to say *No*, and then didn't. He didn't want Jim Caswell to get involved any deeper, but he couldn't really help it. Blagg on his own around London was a babe in the woods, even if he thought of himself as a two-gun tiger, as he probably did. Under Jim's eye in the country he was as well hidden as they could hope for.

He still didn't like the risk to Caswell, and took it out on Blagg. "Corporal, don't let anybody, including yourself, tell you you've been anything but a bloody twallop. You might still come out luckier than you deserve – *provided* you do what Jim and I tell you. But if you do anything clever and land Jim in it, then I'll go straight to the MPs and tell them everything you've told me. Have you got that?"

"Sir," Blagg said stiffly. "But you will talk to . . . ?"

"I'll do what I can. But you've been dealing with some funny people. Jim – ring me if you need to. Just as a precaution, call yourself . . . say, Calloway – and leave a message. I'll ring you back."

"I'll do that. Don't worry about this end." The atmosphere had become formal, more like a company office at a time of serious decisions. It was a good mood to leave with them.

Caswell ceremonially escorted Maxim to his car and, still in uniform, saluted as he drove away. When he got back to the armoury, Blagg had found a broom and was poking at the pitted, oil-stained concrete. Caswell nodded approval and lit another cigarette.

After a while, Blagg said: "He was the one that lost his wife, didn't he? Out in the Gulf, was it?"

"That's right. Some wily oriental gentleman put a bomb on board her plane. I was with him. He saw it."

29

"Jesus," Blagg said thoughtfully. "Something like that happened to me, I'd sort of want to kill somebody."

Caswell put his clenched fist to his mouth, as if politely masking a yawn, and drew hard on his cigarette. "He did, lad," he said in a slow smoke cloud. "He did."

Chapter 4

Monday morning was another perfect day and George Harbinger arrived at Number 10 Downing Street already in a foul temper. He perched on the edge of the desk of the Principal Private Secretary and growled: "The Broad-Rumped Nikon-Tufted Tourist seems to have bred particularly freely this year. There is a positive *infestation* of them outside. I even saw one without a camera."

"Really? I wonder that he got past Immigration at Heathrow. Coming in without a camera seems proof positive that he intends to settle here illegally." Jeremy was tall, with a natural elegance that would never decay into dandyism and always scrupulously polite, having been to that school which believes that it is manners, rather than God, that maketh man, though a spot of money also helps.

George grunted. On Monday mornings no remarks were funny but his own, and he usually regretted even those by the end of the day. He was one of the six private secretaries who – Jeremy included – formed the Prime Minister's Private Office. His own special responsibility was defence and security, although they all sugared each other's tea in busy times. Today looked like being one: on Saturday afternoon the Prime Minister had cancelled a speech he was to have made at an agricultural show in his Scottish constituency and taken to his bed there. He hadn't got up yet.

"How *is* the Headmaster?" George asked.

"Coughing hard but fairly cheerful in the circumstances." Jeremy had flown up and back on the Sunday.

"What are we telling the press?" After the revelations by Churchill's doctor that he had suppressed news of several strokes, and seeing other prime ministers leave the job by

31

ambulance, Fleet Street had become over-sensitive to any hint of illness in Number 10.

"One of these persistent summer colds that they're trying to stop going to his chest. I assume it's bronchitis but Sir Frank won't commit himself. I've suggested they get in a reference to his old war wound."

In May 1940 the Prime Minister, then a young lance-corporal defending a section of the Maginot Line, had taken a mortar burst that peppered his chest with fragments of metal and concrete. The wound might even have saved his life, since he was back in an English hospital when the remains of his battalion surrendered in the wreckage of St Valéry-en-Caux a month afterwards. But over forty years later, most of them spent smoking heavily while the cameras weren't looking, his scarred lung could still turn a simple cold into something that needed to be talked down, and bits of metal were still wandering around his body and occasionally needing to be picked out. I wonder, George thought irrelevantly, if he *pings* as he goes through an airport metal-detector gateway? But as PM he never has to go through such gateways – George had flown with him many times – so probably I'll never know. Bother.

"Have they done an X-ray?"

"At the local cottage hospital. It apparently didn't show anything alarming."

"But he's not likely to be back this week? Is Tired Tim taking over?"

Jeremy smiled painfully at the Deputy Prime Minister's nickname, took off his reading glasses and looked up to consult some Wykehamist deity that apparently floated a few feet above George's head. It was a gesture that annoyed George intensely.

"He will be taking Questions tomorrow, yes. Most likely he'll be chairing Cabinet on Thursday. And he'll be dropping in later today to see if there are any flies in the soup. I'm sure you'll try and limit their number."

"Have no fear." George was going to offer Tired Tim as few decisions as possible.

"And perhaps," Jeremy put on his glasses again, "those of

us too old to relish change might direct our prayers north-wards."

"You mean that if the Headmaster goes I'd be hove out on me ear before his taxi had turned the corner?" It was a thought that hadn't really occurred to George before. His father owned a large piece of Gloucestershire, and the Whitehall whisper was that once Harbinger senior was six foot under and some-body had been contracted to haul away the empty brandy bottles, George's wife Annette would have him out of London and into a country squire's gumboots before he could catch his breath. It could be any day now, the whisper added, and there was enough truth in it for George not to have thought of leaving Number 10 except of his own choice (or Annette's, of course).

Jeremy bent to his paperwork, murmuring: "As ever, George, you go straight to the heart of things."

"I'm not sure I'd want to stay." George wandered away through the almost-always-open door to the room he shared with three other private secretaries and the duty clerk. It was tall and elegant, with big windows looking out over the garden, and their desks seemed something of a crude anach-ronism; George looked at it all with sudden appreciation – and regret, because it could end so soon.

Only the clerk and the young man who kept the PM's engagements book were in, the latter busily telephoning round to cancel or reschedule the appointments; he gave George a despairing grin, and the clerk brought across a bunch of messages, including one from Major Maxim.

"The Major called down before you came in. He said it was only *fairly* urgent."

"And merely *slightly* sensitive," George read. "A very proper sense of values, has our Harry. Well, I'll go up slightly soon and fairly quickly. What else is new?" Suddenly in top gear, he charged into the paperwork, returning the more important phone calls at the same time as he scribbled com-ments on letters and redirected files to other desks in the house. After an hour, the high tide of Monday morning trouble had been pushed back to the normal waterline and he called Maxim to say he was on his way up.

By the time he had climbed the two flights of stairs to Maxim's room, George was breathing hard but only through his nose, which didn't count. In his middle forties – oldish for a PM's private secretary – he looked somewhat like a prince who had only just begun to turn into a frog when the wicked witch lost the recipe. He had a squat face with prominent eyes and a wide mouth, not much hair, a chubby body and thin limbs. But the clothes were still princely, if princes still spent their days at small yet exclusive country race-meetings: a beautifully cut lightweight grey check suit, hand-made brown brogues, a Cavalry Club tie. George usually dressed like that, not particularly because he wanted to, but because that was how his wife told his tailor to dress him. George's only stipulations were that he shouldn't look like a banker (his brother-in-law banked) or a civil servant (which he was). It didn't really belong in Number 10, but many people thought that George didn't either, which was one of his strengths.

He pushed open the door to what had once been a small boxroom, said: "And the top of the morning, or at least this bloody house, to you," and slumped into a chair. He made the room look crowded.

Maxim swung carefully round on a creaking desk chair. He was already in shirt-sleeves, although the single window faced north. "Morning, George. You look quite fit, for a Monday."

"I swear to you my father-in-law waters his whisky. Next time I'm going to take a hydrometer and expose the old – Good God, have we got you cutting out paper dolls already?"

Maxim had been clipping stories on defence from newspapers and magazines. He flashed his quick, protective smile and pushed the papers aside. "Can I do you a cup of tea? Instant soup? Nothing? How is the Prime Minister?"

"Everybody I meet today is going to ask me that. And tomorrow and tomorrow and tomorrow . . . We just don't *know* yet. We hope –" he looked quickly at Maxim and then remembered that this was one man at Number 10 who didn't gossip; who didn't, as far as he knew, have anybody to gossip to " – we just hope it's nothing worse than bronchitis, though when you're well past sixty . . . Anyway, what's this 'fairly urgent and slightly sensitive' weekend you've been spending?"

"A sergeant I had in the SAS," Maxim began carefully. "He got a disability discharge. He gave me a call. He's got a chap, a corporal, who's gone AWOL from Rhine Army. I met this chap –"

"A deserter?" George wriggled himself upright. "You met a deserter and didn't report him?"

"I'm reporting him to you."

"Go on, Harry," George said thinly. "And try and make it good." He slid down in his chair again and started listening seriously.

He was a good listener. When Maxim had finished, George just murmured: "Harry, what *have* you got yourself into?" but without anger or even expecting an answer. Then he just sat, shuffling the story in his mind like an incomplete pack of cards.

The internal phone rang; Maxim answered and handed it to George, who listened for a moment and said: "Can't you try Jeremy or Michael? I'll be down in a minute." He gave the phone back. "You'll never know, I trust, what it is to be both beautiful and indispensable. What have you done about this so far?"

"Nothing."

"That's always a good start."

"I thought you might approve. Anything I could think of would just show I knew something that I shouldn't: call his battalion in Soltau, ask about a murder at Bad Schwarzendorn, snoop around his regimental depot, check with the Military Police that they're really looking for him . . . Even look up his records."

George nodded. "The amount you *haven't* done in a mere thirty-six hours must stir green depths of envy even in Whitehall. Nonetheless, I'm not sure you mightn't have managed a little less. When you agreed to meet comrade Blagg you didn't know anything about the business in Bad Schwarzendorn or the involvement of Six – if that's true. You only knew he was AWOL but must be a good chap really because he'd once been with your Hereford Hell's Angels. You could have asked me first."

"You'd have said No."

George made a throaty rumbling noise. "Well, spilt milk . . . For the moment we'll assume it's all true; the worst usually is –"

"I can check with the German papers . . ."

"You've got the time?"

Maxim smiled sardonically and gestured at the meaningless clutter on his desk. For the past three weeks he had been doing little but attend lectures and short conferences – dogsbody jobs, he suspected, invented by George to keep him looking busy.

"Yes," George said, "our lords and masters *do* seem to have been behaving themselves of late; there must be *some* scandal lurking just around the corner . . . Right, you read German, don't you? Their embassy keeps *Die Welt* and *Frankfurter Allgemeine Zeitung* and the *Suddeutsche* – no, they wouldn't bother with it."

The extraordinary details George kept in his head. One phone call Maxim had allowed himself that morning had been to establish which, if any, newspapers the Germany embassy did file.

"Of course," George went on, "if they've had ten days and not found any link with a British soldier – and we'd certainly know if they had – then it may never happen. Just blow over."

"Blagg would still be a deserter," Maxim pointed out.

"He'd given himself a rather limited choice of futures. I imagine he wouldn't rather be a murderer."

"I got the idea," Maxim persisted gently, "that he feels much worse about the desertion than the shooting."

George went frog-eyed. "Harry, he *killed* somebody."

Maxim nodded. "Yes. Soldiers do."

George opened his mouth to say something, then remembered he was talking to a soldier who had most certainly killed people, one of them since he had come to work at Number 10. Quite likely Blagg had killed before, too.

Maxim went on: "Blagg was chaperoning somebody he

knew worked for The Firm. Working for his country. When that German started shooting, he became The Enemy. Now Blagg expects his country to back him up."

"Was there any hint of blackmail?" George asked, suddenly sharp.

"No, I don't think so. He's not a bloody fool, of course – well yes, he is, in a way – but he knows it could be a big scandal that could hurt Britain, and particularly the Army. In a way, that's why he went over the hill: to protect the Army."

"That is romantic twaddle."

"Soldiers *are* romantic," Maxim said evenly. "They watch war movies and like dressing up in funny clothes and calling themselves funny names like Dragoon Guards."

A quarter of a century before, George had done his two years' National Service in a Dragoon Guards regiment. They had been the happiest years of his life – or at least they increasingly seemed so, in retrospect – but *romantic*? He looked at Maxim suspiciously. "Well . . . what did he expect you to do?"

"Wash him clean and send him back to square one."

"Does he know what he's asking?"

"I doubt it. He doesn't know how an atom bomb works, either. He just knows that it does and assumes we do, too."

"Where do such mad ideas originate? All right: you pop round to the embassy and see what you can turn up. Do nothing else. We'll have to play this hand ourselves – I can't tell the Headmaster and I'm certainly not bringing Tired Tim into this." He paused with his hand on the doorknob. "*Romantic?*"

When George had gone, Maxim rang the German embassy and made an appointment to visit the press office files. Then he filled in time by filing his cuttings and tidying the desk generally. It was a new desk: the Housekeeper's Office had just got around to replacing the old rolltop that had been there when he first joined Number 10 nearly six months ago. He had spent most of those months complaining about it, with its drawers that were the wrong size for standard files and usually jammed anyway, but now he missed it. Now he had an indestructible grey metal box, just like a quarter of a million civil servants, and it was trying to digest him, to turn him into a civil soldier.

That was a childish (or romantic?) thought, but he was feeling the itch of a problem he wasn't supposed to scratch. Abruptly, he picked up the phone and asked for the Bradbury Lines at Hereford, and then for the adjutant of 22 SAS. They knew each other well, and the talk was cheerful, rambling, casual. But when he rang off, Maxim had learned that Captain Fairbrother had finished his SAS tour and rejoined the Brigade five months ago. For the last six weeks he had been in Alberta liaising with the Canadian Army about the live-ammunition exercises to be held there later in the summer.

"Bugger it," Maxim said aloud. Somebody had been lying. Probably everybody had been lying to some extent — that was only to be expected — but bugger it nonetheless. He sat frowning down at the desk and it crouched there, square and smug, knowing there were already more desks than soldiers and that all it had to do was wait.

Chapter 5

Bush House was both different and the same in unsettling ways; always they changed the things you didn't expect and kept the things that should have changed long ago. Security was much stricter: now everybody walked about with security passes clipped to their lapels showing a coloured photograph of themselves. Visitors got a sticky label like a large coin. All ridiculous, of course – but then she remembered the Bulgarian and the Libyan who had worked for the BBC's External Service, both murdered. They never caught the killer of the Bulgarian; 'The arm of justice is longer than the legs of a traitor'. She shivered and asked for the lavatory and there finished the last of the brandy, then tried to wash the smell out of her mouth. She should never have come, and anyway, Leni couldn't still be here.

But incredibly, she was. After a lot of reluctant telephoning around, the man at the reception desk grunted that Leni was coming down and wrote out her own sticky label.

Dear sweet Leni, always small and frail, now smaller and frailer, but the blue eyes still bright behind the big glasses and the thin white hair carefully set in tight curls. And of course the long drooping cardigan that was almost a BBC uniform.

They hugged each other, close like men, not standing right back so that their breasts wouldn't touch, and tears were already trickling from under Leni's glasses. "Darling Mina, you should have called me . . . why didn't you let me know . . . I thought you must be dead . . . Oh, Mina, Mina, it's so good to see you, but you should have called, you were lucky to catch me, I only come in on Mondays as a relief, just to give the young ones a full two days off . . . Oh, to see you again, why didn't you call? . . ."

The corridors were different ones but comfortingly still the same: roofed with all sorts of meaningless pipes and cables, walled with flimsy wood-and-frosted-glass partitions covered with junction boxes and noticeboards. How the BBC loved noticeboards! – she had forgotten that. All the dreadful warnings about fire and flooding and abandoned parcels, the cheery invitations to disco evenings, hockey clubs and hiking holidays . . .

At the door to the office Mina suddenly stopped and seized Leni's thin arm with her twisted hand. She saw Leni look down at the hand, then quickly up again. "No – Leni, I don't want to meet anybody. Just you. I came to see just you."

"Nobody will know you. They're all gone, they change so often . . . Only old Hunke. They won't know your name. Tell me – do *I* know your name?"

Mina ignored the question. "Somewhere we can talk together, just you and I."

"Of course." Leni led the way along the corridor, trying doors until she found a small empty room. She shut the door and started rummaging in a cupboard while Mina stared uncomprehending at the data system screen and the purring teletype. Leni came up with a half full bottle of vodka and two dusty glasses. She poured two tots. "*Prosit.*"

They sipped, and Mina asked: "The machines – do they do all the work now?"

"They can't translate. Not yet, anyway." Leni smiled, still moist-eyed. "Do you hear us?"

"Oh yes, I hear it when I can. But where I live –" she stopped abruptly, shaking her head. "And now I don't know any of the voices . . ." Leni herself didn't broadcast. "Do they still jam you?"

"The Russian service. And they tried to jam the German, since the strike, but now we have this big Army transmitter in Berlin, on 90.2. It isn't so easy to jam that."

"The strike . . ." Mina took a quick drink. "What do they say about Gustav?"

"He's a big man, now. One of the new members of the Secretariat."

"Oh. That is important?"

Mina had always been totally vague about political structures, even one she had lived with for years. Leni said patiently: "It is the most important, the Secretariat of the Politbureau. There are now only eight members, including Manger who will not last more than a year, and your Gustav is one of the youngest. He has moved up fast: he came onto the Politbureau only five years ago. In a few years, who can tell?"

"Oh." Mina looked terribly serious, perhaps haunted. "And Manfred?"

"We don't hear so much about him. But we believe he's a full colonel – he's young, for that. So he pushes, Gustav pulls – you know how it goes."

"Oh yes." Clearly Mina didn't. "So Gustav could be very important."

"Yes, yes." Then Leni suddenly saw Mina's fear. "You haven't been in touch with them?"

"No." Mina shook her head and got a spasm of dizziness. She clutched at Leni. "It's all right . . . I have to take pills . . . They make me . . . No, they don't know about me. Leni, please don't tell anybody. Not anybody."

"Of course, of course." Keeping one arm around Mina's shoulders, she poured them both more vodka. "I won't tell. But now they wouldn't make any trouble. Your coming was too long ago. For Gustav to be where he is, it shows they've forgotten it, they *want* to forget it."

"I don't know . . . there was another man . . . Walter . . . Walter somebody . . . He got very important and they ruined him."

"Walter Dürr. That was years ago. He had an affair with the daughter of another member and Frau Ulbricht broke him. But that was morality, Mina; *you* were political – darling Mina who is the least political thing I have ever met!" She laughed, found they had both finished their drinks, and poured more.

But Mina would not be appeased. "When I first came over, they did things . . . voices on the telephone, saying I was a traitor and they would break my hands . . . messages that were wrong, that sent my luggage to somewhere else or made

41

people believe I had cancelled a recital . . . they followed me, I know, they let me see . . ."

"You never told us. Did you tell the police?"

"No. No, I was afraid they would think I was a crazy woman and send me back."

Leni had been broadcasting from London since wartime days and had listened to literally thousands of stories from refugees and defectors. She knew all about the techniques of the secret police and secret services, the little touches to keep you walking in fear, isolated and suspecting your own sanity. Cruelty doesn't change, only the politics behind it.

"Oh my poor Mina . . ."

"So you won't tell anybody you've seen me?"

"Of course not. But do you feel safe now? Do you have a new name?"

"Yes," Mina said slowly. "I think I feel safe now, seeing you. I have a new name."

"Don't tell me if you don't want to. But Mina – write to me sometimes, please? I will give you my address . . ."

Gradually the gloom and the vodka seeped away, and the memories began. They giggled like schoolgirls at incidents of more than twenty years ago, at characters now dead, retired or gone home to the richer pickings of West German radio stations. Leni was a great mimic, bringing back every voice in every accent until, when the bottle was finished, they were both light-hearted and weeping with laughter.

Then Leni had the idea. "Mina – play something for me!"

"Oh no. No, I can't."

"You must. Just for me, only for me . . ."

"But – you've seen my hand." Everybody saw her hand, but she would have mentioned it to nobody but Leni.

"Just one thing, one little *Kinderszene* . . ."

They rushed along the basement corridors, searching for a studio with a piano, persuading a reluctant engineer to take a recording without worrying too much about his beloved 'balance'.

In fact, at that time of day and after that amount of alcohol, her hands were probably at the best they could be. And though the piano was tuned too hard, with Leni watching enraptured it was easy to turn back the years and forgive herself the little errors and awkwardnesses she knew would come. She took a deep breath and laid her tired old hands on the keyboard.

Chapter 6

Maxim lived in a gloomy first-floor flat in a late Victorian terrace on the edge of Camden Town. His landlady was a musty old widow who constantly threatened that if They didn't Do Something About It, she was going to sell up and go and live with her son in New Zealand. But it was too late, whatever New Zealand might think, and on her worst days she must have known it. The house had been let go too far: just too many years of patching instead of repairing, so that anybody coming in would have had to borrow the value of the house over again to pay for new woodwork, plumbing, wiring and the ripping out of the flimsy partitions and extra gas meters that marked out each of the flats. And anybody who could borrow that sort of money wouldn't have spent it on that sort of house anyway.

He took a can of lager from the refrigerator and sat down at the typewriter that lived on the window end of the table. It was a light and slightly flimsy portable that had belonged to Jenny. Almost all the things around him had once been hers or presents from her. In ten years of marriage, and eight different homes, they had bought only small, movable things. One day they would begin to wear out and need replacing. Would he mind that? – or by then wouldn't he care?

He wound in a piece of paper and began typing.

GEORGE HARBINGER FOR YOUR EYES ONLY   NO COPY
From Major H. R. Maxim.
1   The first mention appeared in both Die Welt and Frankfurter Allgemeine on the Monday, in a manner which suggests that the Sunday papers carried a full story. The embassy files no Sunday papers. There were

follow-up stories on the Tuesday and Wednesday, but nothing from then to the end of the month, which is as far as I checked.

2   Two people died of gunshot wounds on the Friday night in Bad Schwarzendorn.

3   The man was Alfons Hochhauser, aged 59, the town Standesbeamte (registrar). A widower for thirteen years. One son, one daughter, both married.

4   The woman ('Mrs Howard') carried a driving licence identifying her as Frau Gertrude Sailer, aged 46, with an address in Oldenburg. The licence was a forgery done with a stolen blank. No other identity has been suggested.

5   The only mention of a third person was that the police were still investigating a report that a 'young man' had been seen running across the park soon after the shooting. The impression given is that the police are not taking this very seriously (but see 8 below).

6   Wounds: Hochhauser had four (Die Welt) or five (FAZ) bullet wounds, including one in the head which must have been immediately fatal. The woman had three bullet wounds, all in her body.

7   Guns: he had a Mauser 1910 self-loader in 7.65 mm calibre. She had a 'Spanish revolver' in .38 Special calibre, which is the same as the gun Blagg had. No mention was made of how many shots each gun had fired.

8   This could be important, as could the number of wounds Hochhauser actually received. If it turned out that Mrs Howard had fired fewer shots than Hochhauser had wounds, it obviously proves there was a third pistol, and person, involved.

9   The same would be true if the forensic laboratory could prove that one or more of the .38 Special bullets was not fired from Mrs Howard's gun.

Maxim took out the page and read it over while he drank the last of the lager. George would snort and mutter at all that stuff about bullets, but it could be crucial.

He wound in a fresh sheet and typed on.

10 It was reported that the bodies had not been robbed.

11 The forged driving licence aroused suspicions of a terrorist link, but by the time the story was dropped this appeared to have been discounted and the investigation was in the hands of a public prosecutor from Paderborn.

12 It seemed that a Sunday newspaper had speculated that the shootings could have been a duel, arising out of a love affair the two must have been having. Alternatively, it was suggested that as keeper of the town records he could have known her true identity and something about her past and have been blackmailing her. There was no speculation about a third party or any international aspect.

13 Hochhauser's past: he was born locally and worked for the town since 1951. During the war he was a non-commissioned clerk in the Luftwaffe. He then worked for the Control Commission for three years. Neighbours say he was diligent and rather aloof, especially since his wife's death.

14 Both papers printed the driving licence photograph of Mrs Howard/Sailer, so there must be a possibility that somebody will come forward with a new identification.

15 There was no mention of the car.

And that was about it. He signed the second page *Harry*, folded them up and put them in his hip pocket. Then he went through to the tiny kitchen and took out another lager and tried to get interested in the idea of making dinner.

The matter of the bullets still worried him.

"Quite likely Blagg missed," George said. "With a pistol – an unfamiliar one – from about thirty yards *and* at night . . . he'd be lucky to hit the *Gradierwerk*. The thorn wall." Trust George to know the right name for it.

"He missed with some," Maxim said, "but he said he stopped shooting because he knew he'd made a head shot. And we know Hochhauser *was* shot in the head."

"She was still a lot closer and shooting as well. Perhaps he didn't shoot at all, got cold feet."

"He says he fired. I believe him."

46

"Harry," George said gently, "I am doing my humble best to make your little chum out *not* to be a murderer. Why does this charitable task incur your displeasure?"

"He believes he killed, at least helped kill, Hochhauser," Maxim said doggedly. "If somebody else starts believing it, we could have a problem."

For a time, George said nothing, just went on taking deliberate steps as if pacing out the length of Number 10's lawn. It was a morning of bright nursery colours: the blue-and-white sky, the vivid green grass, the simple reds and yellows of the flowerbeds. All rather childish, and childishly secret behind the high wall that shut out all but a faint buzz of noise from the city beyond. Although there were more than fifty windows in the back of Downing Street and the Cabinet Office, they were all shut, even in that weather, politely unseeing and unhearing. With the garden just to George and himself, Maxim felt both cosy and superior, a part of that higher world behind the windows that knew but never, never told. Then he wondered if that was just how George wanted him to feel, and began to feel wary instead.

"Do you think the police are using this as a holdback?" George asked at last. It was normal to keep one piece of evidence, something only the murderer would know, secret from the newspapers. It helped weed out crank confessions, it could lull the real killer into thinking the police had missed it.

"I don't know . . ." Maxim said slowly. "It seems a rather vital thing to sit on . . . Quite possibly they just haven't found all the spent bullets, or just haven't bothered with comparison tests. A .38 wouldn't normally stay in a body unless it hits bone. And you can have the best pathologist in the world, but he isn't the one who gets down on his hands and knees among the sweetie papers and dogshit; that's done by the local copper. In the end, your lab reports are only as good as what he turns up."

George was realising just how many Army officers must have become familiar with the dreary rituals of murder since the Northern Ireland troubles began.

"Yes," he said, "and from their point of view, they have a pair of corpses who have indisputably been shooting each

47

other, giving them a murder – two murders – that happened and were solved in the same moment. It sounds like a detective's dream. If they had suspicions of a departed party of the third part, they'd be strongly tempted to keep quiet about him unless they looked like catching him. And as far as we know, there isn't anything to connect Blagg with Bad Schwarzendorn?"

"I can't think of anything. His battalion's at Soltau and that's a hundred miles away. Even if they were looking for a British soldier there's thousands far closer."

"Good." George beamed, bright as the morning again. They had reached a slatted bench placed so that you could sit and stare at the flowerbeds under the wire-topped wall. George rested a foot on the bench and used Maxim's report to swat dust off his shoe.

So *that's* how it is, Maxim thought sadly. He tried one more time. "We might be forgetting something: Mrs Howard. She had a fake identity. The police are bound to follow that up –"

"Some distance, only some. Forged papers aren't unheard of in Germany."

"Perhaps. But she wasn't hiding her face: she was in cafés and so on, she got that car from somewhere, and now her picture's in the papers. If she's passing as a German she most likely *is* a German, and somebody could easily recognise her."

George waved the report in a loose gesture. "She was obviously something of a professional. She must have known the risks involved."

"She wasn't counting on ending up on a shelf in the deep-freeze."

"How charmingly you put these things."

"And she *was* working for Six –"

"She only said she was," George said quickly.

"She was carrying 3,750 Deutschmarks of somebody's money. And she knew where to find Blagg, where his battalion was."

"You can read where battalions are in the papers. Those things aren't secret. But Six uses a lot of part-timers, they have to. And what they do with the other part of their time . . .

48

some of them are most certainly not the type one would want to take home for tea with mummy."

Maxim walked stiffly around the bench at slow-march tempo. "I grant you she didn't have to get Blagg's address from Six. And she lied about dealing through Captain Fairbrother –"

"Unless Blagg did. Invented that to justify himself."

Maxim halted, staring at his feet. "Is there any way, anybody, you can ask? Or I can? Find out if she really . . . ?"

George was all sympathy and understanding. "Harry, you must bear in mind that – assuming for the moment that The Firm actually was involved – the whole thing represents a quite monumental cock-up. There would have been one mad rush to bury the file deeper than did ever plummet sound, and a general issue of blank stares and short memories. And as an organisation they are actually designed, in large part, to do just that sort of thing. So then what could we offer? – that we heard the story from a deserter who claims also to be a murderer? We have quite enough trouble with the creepiest and crawliest of Her Majesty's servants already. The Headmaster is vulnerable enough without me suggesting we go about believing comic-book stories – and that has nothing to do with whether or not the story happens to be true."

He remembered the report and offered it. "A very sound piece of work. Thank you. Will you burn it or shall I? And any notes, of course."

"You do it. What do I tell Blagg?"

"You get word to him – don't tell him, get word to him – that the only course is for him to turn himself in. And if he doesn't mention Bad Schwarzendorn, nobody else will."

"Two weeks AWOL is going to hurt. He'll lose his stripes and won't get them back for a year. Or more."

"I'm honestly sorry about that, but the involvement of Number 10 with a deserter is very much more a threat to our peace of mind than any happening in High Germany. If you recall, you came here because the Headmaster wanted somebody to help stave off security scandals. At present, the only connection with this one is through you."

Maxim took a slow breath and nodded.

"And tell – no, let Blagg know – that he can hang onto the rest of the money. No questions will be asked."

"Are you sure it'll be enough?" Maxim asked in a blank tone.

"To make up for the damage to his career? No, I'm sure it won't. I'm also sure I'm putting the Headmaster's interests ahead of anybody else's. That's why you and I are here."

Suddenly brisk, he bounded away up the steps onto the terrace and in through the french windows of the Cabinet Room, away from the sunlight.

Maxim went out early for lunch and called Jim Caswell from a box outside the Treasury building. Blagg wasn't there: Caswell had him doing odd jobs around the garage to keep him from brooding, and he'd gone out on his motorbike to try and fix a non-starting car.

"His motorbike?" Maxim asked warily. "I didn't know he'd got that with him."

"It isn't really his. He left his own with a mate in Rotherhithe when he went to Germany; he was going to take it over later. When he came back, he borrowed the mate's bike. So the number wouldn't give him away."

"Umm." That made a sort of sense. "When can I get hold of him?"

"I wouldn't think he'll be back until after lunch. But I can tell him the bad news."

There must have been something in Maxim's tone that had given it away. "I'd rather tell him myself. But it could be worse: nobody seems to think he's connected with you-know-what. If we can dream up some girlfriend trouble for him and get him to turn himself in over here . . . Does he have a real girlfriend, d'you know?"

"Nobody he's mentioned. Goes in for one-night stands, I should think. He doesn't want to be involved with anything but the Army. Stupid sod." It was said gently. "So they wouldn't play?"

"You know who we're dealing with – *trying* to deal with."

"Bastards."

"Yes. I'll call this afternoon."

Maxim put the phone down and pushed out of the sweaty box. An American couple pounced at the phone. As the woman started dialling, the man said: "Hey, excuse me, sir, but could you settle something for us? Big Ben's the bell, right? – not the tower?" The woman stopped dialling.

"That's right. The bell."

The woman stared evenly at Maxim. "Sure. Now let's ask a woman."

He walked across the road and back up the other side, feeling itchy and irritated. He had never spent a summer in central London before; now he saw how much it became Us and Them country. There wasn't much grandeur or elegance in Whitehall to start with, but the way these people drifted aimlessly around and just *peered* at it made the whole shebang seem like a second-hand clothes shop. And turned his own job into selling worn pairs of trousers that didn't fit. He could see why George, after all these years, went psychotic just at the mention of Tourists.

My God, he thought: no wonder the world hates the British. We've done four centuries of *peering* all over the world, fingering people's lives and hoping for a bargain. The sins of Drake, Raleigh and Thomas Cook had finally come home to roost on Major H. R. Maxim. In a mood of gloomy cowardice he went and lunched with his own kind at the Greasy Spoon in the basement of the Ministry of Defence.

That afternoon George had to nurse Tired Tim through Question Time, so he sent Maxim to report back on a briefing being held at the American embassy. The speaker was a visiting CIA analyst who believed he had detected a shift in focus of Moscow's short-term goals as a result of the shake-out in East Germany. It was a good year for detecting goals shifting their short-term focus; certainly nobody was spotting revisions in interim stragetic themes any longer, at least not if they wanted to keep on flying the Atlantic first class. Maxim sat quietly through the briefing and an hour of questions afterwards, then stayed on for a drink with a new friend from the Army attaché's office. He came out at five o'clock with a frost-bitten hand as evidence that he was just a non-transatlantic yokel who didn't know enough to use a paper napkin to hold a glass of deep-frozen bourbon. Then it took a quarter of an hour to find an empty phone box and call Caswell.

George was still at the House; they met below the statue of Northcote in the crowded, echoing Central Lobby. Maxim said flatly: "Blagg's gone. Run away."

"Do you know where?"

"No, except probably Rotherhithe way. He borrowed a motorbike off a mate there, and the mate seems to have called him in the country just after lunch and left a message asking him to call back, and he must have done that and then packed his bag and gone. Just a note saying thank you for having me and leaving a few quid."

"Umm." George frowned down at the stone floor, letting Members and their constituents find their own ways round him. "Rotherhithe's the one place the police will be looking for him. You've no idea who this friend is?"

"His name was Jack. He'd lent Blagg his motorbike, but I don't have the number." Jim Caswell had been furious with himself for not noting that. He could describe the bike, as any good garage man should, but the number . . .

"Well, then . . ." George waved his usual handful of papers. "I suppose that endeth the last lesson. We just hope that when he gets picked up he's got enough sense to plead guilty and forget any names and details."

"I'd still have liked . . ." But he wasn't quite sure what, by now.

"Does you credit. But this is one time to imitate the action of the clam and hope that the chowder will pass us by."

"I suppose so."

George put on his stern–but–kindly look. "Harry – don't do anything romantic. We'd miss you."

Chapter 7

The next morning, Maxim came into Number 10 fizzing with the nauseating good humour of a breakfast cereal advertisement. He gave George a perfectly typed report of the CIA briefing, cross-referenced to recent papers and articles on the subject. He passed on some hot gossip about tactical nuclear command picked up from the Army attaché's man, and then he started retelling what Chris had said on the phone about how well he'd done in the house cricket match.

George was suspicious of enthusiasm, particularly in the mornings, but a second-hand description of a prep school cricket match broke his nerve completely. The Blagg affair seemed to have blown over, he had Tired Tim's performance at tomorrow's Cabinet and another Question Time to worry about, so he readily agreed to Maxim taking the afternoon off to attend a lecture at the Royal United Services Institute. After all, he told himself, Maxim wasn't fool enough to go wandering around Rotherhithe with no better lead than a man called 'Jack'. If he'd bent his distracted mind to it, he might have realised there were one or two other little clues, but the very idea of tramping the streets asking questions of strangers was so far outside George's experience that he couldn't imagine anybody he knew doing it anyway.

Rotherhithe's whole history had been the Thames, but now the river was hidden behind clumps of derelict warehouses and shaky fences that sealed off the abandoned dock basins. Maxim had never realised just how complete the closure of the up-river docks had been, nor how total its effect on the neighbourhood. This wasn't the tough, rowdy waterfront, but a district left dazed, uncertain and incomplete. The buildings didn't seem to fit; a run-down Victorian terrace, a row of neat little dolls' houses with varnished doors and gardens only big enough to park a motorbike, then a low block of modern flats, already cracked, with overgrown lawns and skeins of washing. There were gaps where houses had been torn down, several filled with second-hand cars plastered with garish Bargain Of The Week stickers.

Only the pubs remembered the sea: the Lord Nelson, the Warrior, the Jolly Caulkers, the Albion. The rest was churning cement lorries that scattered a fine dust in the sunlight, making Maxim hawk and spit every few minutes.

He tried the first motorcycle shop he came to. He was looking for Ronnie Blagg, chap he'd known in the Army. He rode a Honda 400N but a friend said he'd been around on a silver Yamaha XS500, two years old.

"He talked about coming back to Rotherhithe on his leaves," Maxim went on, "but he doesn't have an address here. He was an orphan, the Council brought him up."

The proprietor looked both suspicious and blank. "What did you want him for?"

"I thought if he was out of the Army now, he might be looking for a job."

"You come down here just to offer him a job?"

"I'd go a lot further to find a man I know's been properly trained and I can trust to work by himself. Some of the kids you get these days – well, you must know it yourself."

The proprietor, who was about forty, nodded sympathetically. His suspicions were gone, but he still didn't know Ronnie Blagg. Maxim left his home phone number and the name Fairbrother. Blagg would certainly want to speak to *him*, no matter what he felt about Maxim.

It was the same at the second shop. Of course, Blagg didn't have to have bought his Honda in Rotherhithe; more likely he'd got it in Hereford during his three years with the SAS. And friend Jack might have got the Yamaha elsewhere, too. But he plodded on. At the third shop he got a nibble.

There were two of them, and they could have been father and son. The younger one said: "I think I know those bikes. The Honda's blue, is that right?"

Maxim didn't know.

"I remember the bloke. He's been riding those two the last month or so. He's one of those that comes around Saturdays, just for a natter with the other bikers and buy something small. Jack something. But that other bloke, Blagg, I don't know him."

The father figure was leaning on one end of the counter patiently poking at a lump of electronics. He said quietly: "The name rings a bell. Are you a friend of his?"

Maxim went into his act. At the end, he remembered something else: "He was a bit of a boxer, at one time."

"That's it," the father said, "That's where I heard it. I remember Billy talking about him. It was before your time," he said to the young man. "He must have gone in the Army nearly ten years ago. I remember Billy thought he could've been a contender."

"Billy?"

"Billy Dann. He runs the gym up at the Lord Howe. He manages Rance Reynolds; he's a contender. But you don't follow the fights?"

"I've been abroad too much. Will Mr Dann be there now?"

"Should be." They gave him directions and he left his real name this time, just in case Jack whoever came by.

The Lord Howe stood on a wide street corner, a tall, confident square of red brick and ornate stonework from the great days of Victorian sin and gin. Now almost alone in the afternoon sunlight among the boarded-up houses and second-hand car lots, it looked as wicked as a kitten stealing cream.

The dim corridor at the top of the stairs smelt of embrocation and shook slightly with the distant rhythms of somebody skipping and the rattle of an overhead punchball. Maxim hesitated, then walked towards the noise. He was almost there when a door opened behind him and a chunky man aged fifty-something bustled out and gave him a hard look.

"Is Mr Dann about?" Maxim asked politely.

"'She expectin' you?"

"No, it's about –"

"Why'nt you give 'im a ring, then?" He pushed past, his belly bulging his thin tee-shirt. "He's busy."

"It's about a boy he trained once. Ronnie Blagg."

"Never 'eard've 'im." He had his hand on the gymnasium doorknob.

"Next time," Maxim suggested, "pause a moment before you say that. It'll sound much more convincing."

The man turned slowly around.

Maxim said: "I'm not the Military Police." He already knew he couldn't be mistaken for the ordinary police: no plainclothes detective would be fool enough to be the only person wearing a dark suit in Rotherhithe that warm afternoon. He held out his ID card.

The man peered at it. "Woddaya want, then?"

"A word with Mr Dann. You've already told me I've come to the right place, but I don't necessarily have to tell anybody else – if I can get a word with Mr Dann. Would you ask him?"

The man looked very suspicious, then hurried through the door, letting out a brief draught of light and noise. Maxim waited. A boy of around eighteen clattered up the stairs carrying a sports bag labelled LONSDALE, smiled uncertainly at Maxim, and went into a side room.

The gymnasium door opened and the chunky man jerked his head at Maxim. "O'right, Major, you can 'ave yer word."

It was a high room, clean and busy and very bright, with big windows around two walls. It had nothing to do with the boxing gyms of the movies, or with the tired, almost empty pub downstairs. There were over a dozen men in the room, but with two whole generations missing. The boxers were all young, barely twenty, wearing vivid coloured tights and tee-shirts, thick leather head-guards and big groin protectors. The next age up was at least fifty, and a handful sitting on hard chairs beneath the windows and sharing the sports pages of the *Standard* were obviously old-age pensioners.

Billy Dann was about fifty-five, tall, very solid, with a square calm face and longish white hair. He wore a cloth jacket like a hospital porter's, with big pockets, and was leaning on the ropes of a boxing ring that filled one corner of the room.

Two boys, one white and one black, were sparring in the ring, their feet going hiss-hiss-hiss as they slid flat-footed across the canvas.

The chunky man said: "'Ere's the officer, Mr Billy."

Maxim said: "Major Harry Maxim." Billy Dann gave him one quick glance and a nod and went back to watching the boxers. His eyes were a pale, cold blue.

"You've been asking about Ron. Why?"

"He's AWOL. I saw him in the country, last weekend. He told me about it. Then he vanished. I want to talk to him."

"You want to take him back. Are you his CO?"

"No, and I've no power to go around arresting people. I just want to talk to him."

"Suppose he goes back – what'll happen?"

"It depends on his story. He'll get a few days in cells, probably, and lose his stripes for a while. But he'll live it down."

"It could take a long time." Dann took a stopwatch from his pocket and called: "Last ten," and the boxers speeded up to a flurry of blows. After ten seconds Dann said: "Time." The boxers stopped and took sips from a communal water bottle. Dann went and talked to each separately, demonstrating with a dropped shoulder, a jabbing hand, a weaving head.

"Looks pretty busy," Maxim commented. Other boxers were pounding at the heavy bags, skipping, one was dancing poncily in front of a full-length mirror and another lying down doing sit-ups with a trainer standing on his feet.

"Busy?" the chunky man snorted. "You should see it five o'clock of an evening in the fights season." He indicated the black boy, who was listening carefully to Dann, nodding his head at each point made. "You know 'im? That's Rance Reynolds. He's a contender."

"What weight?"

"Welter. You ever fight?"

"Not boxing."

"Karate, I suppose."

"Something like that."

Dann came back and called: "'Way yer go," then glanced at his stopwatch. His whole life was chopped into sections of three and one minutes, and looking at the watch was merely a gesture by now. The fighters moved in on each other, hiss-hiss, hiss-hiss.

"What's Ron to you?" Dann asked.

"A useful soldier. An investment, if you like."

Dann watched the fighters for a while. "He came here when he was just fourteen. I couldn't take him in properly, but I had a word with the Council – you know about his background, of course? – and they said they'd rather he spent his evenings here than on the street. He'd started fighting in his youth club and he'd beaten everybody there twice over and they didn't much want him back. He was looking for something bigger, and it could've been sailors with a month's pay in their pockets coming out at closing time. He was good enough to sort them out sober, let alone half cut. At fourteen. But he didn't really need the money, not if he hadn't got the time to spend it. Keep kids busy and they don't need money. You got any kids?"

"One. But I just want to know –"

"So I let him come here any time I was open. He swept up, he washed bandages, posted my letters. I taught him the exercises and let him get in the ring with some of the bigger lads."

"Bigger?"

"The little ones would've chopped him up, just to show who's boss."

"'E was a cocky little bugger," the chunky man said, smiling.

The hiss-hiss from the ring suddenly became sharp howls as the white boy lost his temper and both boxers started throwing real punches from a solid footing. Reynolds snaked out three right jabs, each tearing through the other's guard and snapping his head back sharply.

"Now, now, now," Dann called.

The white boy backed off, head hunched down and angry. Reynolds moved smoothly after him, the hunting cat who knows it's only a game – until he wants it to be something different.

Dann caught something in Maxim's look and smiled briefly, for the first time. "You can't have him, Major. He could have a big future, that boy. The other one, he's a street fighter. Ron Blagg was a street fighter, to start with. He learned; he learned a lot, then he joined the Army."

Maxim said: "It's kind of you, but I don't really need all the background. I just want to get a word to him."

"I'm telling you something about him. Before you knew him. I could only get him for, maybe it was two hours a day. He wanted more than that. He wanted a family. A fighter ought to have a family. I don't mean married. I don't want any married fighters. Give me a kid from a big family, a poor one, but solid. I couldn't be Ron's family. Maybe the Army was. I hoped it would be. Now, I don't know."

"He was doing pretty well."

"Yes – he used to drop in here when he was on leave. I dunno . . ." He looked at the watch, called: "Last ten," and watched the fighters speed up for the finish. The white boy came out of the ring, Dann had a few words with him, and called over another to take his place.

"'E stopped boxing," the chunky man said. "'E said he'd stopped, Ron did. Couple of years ago, that was. Said 'e wouldn't get in the ring, 'e was afraid he might hurt somebody. *Well* . . ."

Maxim felt vaguely relieved that Blagg, freshly trained in the SAS's version of unarmed combat, had known himself well enough to stay out of the formal boxing ring. Perhaps the Hereford course was really what he'd been looking for all along. It was lucky that Her Majesty had more jobs open for street fighters than true boxers.

Dann said: "'Way yer go," and the new round started. "So what do you want with Ron, then? Try to make him go back?"

Maxim took a calming breath. "That has to be part of it. Every day he stays away makes it worse. But I want to talk to him first."

"You could write him a letter."

"This isn't something I want to put on paper. It's all a bit unofficial."

The door to the corridor opened and another fiftyish man with a broken nose came in and up to Dann and said: "All okay, Mr Billy. It's all right." He went away again, passing within two feet of Maxim and not even glancing at him. In fact, being careful not to see him at all.

Maxim felt a retch of sick anger. "You *arseholes.* He was

here, wasn't he? – when I came in. And you kept me gabbing away while you smuggled him out the back or something. And you think you've been so bloody clever and all you've done is screw the boy's life up a bit further, but you're all right, Jack. No dirt on your hands."

Dann gazed at him with cold, mild eyes.

"D'you want to know what happens to a deserter?" Maxim demanded. "He becomes a non-person. He can't get a National Insurance card so he can't get a real job. He can't sign his name to a cheque or a lease or hire purchase deal. He daren't even go to a doctor because he's got no medical records. Had you thought of any of *that*? He's got to move away from here to some place he doesn't know, and to live he'll probably have to go crooked, even if he doesn't want to. And since he's no good at it he'll get nicked and then he'll have a criminal record *and* be dismissed from the Army because of it. You've just given Blagg a great start in life, Mr Dann, and without even it costing you one penny!"

He had suddenly become the main event of the afternoon. The boxers in the ring had stopped and even the pensioners by the windows were staring at him. And everybody had the same expression of Nobody-talks-to-Billy-Dann-like-that-and-least-of-all-in-*here*. The Fight Game had abruptly become a seminar of shocked spinsters.

Maxim scribbled his home number on an Army calling card. "Get Blagg to call me at that number. Don't have any more bright ideas of your own, just get him to call *me*."

One of the boxers drifted over from the punch-bags, wearing only the protective bandages on his fists. "D'you want me to see 'im out, Mr Billy?"

Maxim ignored him. "And don't send any of your *Palais-de-Dansers* after me unless you want him back in a hamburger bun!"

He brushed past the boxer and slammed out of the door. Dann gazed after him, his face still mild. He took the stopwatch out and looked at it. Beside him, the chunky man was turning purple and spluttering at the room: "Did you '*ear*? Did you '*ear* 'im?"

★

Maxim walked a fast quarter of a mile, breathing quickly. Oh, but that had been clever, that was really cool. You sneak out to make a few discreet enquiries under an alias and you end up being so discreet that they'll probably rename the bloody street after you. Your real name, too.

All right, then. Now we really will be cool. As a penance we will now do everything *exactly* right. Pretend we're back on the Ashford course and been sent up to town to check a dead letterbox, make a brush exchange, all the tradecraft and with the experts watching and eager to make a banquet out of your mistakes. We'll go by the book, we'll go by the book down to the full stop at the end of *The End*.

For the next twenty minutes he was Harry Maxim, Super Secret Agent. When he crossed a road he looked both ways – but not for too long, and crossing only when he needed to. He walked against the flow of a one-way street, to shake off any tailing vehicle, but only because it led in the right direction. He found a telephone box on a corner and called Number 10 to check for messages, giving himself a chance to gaze innocently around and spot anybody who might be loitering. He crossed an open park, forcing a foot tail well back – but again only because it was a short cut. And he used the reflections in shop windows to check the other side of the street, but only with shops that Harry Maxim (non-Super Secret Agent) would logically look into.

At the end of that time, according to the Ashford book, he should have lost – seemingly by chance – most of any team following him. More important, he should have established whether or not he really was being followed.

And he was.

One thing was certain: it wasn't anybody from the Lord Howe gym. These people were real contenders, and that needed some thinking about. But first of all, he had to reassure them, certainly not lose any more of them. So he caught a bus up to London Bridge station; it was impossible to lose a man travelling at the glacier speed of a London bus.

The real question was whether they knew who he himself was. Were they following him to find out where Harry

Maxim went, or had they picked him up in Rotherhithe and were following to find out who he was? If they didn't know, he didn't want to tell them, but if they did then he mustn't do anything blatantly un-Harry Maxim that would show he'd spotted them.

Damn. He should have started playing spies a little earlier. Or rather, he should have remembered the Ashford instructors who had told him often enough – no, obviously not often enough – that this wasn't a game, something to be stopped and started. It was a way of life, till death did you depart.

With the Underground map in his diary, he worked out a route that involved two changes of train and landed him at Finchley Road station – near enough to home that he might have detoured to visit the big shops there. At Ashford they'd told him to assume that any fan club would be working by radio – in their cars, on their motorbikes, in their pockets. But going underground through central London would shed all the wheels, and radio doesn't work down there. In theory, every time he changed trains somebody should flake off and go up to the open to broadcast his new direction. The final trick was to make sure you shed the last of your fans as fast as possible when you came up for air yourself, before the vehicles could be homed in on you again.

But you can never be sure it's really worked.

Chapter 8

Maxim settled down for a gloomy evening. He daren't yet tell George – or anybody – that he was being followed. It was an Unmentionable Disease, and he'd caught it because he'd been to an Unmentionable Place and so it served him right, but that didn't make it any less sore. If they were still with him at the end of tomorrow, he could complain, but not until then.

There was nothing he wanted to see at any of the nearby cinemas, he'd be irritable company in the local pub where he was a contender in a small bar-billiards school, so there was nothing for it but to spend the time watching television with the other sinners.

The phone rang at just after seven. A youngish, roughish voice asked: "Is that Mr Maxim?"

"It is."

"Me name's Dave. Dave Tanner. Er – I heard you was looking for Ron. You know – Ron. Er – am I right?" He sounded nervous, but it could just have been his telephone manner.

"Yes. Are you the chap that has his bike?"

"Er, yes, that's right. He had me Yam."

"Thanks for calling. Can you get him to call me? – or meet me?"

"Er. Yeah. No, I mean – could you come up here? I mean we could have a talk."

"Of course. You mean to Rotherhithe?"

"Yeah. Er – you know a pub, the Golden Hind?"

"I can find it. It shouldn't take me much more than half an hour. How will I know you?"

A pause . . . "Er – I'll be in the Public. I got on me jeans and DMs and me leather."

Black leather jacket, fat Doc Marten boots and jeans. As distinctive as ninety per cent of Rotherhithe's young men, and a fair number of its girls, most likely.

"I'll ask for you at the bar," Maxim said. "Half an hour – okay?"

In practice, it was a bit more. He took the car and the warm evening seemed to have brought out hordes of motorists who were just strolling, and he chose a zigzag route to throw off any fan club.

The Golden Hind was smaller and a lot more cheerful than the Lord Howe, a busy little place with an obvious hard core of regulars wedged into their favourite corners. Maxim stopped just inside the door to the public bar and looked around. As he'd expected, there were four young men dressed as Dave Tanner, but only one of them was interested in who might be coming in. Maxim stared at him, in a friendly way, until he slid off the bar stool and came over.

"Dave Tanner?"

"Yes. Er – it's Major Maxim, innit?"

"Harry. Can I get you a refill?"

"Er, yes."

They moved to the bar. Tanner was drinking lager, and Maxim wanted one as well, after the warm sticky cross-town journey, but he didn't want a long, bulky drink in his stomach. Dave Tanner was a bit too nervous for a man on his own territory. Well, all right, technically he was concealing information about a deserter – although nothing like the scale on which Major Maxim was doing it – but civilians don't take desertion seriously. If you can afford to walk out of your job, walk out, why not?

He ordered a single vodka with ice, no tonic.

"Were you at school with Ronnie Blagg?"

"Er, yes, that's right."

"Did you box as well?"

"Me? – never." Tanner seemed amused. He had a long pale face, fashionably spiky fair hair and a pleasant smile. He was probably Blagg's own age – twenty-five – and he had a gold signet ring on a hand that was already worn and scarred by work at some machinery. "I was never into boxing, but Ron, he always wanted to be fighting something. No, we just sort of hung about together. He stayed with us, sometimes, when he come on leave. He was having it off with me sister at one time. You know – just when they hadn't got nothing better going."

"Can you put me in touch with him now?"

"Er . . . I mean look, what I can do . . ." Tanner seemed even more nervous, taking a sudden gulp at his lager. Maxim took a casual look around. They were jammed in a pack at the bar, having to talk loudly at eight inches' range. They certainly couldn't be overheard, but in that crowd anybody could be watching them. "What I'll do," Tanner said again, then asked: "You haven't got no idea of where he is yourself?"

"Of course I haven't. I thought you knew."

"Yes . . . look, there's somebody wants to talk to you, right?"

"Somebody who knows where he is?"

"Er, could be. He just wants to talk."

"All right." Maxim finished his vodka and sat waiting. He was fairly certain now that he was walking into a trap, and wished he'd come armed. That way, nobody need get hurt. *Now there's confidence for you, assuming that if anybody gets hurt it won't be you.* No, it wasn't really that: it was being trained to get hurt, knowing he could stand it.

Tanner quickly swallowed the last of his lager and led the way. Outside, the sky was still a brilliant clear blue, but the side streets were full of long shadows. Maybe there was half an hour of daylight left.

They turned away from the main street, towards the river and the closed docks. The road was a narrow canyon turning between high walls that protected the now-derelict warehouses, and by its nature must be a dead end. Tanner walked at a hurried, unnatural pace.

"I thought you didn't go to the bike shop except on Saturday?" Maxim asked pleasantly.

"The bike shop? No, I don't. What d'you mean, the bike shop?"

"Where you got my name and phone number."

"The bike shop? Oh yeah, the *bike* shop." Tanner pretended to remember. So where *had* he got the number? Maxim took off his silk scarf, wiped his brow and put the scarf in his pocket. In a fight, it could become a noose.

They passed an elderly Cortina II parked half on the pavement. There were people in it. He was several paces past when he heard the car doors open and realised just how outnumbered he was.

He hit Tanner in the stomach, a short punch to wind him, then snapped him around in a half-nelson and throat-hold. There were five others, four whites and a black, and he thought he recognised a face from the Lord Howe gym. They were the right age, anyway, and they moved like athletes.

"The first thing I do is break his arm," he announced.

"Break both," one of the fighters suggested. They came steadily on.

Tanner gasped: "You bastards," and Maxim chopped him under the ear and dropped him. He got his back to the wall as they swept over him.

Maxim tried a roundhouse kick that missed, turning with it to launch a back kick that dropped one of them. But the others were too close. He grabbed one forearm and broke it, then a blow on the forehead knocked his eyesight out of kilter, another thumped his ribs and he gave up, sliding hunched down the wall trying to keep his groin and kidneys safe. There was no point in getting hurt any more.

They tied Maxim to a wooden chair – just like the scene they'd watched a dozen times at the cinema – in the loading bay of a deserted warehouse. There was no light except hard bars of sunlight shafting almost horizontally through the broken windows, and the concrete floor gave the place a gloomy chill even on that evening.

The boy with the broken arm had fainted once; now he was sitting against a wall, crying. The black, who had stopped the back-kick, sat beside him with grey lips, holding his stomach and only semi-conscious. The other three seemed uncertain what to do next; Dave Tanner hadn't come with him, though he had been on his feet again when Maxim last saw him.

"Christ," said one of the others. "You really buggered them up."

"Did you break his arm?" another asked.

"What do you fucking *think*?" moaned the boy most likely to know.

"It's broken," Maxim said. "Hospital job. And him, too." He nodded at the black boy, who wasn't listening.

"Now," one of them said, "we're going to talk to you. I mean you're going to talk to us. We want to know where Ron Blagg is, see?"

Another slapped Maxim across the face, but not very hard. "We can keep doing that 'til you tell us."

Maxim goggled at them. "Bloody hell! I came down here to try and find him. If I knew where he was I wouldn't have come. I thought you were hiding him."

"Don't give us that shit."

"If I knew where he was *why would I come here*?"

He was slapped again, still without much conviction. "You just tell us where he is."

"I don't know. You had him at the Lord Howe, that's the last I know. I'm an Army officer and all I want to do is persuade him to go back to the Army."

"Well, if you don't know where he is, where is he?"

Maxim stared back wearily.

"We're going to torture you," one of them decided. "I mean like stick cigarettes in your face until you talk."

Maxim did his best to shrug inside the ropes wrapping him to the chair. "Go ahead. It's a police job already so why not give them some solid evidence like burn marks?"

"Stuff the police."

"They're involved, from the moment you get those two to hospital. Unless you just leave us all here to die."

The black boy suddenly keeled over and his head hit the concrete with a startling crack.

"Oh Christ," the torturer wavered. "Is he going to be all right?"

A door banged, echoing across the empty bay, and footsteps clattered towards them. The boys stepped back, looked hastily around, then just resigned themselves. Maxim tried to turn his head to see, but Billy Dann had already begun to talk before he came into view, with Dave Tanner limping behind.

"Jesus," he said softly. "I have seen some fuck-ups in my time, but *you* lot, and *this* . . ."

Billy Dann's office was long and narrow, almost as narrow as the desk placed across it just in front of the window, but very high because it had been partitioned out of a much bigger room. The walls were lined with old fights posters and photographs of boxers in stiff, ferocious poses, and it had a musty, faded feel to it, contrasting with the bright cleanliness of the gym just up the hall.

By now it was dark, with just two small desk lamps throwing clear-cut areas of light: one at a typist's table halfway down the room where Maxim had finally met up with a pint of cold lager, one at the desk where Dann was listening on the telephone and sipping a small glass of neat gin. The rest of the room was lit only by the dim bluish light from a street lamp below the uncurtained window.

Dann put down the phone. "One busted forearm, one ruptured spleen. They have to remove that. They say they'll be all right. Might even fight again. It's the arm that worries me. If you remember what it felt like, broken, every time you throw a punch . . . I don't much like you, Major."

Maxim just nodded. "What about the police?"

"They've been there. I don't know what they asked, I didn't get to talk to the boys . . . maybe they'll think they filled each other in, I don't know. If nobody makes a complaint . . . What are you going to say?"

"Nothing if nobody else does." Maxim had a sore forearm and stomach, a slight headache and a torn seam in his light-weight jacket. "I'll send you the tailor's bill."

"You do that, Major," Dann said heavily. "You do that."

"And I still want to know where Ronnie Blagg is."

"So do I. I'm not arsing you around, I just don't know. When we got him out of here, a couple of the boys had a cuppa with him at a caff down the road. An hour later, he rings in, he says he thinks somebody's following him. That's all. No-body's seen him. I said something to the lads, I don't know what, like your people had caught up with him . . . They must've got the idea from that, called Dave Tanner and got him to set you up . . . I mean it was stupid, just plain wet-nappy stupid."

"D'you have any idea where he might have gone?"

"He had a mate in the country. Kent, I think."

"I know that one. He's not there."

"Was it your people? I mean the Military Police – what's the Army call them: the Redcaps?"

"Actually the Army calls them 'those fucking MPs'. No, they wouldn't have followed him, they'd have grabbed him. He belongs to them, now. I don't know who it was." He took a drink. "You can't think of anybody else he might go to?"

"Tanner, he'd be the only one."

There was a silence. Dann looked at Maxim's glass, then took a bottle of gin from a desk drawer and refilled his own. He wasn't a drinking man. At fifty-five his stomach was as flat as an ironing board. He took a big swallow and sighed.

Maxim asked carefully: "Did he see you before he went to the country, when he first came back from Germany?"

Dann considered. "Just a minute or two."

"Did he say anything why he deserted?"

"He said . . . This is unofficial? – I really mean that."

"Yes."

"Well, he said he might've killed somebody."

"He told me he had, quite sure."

Dann looked relieved, then curious. "And you didn't tell nobody?"

"Not officially."

"I'm buggered if I understand that Army of yours."

"Me too. But you were never in the services yourself?" Dann was certainly the age for National Service, if not the war itself.

He tapped his left ear. "I've got about twenty per cent hearing in this one, that's what they said last time. That happened in the ring, we didn't have head-guards in those days. When I was just seventeen. That's why I took up PE, training. Another punch and I could've lost the lot."

"Could you have been a contender?"

Dann thought for a moment. "You have to say yes. You have to believe it. But how much does anybody else know about . . . about Ron and this business?"

"I've read the German papers and there's nothing been said, so we don't think they've made the connection. So if you see Ron, tell him if he goes back and keeps shut-up, he'll only have the AWOL to answer for. But I'd still rather talk to him myself."

Dann nodded slowly, then asked:"Who d'you mean by 'we'?"

Maxim grinned suddenly at the idea of dragging George openly into this. "Nobody who's going public on it. So if he does get in touch . . ." He stood up and wriggled carefully. "I'm stiffening up. I'd do better to jog home than drive."

Dann stood up, too. "You did better against those . . . those *twats* than I'd've expected. Some of them must be near half your age. I still don't like you much, Major, but I don't say I've liked most of the best fighters I've trained. In a way, I won't say I like Ron too much, and he could have been a contender."

"In its small way, the Army also contends. You've still got my number in case anything comes up? It could be important. And still unofficial."

He walked slowly towards the hall, stretching at each step like a newly awakened cat. He had an early appointment the next day.

Chapter 9

Agnes Algar had dressed with particular care on Friday morning. She chose a slightly flared skirt of fawn flannel, plain white silk shirt with a demurely high neckline, a jacket in soft pastel-brown tweed with a standing collar, absolutely plain but very expensive Italian court shoes and a matching handbag that was small enough to be ladylike but not so small as to seem frivolous. Around her neck she put a thin early Victorian gold chain, on her right hand a fire opal she had recently had reset in a simple gold ring, on her left wrist the gold Baume & Mercier watch.

Agnes thought of her clothes and jewellery in such terms, just as she thought of her car as a two-year-old 3-door Chevette ES in Regatta Blue with wing mirrors and two radio aerials. She lived in a world of detail and precision, of getting the names right and the appearances correct, and had done ever since she joined the Security Service straight from Oxford fourteen years before. She would have described herself quite objectively as aged 35 and looking neither older nor younger, height 5 feet 4 and usually just under nine stone with a figure that was well kept rather than dramatic. Her hair was light ginger and she had long ago given up trying to curl it; she had a snub nose and blue eyes in an oval face that was cheerful but perhaps forgettable. But being forgettable was part of her job; a jigsaw piece that fitted invisibly into any puzzle.

However, that morning Agnes intended to be neither forgettable nor invisible. Only a few hours earlier an unexpected Meeting Notice had been issued, the agenda being simply 'To consider the conduct of Major H. R. Maxim'. Since her job was to maintain liaison with Number 10, which made Maxim technically a colleague, she was to represent the Security Service at the meeting. She had no idea what that 'conduct' had been – a few early morning phone calls had produced more bad language than information – but she knew what 'to consider' meant in Whitehall, and frankly Harry had had it coming. Not that she had anything against him. She had no prejudice against any of the Army's trigger-happy desperadoes – not in the right place. Number 10 just wasn't that place, and she didn't mind who heard her say so.

But what concerned her even more was that the Notice had shown the meeting would include *two* members of the Secret Intelligence Service. That sounded bad. Long ago, the legend said, the security (or spy-catching) service and the espionage (or spy-hiring) service had been born next door to each other in rooms 5 and 6 of the corridor where Military Intelligence first nested in Whitehall. Nostalgically, the old door numbers still stuck among the mass of code and jargon names slapped on the services since then. Thus the Intelligence Service could be MI6, just Six, or The Firm, The Friends (said with a knowing, slightly twisted, smile) or, if you were one of Agnes's mob, the Other Mob.

That is, unless you happened to be about to meet them across a conference table. Then you reminded yourself that they were a bunch of gilded pederasts who spent what little time they could spare from betraying the country's secrets in stealing the Security Service's territory, influence and share of the Secret Funds. If it had ever existed, the cosy Whitehall corridor was long gone, though Agnes sometimes wondered what it would be like to concern herself with frustrating only other countries' spies. But she always dropped the thought as frivolous speculation.

"The room was swept just three days ago," the uniformed messenger said, and Sir Anthony Sladen thanked him automatically, although everybody knew the remark was meaningless. Listening devices didn't grow like bacteria: they had to be planted. The room might have been 'swept' three minutes or three months ago, but what mattered was what had happened since then. Three minutes is a lifetime to a good wire man.

The complete absence of windows gave the room a sense of

being right out of time and place, abetted by the bland neon lighting and acoustics which made everyone's voices sound flat and small. The walls were covered in oatmeal-covered sackcloth, and in the centre two heavy tables had been pushed together to form a single one that looked absurdly big for the eight tweed-covered office chairs around it.

"Lock the door when you go out," Sladen added. "And tell the coffee ladies that we'd like ours in, say, three-quarters of an hour?"

He looked around for support and everybody nodded, but the messenger became doubtful. "I expect they'll be here when they get here, sir."

Sladen sighed. "Far easier to change our entire defence policy than alter the timing of one coffee-trolley. Very well, then."

The messenger ambled out and for no good reason everybody stopped talking until they heard the lock click.

"How is the PM, do you hear?" Sladen asked George. "It's been almost a week, now." He lowered himself very carefully into the chair at the head of the table. He was a stiff man by nature and now his back had seized up on him. The Assistant Secretary from the Cabinet Office, a motherly woman with very neat grey hair and fashionable spectacles, clucked around him, adjusting the embroidered cushion she had brought along.

"Quite chirpy on the phone," George said. "Probably the worst thing wrong with him is Frank Hardacre." Sir Frank, who had earned his knighthood by making house calls only at houses where there might be photographers waiting outside, had once told George he drank too much. "If he survives that he should be back in town next week."

"In the House? Taking Questions?" the Foreign Office asked. He got Mummy's Chair at the opposite end, the natural place for Sladen to look first when asking for comment.

George shrugged. "Tired Tim's quite happy playing Sorcerer's Apprentice. Why close a show that's taking money?" He had to settle for the seat at Sladen's right hand, opposite the Assistant Secretary. Agnes came next to him and Major-General Sir Bruce Drewery next to her. Across the table, the younger of the two men from Six had already torn up his place card and put it in his pocket as a gesture of security.

The Assistant Secretary gave Agnes an all-girls-together smile and flipped open her notebook.

"Ladies and gentlemen, I must apologise for dragging you in here at such short notice, but as you will have guessed from the Meeting Notice the urgency . . ." Urgent or not, Sladen was experienced enough to give them thirty seconds of platitudes while they kicked their briefcases under the table, tugged at their waistcoats – both MI6 men wore them even on a hot June day – and shuffled their papers, although few of them were prepared to put much paperwork on view. One of two Second Permanent Secretaries to the Cabinet, Sladen's whole life was committees, conferences, meetings. He was a thin, thin-faced man and a bad back suited his dignity. His one concession to the heat was a grey suit in place of the usual Cabinet Office blue, with a Trinity 1st & 3rd tie.

"Chairman –" the first off the mark was Guy Husband from Six "– I'm sorry to be singing the school song so early, but the Meeting Notice was classified merely as 'Secret'. Could my service assume that any minutes would only be distributed as 'Top Secret'?"

Sladen glanced down the table. "Concur," the Foreign Office said cheerfully. That was Scott-Scobie, a swinger from their harmlessly-named 'Research Department'; forty-fiveish, healthily plump, curly dark hair and wearing a rumpled linen suit.

George nodded. "Agreed. But does this mean that our friends from Dixieland –" the Intelligence Service lived south of the river "– are going to give us a hint of what they're up to these days?"

"We hope everybody will be giving hints of what they're up to," Husband said smoothly. His voice was pleasant but characterless, as if he were mostly concerned with avoiding mistakes; a provincial schooling or all the years in the spy business?

"Sir Bruce?"

"By all means. Classify it any way you prefer." He was a big Scottish pussycat with a contented purr of a voice.

"Splendid." Then Sladen remembered Agnes; she gave him a happy smile. "Splendid, then. You'll make a note?" The Assistant Secretary already had. "Good. Now, I think we all know that the matter ·before us concerns Major Maxim, currently attached to the Private Office at Number 10. Guy, perhaps you'd like to . . . ?"

"Yes, Chairman. But first . . ." Husband had the good looks of a schoolboy football star who had reached forty with one mighty bound: a strong nose, high forehead, brown hair set in tousled wiry waves. Even in a service which had a reputation for snappy dressing, he was an exquisite. His Italian suit was a little too shaped, too light in colour and probably too expensive. He adjusted his blue-tinted pilot-style glasses with a hand that wore a broad gold ring backed up by a gold cufflink in the shape of a reef-knot. Agnes disliked rings on men, although to be fair to Husband – which she had no intention of being – she had little trouble in finding something to dislike about everybody from Six.

"But first," Husband said again, glancing quickly at Agnes; "may I ask why our sister service is represented here? – no matter how prettily. I ask only because of the need-to-know principle."

You bastard, Agnes thought. You peacock's prick. She waited for George to answer, but he sat hunched beside her, turning a gold pencil in his fingers. She realised she was on her own; George must be expecting a true Conflict Situation if he was already saving his last bullet for himself.

Our Harry has trodden on some *Very* Important Toes, she thought.

She became the bright helpful little girl, friendly but perhaps just a little out of her depth among all these clever men. "I only know that the Meeting Notice was sent out according to a list drawn up by the Prime Minister."

"Deputy Prime Minister," Husband corrected.

"I really don't know. My Director-General asked me to come along because I usually handle the lower-level liaison with Number 10. But –"

"*Lower*-level," Husband said quickly. "That, Chairman, is precisely my point," although it hadn't been to start with.

Her voice stayed steady, despite feeling sick with anger and humiliation; " – but I imagine the Cabinet Office must have had some idea as to whether this is going to touch on security within this country."

Sladen cleared his throat. "I think we can take it that a representative of the Security Service was regarded as, ahh, fundamental."

"I was solely concerned with the need to know," Husband said with deep sincerity.

Now *there* I believe you, Agnes thought. There is something my service needs to know which you don't want us to.

"If there are no other objections," Sladen was carefully not looking for any, "then I think we can proceed with the meeting as it is currently constituted. Now could we –"

"If it comes to that," Sir Bruce rumbled, "I've no clear idea why I'm here myself. Nor," he added, "why that young man is." He smiled lazily across at the second man from Six, directly opposite.

Sladen sighed. "We hope, Sir Bruce, that you might keep a watching brief on behalf of Major Maxim, and indeed the Army as a whole . . . Mr Sims, also from the Intelligence Service, has specialised knowledge which could help us when we get into more detailed matters."

Mr Sims, if that was his real name, dressed not so much snappily as very cleanly. His dark blue blazer looked as if it was brand new, as did the white shirt with a very faint grey stripe and the steel blue tie. He was in his middle thirties, his square tanned face set in a permanent appreciative smile, dark hair cut neat and fairly short. Although he chain-smoked menthol cigarettes, his hands – remarkably small hands – were un-stained and well manicured.

"Now," Sladen pleaded, "could we please get on?"

Husband had been filling a curved briar from a silver pocket box. He struck a match and breathed a haze of bright blue smoke. "As you probably know, Major Maxim is attached to Number 10 for duties that appear not to be precisely defined but touch on security matters. He works, as Sir Anthony said, directly to the Private Office. This whole matter began when my service became *aware* of Major Maxim at the scene of a surveillance operation that had been mounted."

"In London?" George asked.

"Yes, in London. Initially our agents had no idea of who he was, but as I'm sure you know it's standard procedure to take photographs, and as soon as we compared them and a description with our files, we were in no doubt as to who he was."

"So you stopped tailing him," Agnes suggested helpfully. George made a little annoyed grunt. She ignored it; I've been wounded already in this battle, brother. That makes a difference.

"No, not entirely. A full-scale round-the-clock watch obviously wasn't either necessary or appropriate, but we did something to monitor his movements."

Sir Bruce asked: "Did he notice what you were up to?"

Oh, I love that *notice*. Agnes smiled at the old warrior, and then at Husband: by now, her anger at him had distilled to the warming spirit of pure hatred.

"I believe he was lost from time to time, but that of course is inevitable in a down-market operation. We had no positive indication that he was aware of our interest until yesterday morning."

He paused to relight his pipe. Everybody waited patiently. The Assistant Secretary put a large floppy handbag on the table and took out a small handkerchief. Her security pass was clipped to the strap of the bag, like a paddock pass on a racecourse.

"Major Maxim lives alone. His life seems to have no particular routine apart from his work. That night we had two watchmen outside, just in case. He came out very early, as soon as it was light – about half past five – and drove off to Acton. *Acton*. You may or may not be familiar with *Acton*, one gets a glimpse of it from the train, but it largely consists of railway yards, goods depots, great piles of broken-up cars. All rather like a battlefield."

Agnes felt Sir Bruce stir beside her.

"With hindsight, we now see that our soldier friend was in fact leading our agents into his own sort of country. The two watchmen were in a van, radio-equipped of course, but unfortunately the particular area was under some overhead

77

power cables which badly affect radio for some distance around."

Sir Bruce nodded contentedly.

"In short, Major Maxim lured our watchers into this place and then ambushed them. The driver was *pistol whipped*, as I believe our Big Brothers call it, and left dazed and with the radio smashed – *beyond* repair. The other was kidnapped. He was held at gunpoint, handcuffed, blindfolded and forced into the boot of Major Maxim's car. I can understand soldiers being allowed to play with guns, but I would like to know where he got those handcuffs."

Nobody could think where until Scott-Scobie said cheerily: "Buy 'em all over, gun shops and so on. Big item in the FD market."

"The what?" George asked.

"Female domination. Whips and bonds."

"Good God."

Scott-Scobie grinned. "Do get *on*, Guy."

"Yes . . . then he was driven for, he estimates, about half an hour. He was taken out, in some quiet place, out of doors, and questioned. Or rather, tortured. He was told to say just who he was working for, or he would have ammonia poured onto the blindfold. I assume you all know what raw ammonia does to the eyesight? Bank robbers used to use it quite freely, I believe. You can go blind."

The room was quiet except for a hidden fan that suddenly interrupted its humming with a series of squeaks like somebody rubbing his shoes together. Sladen bent carefully back in his chair and frowned at the ceiling.

"Our man could smell the ammonia," Husband said slowly. "He described quite graphically – to me personally – how he felt with it seeping through the blindfold and beginning to sting and then burn at his eyes so that he was finally forced to open them in order to blink. I do not want to hear anything like that again. Major Maxim then told him that there was no special hurry and that he was to take his time and make his statement complete. I understand that he made it complete."

He paused deliberately.

"As soon as we got him to a doctor – which took some

time – it was discovered that Major Maxim must have held the ammonia under our man's nose while pouring some odourless spirit – quite possibly strong vodka – onto the blindfold in order to produce the stinging sensation."

"At school," Sir Bruce said reminiscently, "they taught me you could go blind from masturbation, never mind ammonia."

"How fascinating. I hate to think what Major Maxim got taught in school – or would it have been the Army?"

"Couldn't say, dear boy, but we do encourage young officers to think creatively."

Husband sat back in his chair and began lighting his pipe for the third time. Sladen looked at George, who reluctantly sat up a bit straighter, and said: "Until your chap did talk, I imagine Major Maxim thought he was being followed by a bunch of Kremlin cowboys."

"I don't see why," Husband said. "Any man with access to sensitive information, such as Major Maxim, should expect to be put under surveillance purely as a matter of routine. By Special Branch, or by a positive vetting team from Defence, or even Miss Algar's own service could quite legitimately decide to check up on his private life. I'm sure *she* wouldn't have taken the matter lightly if it had been her own colleagues who had been beaten up and tortured. Nor do I imagine that Number 10 would have been overjoyed if it had been some young detective constable."

"I agree he acted hastily –"

"He acted very deliberately and to a plan. The ammonia proves it."

"Let's say that he should have come to me first," George said in a heavy, measured tone, "and let me sort the whole thing out. I assume that your service would immediately have acknowledged responsibility?"

"Of course."

Liar, Agnes thought. But George had to accept it.

"Very well. But what do you want now? – for me to send him round to say sorry?"

"We'd certainly like him sent round, but to say a little more than sorry."

"Such as what?"

"We would like to know what connection he has or had with the target of the original surveillance."

Sir Bruce leant forward so that he could see past Agnes to George, but didn't say anything.

George said: "Major Maxim is still working to the Private Office."

"If he was working for the Private Office in South London on the afternoon in question I should be very surprised indeed."

"Whereabouts in South London?"

"Rotherhithe."

Sladen was looking from George to Husband and back again, twitching his head from side to side like a tennis umpire. There was a ball being knocked back and forth, all right, but only Husband and, Agnes now realised, George knew what it was.

"Who is your target?" George asked.

Husband paused, cocked his head slightly and peered at George as if he were assessing his artistic value. "Are you quite certain you don't know?"

The room tensed, but George shrugged and let it go past, perhaps admitting that was a ball he couldn't reach.

Sladen waited nervously for somebody to say something, then asked tentatively: "Well . . . if we aren't to discover *who*, is it possible to find out something about *why*?"

Why so nervous? Agnes wondered, then suddenly realised. As a number two to the Cabinet Secretary, who was the most powerful of all civil servants, Sladen's career was almost in orbit. One final boost and he would be up among the true stars, all guidance systems go for a seat in the House of Lords upon retirement. But final-stage rockets had misfired before, and at a time when people were whispering about a change of Prime Minister and the shake-out that would bring, the very last thing Sladen must want was to be caught up in a brawl between Number 10, the Foreign Office, Defence and the secret services. That way lay nothing but the chairmanship of a minor merchant bank.

"I think Guy might fill in some of the background," Scott-Scobie agreed.

But then there was a knock on the door, the messenger unlocked it and stuck his head in, asking: "Is it all right for coffee now, sir?"

Sladen nodded, maybe a little relieved. "Since it would be now or never, yes, it's all right now." The meeting collapsed into muttering groups. The coffee lady, in a green nylon uniform, pushed in her trolley and began handing out ready-filled cups. Agnes got hers with the pale coffee already slopped over into the two sugar lumps and two hard little biscuits in the saucer. Luckily, she took neither sugar nor biscuits.

"May I have mine *black*, please?" Sladen called. Sims wanted his black, too. The coffee lady sighed loudly.

Sir Bruce sipped, made a face, and whispered to Agnes: "And I thought we suffered at MoD. Have you any idea of what we're talking about?"

"Not a thing. We've heard nothing about this."

He grunted. "Do *they* often set up surveillance operations in this country?"

"I didn't think so. My own service was under the impression that it had the huntin' and shootin' rights in this country. It didn't seem too much to expect, when *they* have all the rest of the world." She was wearing a brave but sad little smile. Outnumbered three to one – if you counted swinging S-S as One Of Them – she might need all the allies available.

Sir Bruce made another Highland noise. "I never could get on with those people; they appear entirely obsessed with sex. They will not get it into their heads that what the military wants is *military* information, not the phone number of some general's girlfriend. I don't believe there's a one of them could tell the difference between a T-72 and a kiddie's tricycle."

Agnes nodded sympathetically. As the coffee lady trundled out, the messenger poked his head in. "Shall I lock up now, sir, or wait until she's collected the cups?"

"Oh Good God!" Sladen almost lost his temper. "It doesn't *matter* about the cups. She can get them when we've finished, if we ever have the chance. Just leave us *alone*."

Husband whacked out his pipe in a big glass ashtray, making a sound like a gong, then walked around the Assistant Secretary to mutter into Sladen's ear. Agnes flashed a smile at

Sims and leant across after it.

"Look – the next time you want to set up a surveillance in London, do remember that we're here to *help*. We have an awful lot of experience in these things, and we can do you quite a big show at very short notice."

Sims smiled back. His teeth were very even and, of course, very clean. "Thank you, but I think we can do all right." He had a faint German accent.

"I'm talking about a dozen sets of wheels, thirty or forty bods. Not just two old men in a van."

Sims stayed impeccably grateful. "You are very kind, but I do assure you we can manage."

"You really are getting that section organised," Agnes said admiringly.

Scott-Scobie suddenly woke up from behind his *Financial Times* and asked: "What was that? What did you say?"

Agnes smiled at him. "Just a little liaising at the lower levels."

S-S stared suspiciously at Sims, who lit another cigarette.

Husband came back, also distributing suspicious looks, and sat down. Sladen tapped his papers together into a squared-off pile, spread them out again, and said: "Miss Algar, gentlemen, can we get back down the mineshaft? I believe Mr Husband was going to . . . ?"

Agnes interrupted. "Could I sort out one little problem first? I gather that the Rotherhithe operation was a full-scale affair, lots of wheels, thirty or forty personnel. Can I assume that it was cleared through the Cabinet Office? Obviously one can check, but . . ."

Sladen's eyes searched for comfort. A few doors down from his own room sat a Co-ordinator of Intelligence whose task it was to try and keep MI6, 5 and the true military organisations from duplicating each other's efforts and spitting in each other's beer. His main control was money, since he turned the taps of the Secret Funds, but that was rather long-term. When relations grew particularly bad he became the child go-between in a household of warring parents: "Ask your father if it would break his heart to change channels so I can watch the news." By the unwritten laws of an unadmitted game, Six should never have sent a war-party into Five's tribal land without at least telling the Co-ordinator.

"Or perhaps," Agnes added, "they went through the Yard?"

Everybody knew they hadn't. Nobody told Scotland Yard anything they would mind seeing as next day's headlines.

Husband wriggled himself comfortable and reached for his pipe. "Dieter?" he said to Sims.

"I arranged for the surveillance," Sims said evenly. "It was done from my section and I am afraid I did not ask for sufficient permission. I am sorry."

The can is carried here, Agnes thought.

"I think Dieter's been a bit naughty," Husband puffed, "but it was a direct follow-up to an incident abroad, so you might say it came under the doctrine of 'hot pursuit'."

"But if my Director-General asks what happened to the agreement that no operation of anything approaching this scale was to be mounted in this country without our knowledge . . . ?"

"You don't *know* what scale it was, but you can tell him Dieter says he's sorry." Husband waved his pipe, making brief smoke trails.

George muttered: "Drop it. Leave it lay."

Agnes stared at him, amazed. This was just the sort of thing – a secret service playing God – that usually had George registering 9 on the Richter Scale. But then it came to her just how much of George's power flowed from the Prime Minister in person. Now that the PM was on his Scottish sickbed, George was a near-flat battery, hoarding his last sparks for really crucial issues. Scott-Scobie's strength was that of the Foreign Office, faceless but continuous while PM's came and went like lantern slides.

"I'm sorry for the interruption, Chairman," she said bleakly.

"You can also say," Husband added, "that the surveillance has been discontinued – hasn't it, Dieter?"

"Oh yes."

Sladen said: "Now we've got that settled, perhaps Mr Husband, you'd like to . . ."

"It's Dieter's section that's been handling this, so I'll let him fill in the background."

Sims ground out his cigarette and began. "You will all be aware of the changes in the Politbureau in the GDR since the railway strike. Especially one of the new members of the Secretariat of the Central Committee, Gustav Eismark."

Sir Bruce wasn't sure he'd read that issue of *The Economist*.

"He is widely regarded in the West as the token liberal," Sims explained. "Just as there must be a token Jew and a woman. We believe he could be more than this. His background is with shipping, first in the yards at Rostock, then with the national shipping line. He stopped the seamen and dock workers joining the strike, but he did not take too hard a line. We prefer to see him as we think he sees himself: a pragmatist."

"The great thing to be in East Germany right now," Scott-Scobie announced. "It marks you as one of the techno-crats – what a ghastly word – and they're the class that counts. The politicians may say Blah but the computers go on saying 01 10100 or whatever it is, and it's the people who can make sense of *that* who'll be in the top bunk when the dam breaks. Also Eismark's only sixty-odd and that's a mere youth in the GDR. Ulbricht died in office when he was gone eighty, didn't he?"

"That is so," Sims said, smiling – apparently grateful for S-S's help. 'Filling in the background', Agnes saw, didn't include delivering the punch lines. "We believe he may be, in the long term, a very important man. And we also know of his early life something more than the official biography, since, thirty years ago, his sister defected to here. She was a pianist, and used her mother's name, Linnarz. Wilhelmina Linnarz."

"I remember her," Sladen pounced, thankful for something he recognised at last. "She used to play a lot of Schumann. I didn't always agree with her Chopin, and her Liszt was a disaster area, but I'd listen to her for a long time if it's Schumann. What happened to her? – is she dead?"

"We do not know. She left this country twenty years ago, and we have no trace."

There was a moment while everybody thought about that,

probably for no good reason except that they didn't like to see twenty years go by without offering up a few seconds' respectful silence, then Sir Bruce asked: "So she didn't go back to the GDR?"

Husband said: "We're very inclined to doubt it. They'd have put her in the freak show, confessing how misled she was by capitalist gold. One defector that repenteth is better propaganda than nine-and-ninety loyal party workers, isn't that so, Dieter?"

But of *course*, Agnes realised, Sims – or whoever he'd been born – must once have been on the far side of The Wall, too. She'd been slow to see that, and tried to make up for it by saying quickly: "Her jumping over can't have helped Eismark's career."

Sims nodded, thanking her. "That is so. But he was only young then, about thirty, and he did not have so far to fall. And also his background was very good. His father had been killed in the Rostock riots of 1931, and it seems that Gustav himself had for certain been a Worker Youth."

"In 1945," Husband said, "they were trading cigarettes – which were better than gold in those days – for Party cards and affidavits that they'd always been true Worker Youths – once they found themselves in the Russian Zone. There were – are still, I'm sure – plenty of overnight heroes of the Resistance with Hitler Youth uniforms buried in their cellars."

"Yes, yes, yes," Scott-Scobie said with cheery impatience. "But we can accept that our Gustav wasn't one of those. Apart from anything else, he wasn't even in the Russian Zone to begin with. He actually went East soon after the war ended, if Guy's files mean anything. So his wicked sister's vanished and now he's big man on campus. Let's read on."

"In the war," Sims said, "Gustav had married. He had a son, that is now Manfred, who is a colonel in the SSD. But Gustav's wife was killed at the end of the war. His sister then helped to bring up the child while Gustav was in Moscow for two years, at the university and taking the political indoctrination. He did not marry again until much later, when he was coming back to political life after the economic changes of 1962, which made the shipping more important. Politically, it is important to be married. It is normal, and the Democratic Republic is very modest."

"An absolute hotbed of puritanism," Scott-Scobie cut in. "Rife with morality. When Frau Ulbricht was den mother she ran the Politbureau like a convent school."

"So when Gustav Eismark came to the Secretariat," Sims went on, "naturally we looked in the files about him. There was not much; we do not have the money to research every politician in the Republic. But now, we said to our people, if anybody has something about Eismark that they had not the money to explore, now we can unlock the money."

"Standard operating procedure," Husband said, quickly smoothing over Sims's full-frontal use of the word 'money', even though there was nobody there from the Treasury to hear it.

"And one person said yes, she thought she had something."

"Something interesting or something dirty?" Sir Bruce asked.

Scott-Scobie grinned at him. "Both, we hoped. It's the dirty bits that make the world go round, don't you find, General?"

"*Please* . . ." from Sladen.

"So we said to go on, to investigate. She reported that she was sure she would be able to prove something, but it needed just one operation, with more money. It was to be in a small town called Bad Schwarzendorn."

"Do you know the place, George?" Scott-Scobie called.

"A spa with a *Gradierwerk* down near Paderborn. I toddled through it when I was with Rhine Army. What happened then?"

Husband said: "It went wrong, badly wrong," then lit a match and Sims found he was holding the ball again.

"There was a shooting. Our agent was killed, so was the town registrar. If you read the German papers, it was in there. We lost the money, we did not get the proof."

"Oh *dear*," Agnes said brightly.

Sims's smile stayed as bright and unchipped as his teeth. "But the identity of our agent was not discovered and the police seem to think it was a crime of passion without any third person involved. We do not expect any blowback."

"Ah, that *is* lucky," Agnes helped. Husband glared at her.

Scott-Scobie also gave her a look, then past her at George. "I have to say that we in The Office put the highest, the *very* highest priority on acquiring this proof – *if* it still exists."

George asked: "Knowledge of what? And in what form?"

"That," Husband said, "is what we would like your Major Maxim to *toddle* round and tell us."

Chapter 10

The cricket ground was wide and shapeless, surrounded mostly by the back gardens of houses, but one stretch gave onto the main road, where the taxi from Littlehampton station dropped Agnes off. She walked up a gravel drive crowded with large cars, past an old-fashioned wooden pavilion and two clay tennis courts, ignored the adult game going on in front of her and started around the boundary to the second and much smaller game in the far corner.

Maxim was sitting on a wooden bench in the uncertain shade of a row of poplars and chatting to two small schoolboys in fresh whites. He stood up as she got near, taking off his sunglasses politely, and they shook hands. He wore a loose cotton blouson buttoned at the waist over a blue tee-shirt and faded khaki slacks.

The bench was cluttered with cricket gear; Maxim asked the boys: "Could you find us a couple of chairs, do you think?" They rushed away with competitive enthusiasm.

"The word of command," Agnes said admiringly. "An Army training has its uses after all."

"For finding a place to sit down, consult us first."

"Was one of those your boy?"

"No, he's batting now."

"Oh. Which one?" She put on her own sunglasses and looked out across the worn pitch. The umpires looked very big and the ten- and eleven-year-old schoolboys very small, like squat white fleas that stayed still or suddenly hopped about and often fell over.

"The bowler's end. Not taking strike."

The other two boys hurried back, each with a folding wooden chair that was probably less comfortable than the bench but certainly newer. Maxim had them set up a few yards away, thanked the boys gravely, and they sat down.

"It's a very nice rig," Maxim said, "but you didn't really need to get into your Number Ones."

"Thank you, kind sir, but I didn't dress for you. I dressed for a meeting whose minutes will be classified Top Secret."

"Ah. Sorry."

"You were one of the main items on the meeting paper. Afterwards, George asked me to come down and see if I could talk some sense into you. From what I learned at the meeting I can't see why he thinks I'm up to such a task, but maybe *la bête a ses raisons que la belle ne connaît pas.* Do *you* think you can have some sense talked into you?"

Maxim frowned out at the cricket. "You can always try. What did he say?"

"Do you want it with or without the four-letter words? Let me warn you that without them, it's very short."

"I think I got most of those yesterday. Go on."

"Do you have any information – I imagine it would be in documentary form – concerning a certain East German politician?"

"What?" Maxim looked convincingly blank.

Agnes sighed. "I should have known it wouldn't be that simple." She took off her pastel jacket and hung it on the back of the chair. "Aren't you rather hot in that blouson?"

"I'm fine." But he did look a little overheated, so why didn't he at least unbutton it? Because he had a shoulder holster on underneath, of course. Having the hounds from Six on his trail had made him wary – perhaps especially so around his only child. But, she realised, there was a pleasant incongruity about watching *cricket*, of all things, next to a man with a concealed pistol.

"How much did your unwilling informant from Six tell you about Plainsong?"

"About which?"

"He didn't tell you much. Plainsong: that's their codename for the whole operation."

"All he told me was that he was working for the Sovbloc desk at Six, and they were looking for a deserter, but he didn't even have Blagg's name. He knew who I was, and that's about all. He wasn't likely to run Sherlock Holmes out of business."

"No . . ." She sat silent for a while, making a decision. "As I say, this is supposed to be Top Secret, but you'd better know if you're to be any help. You'd know anyway, if you'd got what they think you've got, whatever that is. Have you ever heard of Gustav Eismark?"

"New man in the East German Secretariat. Supposed to be a moderate, but has a lot of support from the not-very-political new managers and so on." Maxim *had* read that issue of *The Economist*.

"Correct." Agnes began to explain what little she had gleaned from the meeting. Maxim listened carefully, but with his eyes on the game. Untypically for his age, Chris preferred to play most of his shots to the off rather than drag everything round to leg. But the opposing school couldn't adjust to his rarity and left plenty of useful gaps in the offside field. So he made 32, including two perfect drives that stayed on the ground all the way to the boundary rope. Then, over-confident, he tried a late cut: there was a click, a squeal of joy, and first slip was doing a war-dance. Chris trailed back, dragging his bat in disgust, but loudly clapped by his team and the little group of parents around the scorer's shack in the corner of the field. In a prep school match, a score of 32 rates with a Test century.

When he had smiled uneasily through the congratulations, and taken off his pads, Chris came down to them. He looked at Agnes with cautious curiosity, and Maxim introduced them. "Miss Algar works for the Home Office and liaises with Number 10."

Chris shook her hand. He had the natural compactness of a good ball player and a Celtic paleness of skin and darkness of hair, with big golden-brown eyes that saw everything as wildly funny or desperately serious. His mother must have been a smasher, Agnes thought; he doesn't get those looks from our Harry. She glanced covertly at Maxim, who was watching Chris with his usual quiet self-protective smile.

She said: "A very good innings."

Chris shook his head. "I should never have got out like that."

"You know what they say in Yorkshire," Maxim offered. "Never make a late cut until September and then only on alternate Tuesdays."

"You've said that before, Daddy."

"I'll say it every time I see you contributing to the Slips' Benevolent Fund."

Chris looked back at Agnes. "Are you talking work?"

"Just a spot," Maxim said quickly. "We'll come over for tea." In front of the hut, several mothers were setting a trestle table with crockery and unwrapping polite little sandwiches.

Who said we'll go for tea? Agnes thought, briefly annoyed. Chris smiled at her and walked away.

When he was out of earshot, Maxim asked: "Did Six actually admit they were involved in that shooting in Germany?"

"Yes, but only on the grounds that it wasn't their fault. Even that surprised me until I found out afterwards that George had known about it all along; I suppose they didn't want to risk him bringing it up first. And of course the woman wasn't really one of theirs, just some distant freelance, and the back-up with her was some nutty amateur they'd had to use at the last moment –"

"D'you mean Blagg? Did he get mentioned?"

"Not by name, rank or number; I got him out of George afterwards, as well. They said he'd lost his head and started shooting –"

"Blagg? They're claiming he started it?"

"Oh yes. George said you'd got a different version."

"Damned right I have. I've read the German accounts of it all, too. Blagg isn't the type to go off at half cock –"

Agnes held up a placatory hand. "I know, he's SAS trained. But don't waste it on me in any case: I wouldn't believe Six even if they told me they were lying. So then Sir Bruce got hopping mad because nobody would tell him who they were talking about, and asked why they were so certain you were involved, and Six – it was that luminous dong Guy Husband and some new pin-up boy who runs the East German section – said they had their reasons and George could explain more.

George just sat there looking like a State Secret. And Sladen didn't know what was going on, either, but I don't think he wanted to; he was just scared that somebody would start throwing coffee cups and he'd get the blame. The FO chap knew all about it, of course, and any time things looked like coming off the boil he dived in and assured us this could be the biggest coup since the Zimmerman telegram. Oh, it was the merriest morning I've spent in a cow's age, and all the work of little you." She beamed happily at Maxim.

A batsman in the distant adult match clouted a ball that sailed right into the middle of the school pitch. There was a flurry of yelps and scurryings but nobody managed to field it and it rolled almost up to Maxim's feet. He collected and threw it back to the pursuing fielder with an easy gesture – then suddenly clutched at his left side. For a moment Agnes thought he must have pulled a muscle, then giggled as she, and she alone, realised he had come close to spilling his holstered pistol.

He sat down again. "So what in the end got decided?"

"Oh, nothing got *decided*, we just provisionally concurred with each other. Except Sir Bruce agreed Six could search your flat –"

Maxim sat up straight. "Did he buggery!"

"They'd have done it anyway. This way, he could send an officer along from the SIB to make sure they didn't nick your spoons. And George had to agree to go through your files at Number 10."

Maxim wondered why he wasn't more shocked at the instinctive distrust implied by that decision, and sighed as he realised it was because he'd been nearly six months in the atmosphere of Whitehall. "Does George – or Sir Bruce – want me back in London now?"

"At the moment, I think it would suit George just fine if you caught a slow boat to Yokohama. He told Husband he'd have to consult with the rest of the Private Office and maybe even the PM before he could agree to them interrogating you; he may actually be doing that, for all I know, though I think it's more likely he's been waiting for his temper to cool before he briefs you. He's had a rough week."

"Well, what's happened to Blagg, then?"

"They lost him, in Rotherhithe, the day they picked up you."

"They *lost* him?"

"They blame you for that, too. They'd already split their team to cover both the gym and some other place, and then split it again to follow you, so Blagg only got the leftovers, spotted them, and took to the hills."

Maxim chewed that over. "They said all that at the meeting?"

"All that except his name and the fact that he was a deserter. I suppose they were scared of what Sir Bruce might say. What *does* the Army do about deserters these days?"

"Gets very uptight and doesn't want to talk about them. We're an all-volunteer force now so you shouldn't have any reason to run away. Mostly it's woman trouble, though there's a few went to Sweden rather than Northern Ireland. Poor bastards." Perhaps they had adjusted to the sanitised neutralism of a Stockholm commune, but it seemed an odd life for men who had chosen to become soldiers.

The cricket stopped. The boys headed for the tea-table, not quite hurrying, with the two umpires strolling behind and a frigid few paces apart. Each a master from one of the schools, they had obviously totally disagreed on some decision.

"Good for Blagg," Maxim added thoughtfully. "Giving them the slip."

"He also did it without use of grievous bodily harm."

"I meant in spotting them at all. I hadn't thought he'd be all that bright at the bogeyman stuff."

"I don't suppose the team was exactly a thousand-candle-power. You spotted them as well." Agnes clearly wasn't going to take Maxim any more seriously as a spotter of fan clubs than she took Six as an organiser of them.

"So the position is," Maxim summed up, "that they assume the dead man, Hochhauser, had some document or other, they assume Blagg picked it up, and now they're assuming he gave it to me."

"Intelligence is mostly assumptions. Tea, however, is fact." Agnes stood up purposefully.

The tea was handed round by a posse of mothers who greeted Agnes in a friendly but appraising way which infuriated her. She knew she was overdressed for the occasion but hadn't realised it would make her look both predatory and incompetently so, since one of the main adult sports at Chris's school was trying to get that nice Major Maxim remarried. That, and trying to recruit him to the Parents' Association committee (which was almost the same thing, as the most active women members were divorcees).

"We only meet about three times a term," one drastically lean lady was telling him; "and the dates are always fixed *well* in advance so all you have to do is *arrange* to be free on that evening."

"The trouble with my job at the moment is that I can't guarantee to be free at any given time."

"Surely it's just a matter of *arrangement*. My brother works for the Department of Health and he can always *arrange* to get away if he knows the date far enough in advance."

"My job just isn't that predictable."

"My brother is very *high* in the Department of Health," she said warningly.

"That's just the trouble," Agnes chipped in. "When you're more junior your life simply isn't your own. If somebody sends you off to – say – Acton or Rotherhithe, you don't have a choice. You just have to go."

"Acton? *Rother*hithe?" The lady looked mystified. "Who'd want to go to those places?"

"Nobody in his right mind," Agnes agreed. "They were just random examples. But I do know the difficulty the Major has in getting away to do his own things. It can be very frustrating."

She could feel Maxim's steady glare.

"Well," the lean lady said, "I still feel that something could be *arranged*. My brother has always found the civil service *most* accommodating . . ." She drifted away, trailing aromatic dissatisfaction.

"Thank you," Maxim said in a sort of growl.

"Any time."

Chris appeared with a handful of rather sweaty egg-and-cress sandwiches and a smaller boy who wore spectacles and had a problem. Chris explained: "James here is our scorer and Mr Marshall signalled four wides when there was a wide and the ball went to the boundary, but the other side's scorer says you can't have *four* wides at once, only one, and the other three must count as byes. What do you say, Daddy?"

Maxim was still wondering what to say when Agnes said: "Certainly you can have four wides off one ball. Look it up. 'All runs that are from a "Wide Ball" shall be scored "Wide Balls", or if no runs be made one run shall be scored.' It doesn't mention the boundary, but it must be implicit. It's Rule 29, isn't it?"

James dropped his pen, adjusted his spectacles and fumbled through the back of the score-book. "Gosh, yes, 29: 'The ball does not become "Dead" on the call of "Wide Ball"' . . . Do you know all the rules by heart?"

"Most of them, yes." The two boys gazed at her with such blazing admiration that she came close to blushing. "When I was your age I spent almost every summer weekend scoring for my father's village team. And pouring jugs of beer and passing bowls of pickles at the 'tea' intervals."

"It must be very useful," James said with utter sincerity, "to know all the rules of cricket by heart."

"Not quite as much as it used to be. I don't do much scoring nowadays."

"Don't you?" Maxim asked.

"We don't get pickles," Chris said, staring at his crumpled handful of sandwich. "Have you finished talking work?"

Maxim and Agnes looked at each other. "Not quite," she said in a small serious voice.

"Are you in a rush to get back?" Maxim asked.

"No-o. I'm just the messenger. I'll have to ring George and my office anyway . . ."

"Why don't you stay on and have dinner with us? – at my parents' place?"

There were a lot of reasons why she didn't want to get involved in Maxim's domestic life, particularly when he seemed to be intent on jumping from the tenth storey of his career structure – but in the end, why not? Curiosity was one of her best-developed talents.

"You're sure it'll be all right?" She glanced quickly at Chris, but he was grinning broadly.

"My mother keeps an open-house policy. Chris is always bringing somebody home."

"Then I'd love to. I'll go and ring George now. The message is, you don't know nuffin' – right?"

"I could ring a couple of people, or go and see them, about trying to find you-know-who, but . . ." He shrugged.

"I don't think George wants you doing any more on your own initiative."

"Then he can bloody well tell me so himself."

"I was under the impression that he had." She grinned suddenly. Her smiles were light, acted expressions, but her grin was wide and uninhibited. "But I'll pass the thought on." She picked up her jacket and handbag and headed for the distant clubhouse. Behind, she heard another parent swoop on Maxim. "Oh, Major, did you get the message about our little wine and cheese party for . . ."

Chapter 11

Corporal Blagg had spent his childhood – those parts of it the local authority hadn't been able to control – in the courts, alleyways and concrete 'gardens' of Rotherhithe's blocks of flats. He had learned to fight there, to ride there, to play football there, and at last how to get his hand inside Betty Tanner's jeans there. He knew those courts and gardens, not just as places and secret short cuts, but as a whole pattern of life and behaviour. And he knew immediately that the two men walking towards him didn't belong, were wrong. They couldn't have been more wrong if they'd worn Father Christmas suits.

But they'd seen him the moment he saw them, so he kept on walking towards them. They might not know him by sight, or might not be looking for him at all. They weren't police; one of them had a rather foreign look. He put his hand casually into his jacket and touched the butt of the Spanish copy of the Colt .38. They were about five yards apart and he was just deciding they weren't anything to do with him when they both took out pistols.

He shot one twice, in the middle, and he collapsed against the other, blocking Blagg's aim. The second man brought up his gun and fired from the cover of his wounded companion. Blagg tried for a head shot and missed, felt a punch in the chest that made his knees fold, but he fired again and saw the pistol fall loose. Then the man was running, and Blagg could have shot him in the back but he had only one round left.

The first man lay there, moaning. Blagg started to run, too, in the other direction. He moved fast and confidently, but when he had gone only three hundred yards he began to feel breathless, long before he should have done, and realised what

97

that one shot might have done. He started desperately to think of a place to hide.

Something in the sea air must act as a mind-blowing drug on English architects, Agnes decided. Mining towns, garrison towns, purpose-built New Towns – all those were fairly hideous in their own ways, but they offered no contest to the English seaside. There, an impregnable first line of defence against any invader with visual taste, stood hundreds of miles of small houses that could have been assembled by retarded monkeys dipping randomly into a box of building styles.

The little semi-det that Maxim's parents had bought when they retired to the outskirts of Littlehampton sported a Georgian bow window, timber cladding above the garage – which had a metal door – and tile-hung patches around the first-floor windows, whose balconies were just big enough for a seagull to stand on. And that was restrained compared with the green pantiles, Spanish ironwork, Provençal shutters and stained-glass leaded windows spattered along the rest of the road.

Or maybe they just didn't have architects within three miles of the sea. Maybe it was all done by builders' baby daughters: "Draw Daddy a nice house and Daddy will build it."

Maxim's mother was a cheerful, bustling little woman; his father wore a moustache, smoked a pipe and said very little but, Agnes guessed, listened a lot. She learned that Maxim had an elder sister – oddly, she'd always assumed he must have been the first child – who had married a Quaker schoolmaster and lived up North, had three children and didn't work, "Except at disapproving of the Army," Maxim added. They were just finishing the apple pie when the phone rang.

Everybody looked at Maxim. Probably his parents didn't get more than half a dozen calls a week, Agnes realised.

Maxim answered it, then said: "Speaking," and mouthed to Agnes: "It's the Fun Palace," and took the phone into the hallway, out of hearing. Nobody else said anything, and Agnes suddenly saw that Chris was pale and rigid with apprehension as he sensed his weekend turning lonely. But his face said nothing; a soldier's face. You poor little bugger, she thought.

Maxim came back and beckoned Agnes out. They stood just outside the front door.

"A gun battle in Rotherhithe. One badly wounded, police looking for two more, at least one of them thought to be wounded. As much as anything, I think George was just wanting to make sure I was still here."

"I'll give you an alibi. What do you think it is?"

"The same as George thinks it is. I don't know how often Rotherhithe goes in for gunfights, but this could be one of ours."

Agnes nodded gloomily. "It's a bit late for bank hold-ups and a bit early for night-club ructions."

"I'd better get back."

"Can you give me a lift?"

She let him go in alone to break the news to Chris. Across the street a lace curtain twitched. The neighbours would be interested in whom that nice Major Maxim was talking to on the doorstep, too.

After driving in silence for ten minutes, Maxim said suddenly: "I was a bloody fool. Blagg told me he'd thrown away the revolver that woman gave him. Soldiers *don't* throw away guns. They join the Army to *get* guns, and they're always in trouble for possessing one illegally or swiping a few rounds of ammunition. It's crooks who throw away guns. I've been thinking like a crook."

"Six months at Number 10 would do that to anybody." Agnes sympathised. "Are you a gun nut as well?"

"You can't be a soldier – not an infantryman, anyway – without liking weapons. And liking some more than others. It's like a pilot having opinions about aeroplanes, nobody thinks that's odd. Don't you get any firearms training in your mob?"

"Oh, we're supposed to know something about handguns, and fire off a few rounds every so often. I usually manage to dodge that. I've only had to carry a pistol once, just a few hours. And I've never used one."

Maxim nodded. They had passed through Arundel and were coming over the ridge at Whiteways Lodge roundabout, heading for Petworth and then the A3 at Milford. It was far the best route into London from the South. He was driving fast but safely and, Agnes noted, not as well as she could have done. Still, she had the training and he didn't. Being able to handle a car was for her far more important than playing Annie Get Your Gun.

"If it is your wandering corporal in hospital, what were you planning?" she asked.

"Oh, I wasn't thinking it would be him."

"Really?" Without glancing at her, he knew she had her eyebrows at full stretch.

"I'd back Blagg at any fun and games of that sort. He could be hurt, but he wouldn't be the one left behind."

"I forgot, he's one of your Hereford Superstars. But even so –"

"I assume whoever-it-was wanted to capture him, not kill him. If they'd got him badly wounded, they'd have taken him away, wouldn't they?"

"Much in what you say," she agreed reluctantly. "So do you have any ideas where Blagg could be?"

"None. I'll just have to go looking."

"Of course. I suppose that would be the one way to make things worse. I should have had more faith in you."

This time Maxim did glance at her; she was staring straight ahead, nodding gently to herself.

"What do you mean?"

"Harry, do you have any conception of the strife you have caused so far?"

"By thumping those two gits from Six?"

"Not just that. If that were all, I'd applaud it as a wise and public-spirited action and I hope it starts a trend. But it was very far from all, wasn't it? Until you came along, Century House was right out on a limb. One of their sections had gone hog barmy and set up an operation that turned into a shoot-out in a friendly country with an apparently innocent citizen getting killed. They'd followed that up by mounting a major surveillance job in London without clearing it with us or the Co-ordinator or anybody. Their private parts were firmly jammed in the wringer and all it needed was for somebody to give the handle a slight nudge . . . So then you came galloping to the rescue. You concealed knowledge of a deserter, you actually helped him stay deserted, and *They* can make out a case for saying you still are. You messed up their surveillance, you beat up their agents, you went in for *exactly* the same unauthorised adventurism as they had – and so let them off the hook. Now if they pull it off everybody'll heave a sigh of relief and their methods will be forgiven, and if they *don't* then it'll all be Number 10's fault and that would probably suit their book just as much as coming good on Plainsong itself."

Maxim took a deep breath and said reluctantly: "I suppose . . . I do see most of what you say. I just thought Blagg was getting a raw deal. And now it seems they're loading the whole blame for Germany on him, and he's only a corporal and the Army's his whole –"

"Forget Corporal Blagg!" Agnes shouted. "Forget *all* the bloody corporals in *all* the bloody Army! Just get it through your tiny 1914-pattern mind that you have started a constitutional crisis! Have you *got* that, or should I send it in cipher?"

There was nothing to cause an echo in the car, already full of engine and wind noise, so it was probably only in their minds that her voice seemed to fade in throbbing waves, as across a vast canyon. Both of them were rather shaken; Maxim slowed abruptly and sat up straighter in the seat.

"I haven't lost my temper with anybody in years." Agnes was speaking through teeth clenched against any further emotion, and fumbling in her handbag. "In my job you're not supposed to. Does that dashboard lighter work?"

"I think so. I didn't know you smoked."

"I don't often. I want to now." She rammed the lighter knob viciously, and lit her cigarette with trembling fingers. "I understand you also told George that you had a rehearsal in Rotherhithe the night before you tried to reform the Intelligence Service by *force majeure*. What was the score there? – one busted arm, one ruptured spleen. Had you thought about how *that* might look in the public prints? Thank God Husband doesn't know about that, not yet, anyway." Her voice was small and hurried. "Stop at the next phone box, would you?"

They drove in total silence for five minutes until they found one.

Agnes got back into the car shaking her head. "Nothing new, but I've asked our people to bend an ear that way." She lit another cigarette, but now her hands were steady; Maxim drove off, changing gears very precisely.

There was still perhaps three-quarters of an hour of daylight left, but the sun was just glimpses of coppery gold between vast castles of cloud stacking up on the horizon. It was only the breeze when the car was moving that made the warm air breathable. Agnes watched the clouds, the incredible impermanent detail of the cumulo-nimbus that had fascinated all the English landscape – and seascape – artists.

"I don't get out of London enough," she said. "You have to get out to see what the job's really about. London doesn't give you enough reasons."

"Were you country?"

"Worcestershire. My father kept a small flat in London and commuted for the week. It made it a weekend marriage, but it seemed to work. I remember loving Friday nights, when he came home . . . I suppose that's usually your set-up, too."

"Usually." But this Friday he was driving *back* to London. "What would you be doing now if you hadn't come down?"

"Cooking."

"Sorry. Did I get your evening wrecked?"

"No, it was only going to be me and Mozart. If I can get three or four dishes into the freezer I can do a dinner party without worrying about being home in time to cook." Realising she'd never invited him, she moved the topic on quickly. "Do you cook?"

"I'm learning."

"Don't they teach you cooking in the Army?"

"A bit, but it mostly seems to be with rats and hedgehogs and seaweed."

"You're joking."

"No. The only cookery I got taught was survival training in the SAS."

"Lord. Do you get used to it?"

"I hope I never know." He took a deep breath. "You mentioned a constitutional crisis. Did you mean that?"

Agnes threw the last of her cigarette out of the window. "So much for preserving the beauty of the countryside . . . I don't think you quite realise how much money's being bet on Plainsong. If they can really get a hook into this Eismark, a member of the Secretariat and likely to be there for years, it'll be quite a coup in its very quiet way. Something the West Germans or Uncle's boys or the French couldn't do. For once there could be enough credit for everybody who wants it. Scott-Scobie, he's one of the most ambitious young men at the Forbidden City. I don't know what he wants, it could be the Permanent Under-Secretary's Department, it might be the next Director-General of Six . . . And Guy Husband, he's new to the Sovbloc desk; if he pulls this off in his first few months, he could become a living legend."

"Does he want to be one?"

"Oh yes. It's their top word. What else can they want if they're in these behind-the-arras jobs? They're never going to get rich or famous, but they love thinking they'll one day be legendary to Those Who Really Know. As for Dieter Sims, I don't know much about him except that he's been building up the East German unit under Husband's wing. Maybe he'll have to be content with merely doing all the work, but there's compensations in being indispensable, too."

She looked at the few cigarettes left in her pack and then impulsively threw them all out of the window. "The hell with the countryside . . . The whole of what's usually called the Intelligence Community's feeling a bit frisky at the moment. I imagine you've noticed that our dear Prime Minister doesn't exactly go a bundle on us, on any of us?"

"That was why he invented my job, wasn't it?" An all-too-nearly-public scandal caused, that time, by Agnes's service had prompted the PM to appoint an Army officer to Number 10, although it hadn't prompted him to decide exactly what Maxim should do once there.

"That's right. He's always been paranoid about intelligence, seeing plots and hidden microphones and leaks to the media . . . he kept the money tight, too. Now it seems he won't be with us for ever. He's not a well man."

"Did George say that?"

Agnes thought long enough for Maxim to glance at her, making sure she'd heard. "No-o, not in so many words. But we have sources of our own. We're supposed to know what goes on in this country, and the PM's health is a national asset, so . . . But he isn't responding to treatment."

"I thought it was just bronchitis."

"By now it's pneumonia. It's probably only that old quack Hardacre feeding him the wrong antibiotics –" Agnes shared George's view of Sir Frank "– but if each course takes five days before they decide it isn't working, it can run on. He's over sixty and he's had chest trouble before. And every day he spends in bed wastes away a little more of his authority: Parliament doesn't like sick leaders, it casts them out to die on the cold, cold slopes of the House of Lords. Quite right too, of course. But that makes now a good time for a little discreet character assassination, suggest the old boy can't even control his own Private Office. That's you."

"They're using me to try and bring him down?"

"They're using anything they can find. Yes, they're using you."

Maxim was silent for a while. "And there's nothing I can do about it."

"You could give up consorting with deserters and street fighting in all its forms . . . I realise it'll be tough, trying to cut it down, but just say to yourself –"

"None of this was *planned*, was it?"

"Oh Lordy me, no. You leave the conspiracy theory of history to the professors, and keep your eye on the opportunists. A sense of timing's always been more important than mere dishonesty."

They were on the choppy, wavelike hills before Milford, a narrow road with too much Friday evening traffic heading south, against them, for Maxim to risk trying to overtake an elderly truck in front. He resigned himself and let the car drift back to a comfortable fifty-yard gap. A fat Jaguar promptly swerved past him, closed up on the truck and started weaving in and out, forced back every time.

"Everybody's a contender," Maxim said, so softly that Agnes had to think for a moment to be sure what she'd heard.

"Aren't you?" she asked sharply. "Don't you want to run the Army? Or even a battalion?"

"I think I did once," Maxim said slowly. "But now . . . now I just don't know . . ."

Agnes let it go at that. He might go on to talking about his dead wife, Jenny, and she didn't want to hear about her. She wanted to know, she just didn't want to hear.

Chapter 12

During the week – and weekends when he was the duty Private Secretary – George and his wife Annette lived in the family set of rooms in Albany, just a few quiet yards from the snarling traffic of Piccadilly. The porter was expecting them and let Maxim park in an awkward position on the forecourt pavement.

It was dark now, but warmer than when they had left the coast nearly two hours before, and the air tasted like something breathed through a hot towel. The weather was going to break, and noisily.

As they walked through the lamplight of the Ropewalk, Maxim noticed a small incised plaque to Lord Macaulay, who had lived there in the 1840s.

"That's the bastard who loused up my promotion chances."

"What?" Agnes stopped and peered.

"He once wrote: 'Nothing is so useless as a general maxim.'"

She chuckled. "Did you run across that yourself?"

"Oh no. There've always been plenty of kindly brother officers to bring it to my attention. We're a very well-read Army these days."

George's rooms were on the first floor; they had the traditional stolidity of a steak and kidney pie and were much the same colour. Annette had never dared touch the dark panelling that George's family had put in eighty years before, nor even most of the ponderous mahogany furniture and the lovingly detailed pictures of dead hares and partridges surrounded by dewy vegetables. She had counter-attacked with bright lampshades and curtains, but she hadn't won.

Agnes knew the room and went straight for the telephone. George was sitting at one end of a vast empty dining table, with a little oasis of bottles, coffee pot and cheeseboard at his elbow.

"Ah," he greeted Maxim; "do I see you refreshed by two days of country air? Revived? Refulgent? More to the point, do I see you *repentant*? Your lad's really done it this time. Port or brandy?"

"Just coffee, please. Who got shot?"

"The man in hospital hasn't been named, but he isn't your Corporal. It happened around seven o'clock, at a place called Neptune Court. Do you know it? No? I thought you knew Rotherhithe like your own back garden."

"I don't have a back garden."

"Neither does Neptune Court. It's a block of council flats, probably one of those redbrick Edwardian things, with a court in the middle and a service road down the back. Front doors open onto long balconies with iron railings covered in damp washing and snotty little kids dribbling on your head through the bars."

Maxim grinned, surprised less by George's attitude than by his knowledge of such parts of London. They were certainly Rotherhithe blocks he was describing; Maxim had seen them.

"It happened in the service road. Five or six shots. Neighbours saw one man drive away and it looked as if he was hurt. Another one running in the opposite direction."

"Running?"

"They said so, but from the blood marks the fuzz think he could be wounded."

"What about the guns?"

"I do not *know* about the guns, Harry. I can't be ringing up Rotherhithe nick asking for details. That would just establish the very connection I'm hoping – despite your assistance – to avoid. All I'm giving you is from the radio and the PA tape. But six shots and a man in intensive care," he added, "makes it reasonably certain that some friend of yours was involved."

Agnes came over and George handed her a gin and tonic. "Thanks. Our people have been in touch with the police, just checking to see if there could be a terrorist element. That would be quite normal. They've got the one in hospital down as Hans-Heinz Lemke, but they aren't entirely convinced.

They're checking him out. He's about thirty-five, dark, five foot eleven, eleven and a half stone. Shoes made in Germany – West."

"Did they say anything about the guns?" Maxim asked. George gave a heavy sigh.

"There were two left at the scene." She glanced at a piece of paper. "A Sauer of 7.65 millimetre calibre and a Walther of short 9 millimetre or .380. Is that right?"

Maxim nodded.

"The Sauer had been fired, probably twice. The other one wasn't fired. And they've picked a .38 Special out of Lemke's liver."

"That could be Blagg," Maxim said. "It was a .38 Special he had at Bad Schwarzendorn."

"Oh hooray," George said mournfully.

A vivid light flared outside, bright enough to penetrate the heavy curtains. Everybody waited, but when the tearing bang of thunder came it was still loud enough to make Agnes jump. She didn't like thunder; it was over-dramatic and showy, like tropical plants.

Maxim finished his coffee. "I'd better get going."

Agnes waited for George, but when he stayed quiet, she said: "Harry, Neptune Court and its purlieus will be absolutely *crawling* with cops. This is the sort of thing they really go to town on: an armed man, probably wounded, probably hiding out nearby. They'll *smother* that place."

"I know."

She was about to ask *How* do you know? and then remembered his tours in Northern Ireland. She looked at George, but he was just pouring himself another glass of port.

"Will you be here?" Maxim asked.

"For a while – if George doesn't mind."

"Be my guest."

When Maxim had gone, Agnes said: "You didn't even *try* to talk him out of it."

George nuzzled his nose into a glass of port. "You haven't been in the Army."

"I'm glad you've noticed."

"There's a wounded soldier out there, or he thinks there is. I couldn't have stopped him with an anti-tank gun. It's the most common form of heroism, risking your life to rescue one of your men. The fact that he's only risking his career – and mine, and the government's – doesn't really make any difference. Not to him, anyway." He gulped his port.

Agnes looked disapprovingly at George's glass. "You're going to have to watch that stuff. We could be in for a long night."

"Why does everybody tell me I ought to watch my drinking when they're all so busy watching it for me? *Some*body in Whitehall has to be looking at something else, and it might as well be me."

"Cheer up. Blagg may be dead."

"With our luck, he's probably shot a couple of coppers as well by now." He reached for the decanter. Beyond the curtains, the rain came down with a sudden clatter on the roof of the Ropewalk below.

The pain wasn't so bad, it was the breathlessness, using all his energy to suck another few seconds of life from a chest that seemed to be wrapped in rusty iron bands. He knew he had a hole in one lung, leaking air and blood that put pressure on the other lung. They had taught him that much in the Army. They had also taught him that the first thing to do with a wounded man was clear his breathing. But how did you do it yourself, and clear something deep in your chest? And by now he was far too weak to move, even to sit up. Unless somebody found him soon . . .

Until then, the only thing to do was endure. Endurance is a soldier's job. A few may turn out to be heroes as well, but a few is all you need; for the rest, what matters is biting down and holding on. The Army had taught him that, too, and the SAS acceptance tests had rammed the lesson home by sending him out over the damp Brecon Beacons with a 55-lb Bergen rucksack knowing he had to cover a certain distance in a certain time but not knowing that when he had done it, there wouldn't be the trucks they had promised but a vague assurance of a cup of tea if he kept on marching a few more miles in *that* direction. That was the real test, what they called the 'sickener' factor.

"*Fuck* you lot," Blagg had snarled at the officer in charge, and set out to march to the end of the world. Now, it seemed he was almost there.

His senses were fading as his whole existence concentrated on taking in the next breath. He had long since stopped noticing the foul smell inside the little concrete box, or the damp grittiness of the floor against his cheek, and he heard only distantly the rolling crash of thunder. But a few minutes later he heard the rattle of heavy rain on the loose corrugated iron sheet hiding the way in, felt the first trickle of water crawling down the floor, and then remembered how long this place took to drain.

He realised that he was quite likely going to drown. For the first time, the first time in his life, he was horribly and totally afraid.

The rain was smashing itself into a two-foot-high mist above the roadway as Maxim pulled up outside Billy Dann's house. It was semi-detached and mock Tudor, in a quiet suburban street lined with acacia trees and unbroken street lamps. In his slow crawl from the corner as he peered for the right number through the flooding windscreen, it had seemed an odd neighbourhood for the Fight Game: well-weeded drives, well-painted houses, the cars as recommended by *Which?* and Ratepayers' Association posters in several windows. Maybe he was just wrong about the Fight Game.

Perhaps there had been a hint of the rain slackening; anyway, it did in the minute he waited in the car. He wrapped a short raincoat around himself and ran up the front path.

Dann opened the door himself, looking warm and sticky in a pink short-sleeved shirt and bright green slacks. Maxim hadn't been entirely wrong about the Fight Game.

"Bloody hell," Dann said, "it's you again. Don't they teach you in the Army how to use the telephone?"

"I just wanted a private word. Are you alone?"

"Well, right now, yes, but the wife's —"

"Hop in my car. We'll drive around a bit."

Dann stared. "Are you totally *barmy*? I mean you had noticed there's a hurricane going on out here?"

Feeling rather like a flasher, Maxim opened his raincoat to show the revolver pointing vaguely at Dann's crotch. "I'll explain in the car."

Dann went wide-eyed and said: "Fucking arseholes," in a reverential sort of voice. Maxim reached around him to pull the front door shut and ushered him down to the car. In the movies they always seemed to make the kidnapped party drive, but Maxim thought about Dann driving his – Maxim's – car into the first acacia while he watched the gun, which seemed to have hypnotised him. It was safer and cheaper to drive one-handed, letting the car steer itself when he changed gear. Why didn't kidnappers choose automatic gearboxes?

When he had turned two corners and gone about a quarter of a mile, he gave Dann the pistol. "Sorry about that: I just wanted to get you out of the house. Be careful with it, it's loaded."

Dann turned the gun in his hands, still staring at it in the passing flares of street lighting.

Maxim went on: "I'm pretty sure your phone's tapped, your house could be wired, and somebody'll be watching it. Are you *listening*?"

Dann woke up and handed the gun back. "Here, you take the bloody thing, I don't know anything about guns . . . Did you mean all that? Why?"

"Oh yes." Maxim tucked the gun away. "Did you hear the news tonight?"

"No, I only listen to the sport. I've got no time for –"

"There's been a shooting in Rotherhithe."

Dann hesitated, then asked: "You mean Ron?"

"It's not him in hospital. But he could be on the run. He could be wounded." He let the car drift to the kerb and stopped with the lights off, watching the rear-view and wing mirrors.

"Where did he get a gun?" Dann asked.

"If it is him, he had it all along. Now: do you have any idea where he might have gone?"

"He might've gone to the gym –"

"I doubt it. That was being watched when I was there. They picked him up there but he shook them off."

"Look, who are these buggers? Did you say they'd got my phone tapped?"

"I said probably. They're Our Side, the Good Guys. Not the police, the ones you're not supposed to talk about. Our Ronnie's mixed up in more things than he knows about."

Dann's outrage was mounting. "Isn't there any bleeding law in this country any more?"

"Yes. There's the one that says you can get up to two years for 'incitement to disaffection'. Hiding a deserter, that means."

"Then what about *you*, Major?"

"Oh, I'm not threatening anybody. I'm so far up the creek myself that when they throw the book at me it'll be the whole library. The point is, we're neither of us in a position to complain. Now – anywhere you can think of? Could he have gone to Dave Tanner?"

"He might have done, if there was nowhere else," Dann said grudgingly.

"Where does he live, d'you know?"

"Place called Neptune Court."

"Damn!" Maxim slammed the steering wheel with both hands, nearly hard enough to break it, certainly hard enough to make both palms sting. "The shooting was there. He must have been hiding out with Tanner, or gone round to scrounge a meal."

Why, he thought, why couldn't Blagg have gone out of town, to some place he knew, like Hereford or . . . Of course not. The only other places somebody who'd joined the Army at sixteen would know were Army places. And as a deserter those were just where he daren't go.

"Anywhere else, at all?" His voice sounded tired and defeated, even to himself.

"We could just drive around Rotherhithe," Dann suggested without enthusiasm.

"A couple of hundred police have already had that idea. I came through and it was blue lights from wall to wall . . . We'd better ask Tanner."

"Hold on. If you said the cops are all over, they'll be all over Dave Tanner."

Maxim switched on the car lights. "Not necessarily. I don't think they know it's Blagg they're looking for, and if they don't know that, they won't know about Tanner. They probably talked to him already, they'd have talked to everybody in that block, just asking if they saw or heard anything. Routine."

A fresh gust of rain bounced off the bonnet as he pulled away from the kerb.

The police had stationed their Major Incident Vehicle, a glorified caravan with radio aerials, temporary telephone lines and a flashing blue light on a small mast, in a small crescent at the end of Neptune Court. There were several other police vehicles parked around, and a small group of men working under floodlights and umbrellas at the back of the court itself, but that was all. If you're trying to catch somebody immediately after a crime, you grab every man you can and smother the area. But after two or three hours and nil results, you have to accept that the trail is cold and you can't justify that level of manpower. Out there on the unpoliced streets beyond the floodlights, other people are getting stabbed, mugged, raped, burgled, sometimes even just run over. A death by gunshot is only one item on the programme of a Friday night. And with luck, it could turn out to be a bit of gang warfare which nobody is – unofficially, of course – going to bust a gut trying to solve.

Maxim drove past and parked a little further on, and Dann said suddenly: "What am I doing here?"

"You can wait in the car."

Dann changed his mind back. "No-o. The kid knows me. I'll come in." It was quite likely that, after Wednesday night, Tanner wouldn't want to be alone with Maxim.

Tanner was distinctly unhappy to see Maxim again. He lived with his wife, a thin and rather nervous girl with ragged blonde hair, in a second-floor flat that belonged to her widowed mother. The rooms were small, warm and smelt damp, filled with brightly varnished furniture that looked well made but nevertheless home-made. A motorcycle jacket and a vivid red helmet lay on one end of the small dining table.

After a couple of minutes' polite talk and the offer of a cup of tea, Mrs Tanner went away to talk to mother.

"We're looking for Blagg," Maxim said abruptly.

Tanner swallowed and nodded. He had seemed pale and jittery ever since they had come in.

"It's for his own good," Dann put in. "The Major thinks he could be hurt."

Tanner nodded again. "Yes. The coppers said he – who-ever it was – could be."

"They don't know it's him?" Maxim asked.

"No, they didn't seem to."

"But he was staying here?"

"Yes. He come round last night. Said could he sleep on the sofa a couple've nights. I mean, he's an old mate. I didn't think anythink like this was going to happen." He shuddered. "I mean, what could happen to me?"

"Nothing, if we reach him first. Now –"

"I mean he's left his gear here, hasn't he? That's his bag in the corner, innit? And the cops standing there asking me if I knew anything and all the time it's his gear they're looking at. I mean –"

"I'll take it away," Maxim soothed him. "Now, any idea where he might go?"

Tanner thought for a moment and shook his head.

"*Think*. We're assuming he's wounded and had to hide nearby. When you're hurt, you regress. I mean, you want to run home to mother. Okay, so he hasn't got a mother. But he might go back to some part of his childhood."

"I don't see him going back to the Council," Dann said banteringly. Maxim shot him a furious look.

"He might not be hurt," Tanner temporised.

"If he's not, he's probably in Norwich by now and still running. But we have to look at the worst possible case. Is there anywhere round here?"

There was a long silence. Then Tanner said slowly: "We had this sort've a gang, once. Just when we was kids. I mean, we had this sort of hideout, meeting place. It was an old air-raid shelter, I think. Only they'd blocked up the way in, like, and you could only get in through . . . I dunno, maybe it was some sort of ventilation thing. If you kept that covered up, most people didn't even know it was there."

"Show us."

Chapter 13

George had switched to drinking coffee laced with cognac – "The complete cycle, the disease and the cure in one simple package," and Agnes had muttered something about vitamin C and gone across the big room to play a Mozart piano concerto on the stereo. She felt drained. It had been a long day at the end of a busy week, but that wasn't all of it. At dinner in Littlehampton she had acted perfectly, had been friendly but not familiar, always cheerful, talking enough but not too much – but always *acting*. There were so few homes where she could relax and, without talking about the hidden things, not be consciously hiding them. It was that, the holding of your thoughts like holding your breath, that broke so many of them in their forties. She had seen it far too often: the self-inflicted divorces, the ones you had to talk to before lunch because the rest of their day was an alcoholic marsh, those shunted to a not-too-responsible job in the Registry or an early pension – Peace hath its victims no less renowned than war. I have perhaps ten more years. Will it all have been worth it?

Suddenly Mozart seemed too busy and clever, and she started sorting in the cupboard under the turntable until she found a record of *Papillons*, and lay back surrounded by Schumann's fluttering primary colours.

George looked around. "If I'm not to be allowed Mozart, why not somebody with an appropriate gloom quotient like Mahler? What are we doing back in the nursery?"

"I suppose it was that meeting. You remember Sladen talking about Wilhelmina Linnarz, the pianist defector? I'd been wondering what made me think of Schumann."

He grunted. "You're regressing, young Algar . . . There must be a file on that woman."

"I'll dig it out tomorrow. *Late* tomorrow."

"Why the hell hasn't Harry rung in?"

"He's probably been arrested."

George glared and said provocatively: "How did you get on with him today? He likes piano music too, I recall."

"Count Basie."

"Pure race prejudice."

Agnes closed her eyes. "George, you're not going to get me as bad-tempered as you are."

"*Me?* Balls!"

But I wonder if Harry has ever listened to Schumann? she thought. And maybe I should try that Basie trio he was going on about. Maybe we . . . Maybe *we* nothing, she told herself angrily. You stay *away* from that man; he is *bad news*. Of all the people you do not want to get mixed up with he is the first and the last. Losing your temper with him was *unforgivable*.

The phone rang and her heart gave a jerk. She got up quickly, since she was nearest.

"If it's Harry," George called, "and he's got any *good* news, just throw a fit and I'll get the general idea."

Agnes said: "Speaking," and listened for a minute, then put the phone down. "The one in hospital: dead."

The dock was fenced off, but not the way it had been as a real dock, with real cargoes to steal. This one was bodged together from old planks and doors from wrecked houses, intended as little more than a defence in court for the demolition company when some child got through and broke his neck amongst the rubble. There were several places kids obviously did get through; Maxim widened one by yanking loose another plank and ducked in. The other two followed, Dann reluctantly. He was wearing Maxim's car coat over his thin shirt, but his shoes were still canvas and the ground beyond the fence was a mudpond laced with sharp lumps of concrete and old iron-work. Maxim had a torch which he used very cautiously, but at least they didn't have to whisper in the steady drone of rain.

"'Ell," Tanner said, looking around. "It all looks sort of different, now."

Indeed it did, to anybody who remembered or could visual-ise it as a busy dock. Level, as all docks must be, it was a soggy wasteland stretching to the edge of the river. Cranes, ware-houses, offices – all had been stripped away, leaving just a small site office and an abandoned bulldozer outlined against the damp glow on the far bank.

"I think it was over here . . ." They followed him. He stooped a couple of times to shift a sheet of corrugated iron or warped plasterboard, but didn't find anything.

He straightened up, shaking his head and wiping rain out of his eyes. "I just dunno. I mean, they could've filled it in. I mean . . ."

Maxim looked around. There were no flashing blue lights – the police would have walked over this ground, but hours ago – and they were well away from any inhabited buildings.

"Blagg!" he shouted. "Corporal Blagg!"

They listened but heard only the steady rain.

"Blagg!"

He had just taken breath to shout again when there was a muffled bang.

"It came from there," Tanner said.

"Over there." Dann suggested another direction.

Maxim wasn't sure himself, but he was sure he had a lot more experience than they in locating the origins of gunshots. He stumbled away in the direction of his own idea; they followed.

When they found him, the water had just reached his nostrils.

Maxim lifted him very gently to a sitting position. The dragging breath and the bullet holes at front and back gave him an easy diagnosis. Thank God there were two, and not too low down. Blagg had tried a brief smile when Maxim flashed the torch on himself for identification, but didn't speak. The Spanish pistol was still clutched in his right hand; Maxim took it away and dropped it in his own pocket.

It took all three of them to lift him out of the reeking waterlogged shelter through an opening just big enough for one of them at a time. It was easy to see why the police would have missed it: from outside, it was just a concrete hardstand, perhaps the foundation for an old shed, and the opening led through a shallow pit that was usually jammed with rubbish and covered by a corrugated iron sheet. But at last, panting steam, they had Blagg propped almost upright in the rain.

"Fireman's chair," Maxim said. "Grip your own wrist, then mine, under his arse." But Dann knew all about that. Tanner was half his age, but Maxim turned instinctively to the trainer for important work. "Dave, you support his back. *Don't* let his head fall forward."

They staggered and slithered the hundred yards or miles to the fence, sweating into clothes already soaked, swearing breathlessly. So now Maxim had to bring the car up. It would have been suspiciously obvious parked near nothing but a gap in the fence, so he had left it by the nearest flats. The three of them stayed just inside the fence while he went for it. By now the rain was easing.

There was just a few yards' walk to the main road, a careful look around, then across it, instinctively choosing the potential cover of a derelict warehouse on that side rather than the dockyard fence on this. Walk a hundred yards, then turn down a side street. He had almost reached that turn when a police car came around another corner three hundred yards ahead.

They had to have seen him. The road was empty and most of the street lamps still lit, outlining him against the shining pavement. And when they reached him, they would have to stop. A lone man at nearly midnight, wearing a thin jacket in a storm that had been blowing for over an hour . . . And when they stopped, they would see the mud on him . . .

He took four strides to the corner, turned it and *ran*. Behind, he thought he heard the car surge forward. It hadn't been a little Panda, either, but a Rover 2600, an 'Area car'. A trouble-hunter.

There was still the warehouse on his left, and a derelict site beyond that, with occupied flats coming up on the right . . . He could dodge two coppers in a car easily. Probably he could dodge the twenty coppers in ten cars that would be there in five minutes, and get clear away. But he didn't want to get clear away. He had to spend those five minutes here.

His own car was a few yards ahead, and he could be in and started before they turned the corner – but not out of sight.

And once they saw him, they'd have him. Even if the cars were evenly matched, he knew he couldn't out-drive the police.

He unlocked the boot, scrambled in, and slammed the lid on himself.

Inside, it was utterly dark. Rain pattered gently on the unlined metal above, and he hoped it drowned his panting breath. He heard the Rover roar around the corner, accelerate past, then squeal to a stop and whine back in reverse. The motor noise dropped to a rumble and feet clattered around his car. He couldn't see the torch being flashed underneath and through the windows, but he felt the car sway as one of the coppers tugged at the driver's handle and the boot. Then more feet, the slam of a door, the surge of power as the Rover shot away to look at the next corner. He turned on his own torch and started wondering how he was going to get out.

One look at the inside of the lock put him off trying that. The bolt was a hook of thick metal that snapped shut around a U-shaped rod the thickness of a pen. He could never get the leverage to force that open, and there was no inside keyhole, of course. He struggled painfully around into a new foetal position and started work on the back of the back seat.

It wasn't, blast it, one of those back seats that turn into a double bed or a discotheque just by twiddling a few knobs and wrenching your spine out of joint. This was just a back seat and very determined to stay that way. He could get it loose in time, but he didn't have any time. If only he had some *tools* . . . Then he realised that all those knobbly things sticking into his kidneys and buttocks were tools. Thirty seconds later, he had the whole U-rod assembly unbolted from the car and stepped back out the way he'd come in.

"What took the time?" Dann demanded, his voice shivery with cold and anxiety.

"Dodging coppers. Get him in the back seat. You go with him. Dave in the front." He left them to it while he roughly bolted the U-rod back on again; driving with a flapping-open boot lid was asking for attention. He pressed it gently shut and it held; loosely and with a slight gap, but it held.

"What were you doing that for?" Dann asked as they pulled cautiously away.

"Long story. What happens if I go left?" Left was away from the place the Mobile had last seen him, away from Neptune Court.

"Sooner or later you hit the Lower Road. Where are we going to take him? He looks pretty bad."

"I just want to get out of the area and reach a phone."

"You can't take him to my place," Dave Tanner said abruptly.

"I wasn't going to." Maxim's thinking had just begun to catch up with why two armed watchmen – the ones outside his own flat hadn't been armed – had suddenly turned up in the service road of Neptune Court. It would be no place to watch from. They must have been coming to collect Blagg, and very certain they would find him.

"D'you work, Dave?" he asked.

"Course I do. I'm a wood machinist, in't I?"

"And your wife?"

"No, not now. She had this job at the checkout in the Co-op, but . . . I mean, what's this all about?"

"Nothing."

"I mean if you think Ron and my wife, well, you can bleedin' well –"

"I wasn't thinking – hold it."

Headlights blazed in his rear-view mirror, topped by a flashing blue light. The Rover closed right up, blatantly harassing him into making one mistake that would give them the excuse to stop him. Maxim began driving like a saint on the way to beatification, but with very sub-saintly feelings in his heart.

It couldn't be the same Rover, because they'd have recognised the car, although he hoped they hadn't stopped long enough to get the number. All he could do now was keep steady despite his growing anger.

"What do we do?" Tanner asked fearfully.

"Keep going. Those *bastards*."

"Hang on, Major," Dann said from the back. "We *are* carrying a deserter who's shot somebody."

"They don't know that! If they stop me now . . ." He took his own pistol from a pocket and jammed it down between his thighs.

Tanner's voice became a squeal. "Here, you can't start using that thing!"

"You can't, Major," Dann chimed in. "You can't start any more shooting."

Maxim never knew what he might have done. The Rover abruptly swung out and roared past, the passenger cop giving them a suspicious but mostly supercilious glare. It turned right at the next street.

A few minutes later they came out onto the bright and still busy Lower Road. It was like sailing into Harwich harbour after a winter crossing on the ferry; you just didn't believe how smooth and easy life could be.

Maxim stopped at the first phone box; Tanner was out of the car well before him. "I'll get me own way home, thanks . . ." And he was gone.

"I know just how he feels," Dann said.

Agnes covered the phone mouthpiece with her hand. "Harry's found him. He's wounded. Can we supply a doctor who knows about bullets and keeps his mouth shut?"

George rubbed his eyes. "*Do* we know such a person?"

She nodded.

"I was afraid we might . . ."

"George, he's got us over a barrel. If we let Blagg go to hospital the cops get him, and he could be up on a murder charge. There's no way he's going to keep his mouth shut throughout that. We just have to go along." She thought for a moment. "The only realistic alternative is to let the boy die, and I can't see our Harry wearing that."

"Nor would I," George said instinctively. "*All* right."

Agnes lifted the phone. "Go ahead."

Maxim said: "Tell the doc it's through the chest, in at the eighth rib, *definite* exit wound at the ninth. Small calibre. There must be bleeding and air in the pleural cavity that's collapsing the other lung. He should be prepared to tap it. I don't think the bleeding's bad in itself. Okay?"

On the phone he sounded crisp and efficient. But if soldiers can't do that, what can they do?"

"Got it. Where are you?"

Inside four minutes she had a doctor, a plain van and a rendezvous. She could be crisp and efficient herself when the heat was on; it wasn't only soldiers who made the world go round.

It was barely dawn when Maxim reached Albany but it was Annette Harbinger who opened the door to him. She was shortish and had an attractive way of cocking her head on one side and looking up with big dark eyes and a wryly amused smile. "Come on in, Saturday seems to have started rather early this week." She wore a belted Japanese kimono that emphasised her cottage-loaf figure and had a warm, rumpled, half-awake look that made Maxim just want to curl up beside her and sleep for a week.

He sagged past into the smell of frying bacon, and she closed the door. "How d'you like your eggs, Harry?"

"Nothing but tea or juice, thanks." Mrs Caswell had fed them all poached eggs and toast once they had got Blagg bedded down. "D'you mind if I start with the cocktail hour? It rather got lost in the rush."

Her head went even more on one side. "A whisky breakfast? Don't tell George: he'll be jealous he hadn't thought of it for himself. You know where it all is."

George was asleep in a big leather chair, making wuffling noises through his open mouth. Carefully not clinking the bottles, Maxim mixed himself a whisky and water, drank it in three gulps, then poured another and began sipping. The lamps were out and the curtains open, letting in an aquarium light that showed up the room for what it really was: a cold, colourless tomb. Maxim shivered and took his drink away to the kitchen.

Agnes was sitting at the table munching bacon and eggs under a bright neon light. "'Ello, ahr 'Arry. Have you got planning permission to carry that much valuable agricultural land around on your person?" She giggled into her coffee.

Maxim's clothes were still sticky-wet, he was splashed to

123

the knees with mud, and as for his shoes . . . With his fair hair, the stubble on his chin showed only as a slight blurring of the normally sharp jawline, but the rest of his face was a bruise of tiredness and strain.

"Don't you taunt the poor man, Agnes," Annette said severely. "Now, would you like to borrow some stuff of George's?"

The idea was briefly attractive, but the difference between George's waistline and his own . . . "I'll manage, thanks." He slumped down opposite Agnes, who herself had changed her delicate jacket for one of Annette's cardigans, and kicked off her shoes somewhere.

Annette put down a cup of tea and a glass of orange juice. "It is lemon and sugar, isn't it? Now you two'll want to talk Top Secrets so I'll go and get dressed." She bustled tactfully away.

"Went the night well?" Agnes asked.

"Pretty well, if he doesn't get pneumonia, but he's full of antibiotics just as a prophylactic . . . It was close. Lucky he was young and fit and all." He took a sip of whisky, then juice, then tea.

"He wouldn't have got mixed up in all this if he wasn't young and fit. Is that your normal breakfast?"

"Not exactly. What happened on the home front?"

"You heard it could be murder? – yes, I told you on the phone. Nothing more from that angle except that the police have asked *us* to check him out, so they're pretty dubious about who he was."

"We know who he was working for, anyway."

"If you mean Six, it really isn't likely," Agnes said. "And I'm not saying that as any friend of theirs."

Unconvinced, Maxim gave a little shrug, then took Blagg's Spanish revolver from his pocket. It was still wet and choked with gritty mud. He emptied out the fired cartridge cases, went across to the sink and washed the gun under the hot tap.

"Where did you take him?" Agnes asked.

"The doc offered one of your safe houses, but I didn't think you'd want to be that much involved. In the end, we went down to a chum in the country." At first, Mrs Caswell hadn't been all that keen, probably because she didn't want anybody dying on the premises. But Jim, bless him, had taken it with as little fuss as if he'd been asked to feed the cat for a couple of days. "The doc's going again today, and I'll get down this evening."

The door clattered open and George, barely awake, stumbled in. He edged Maxim away from the sink, ran the tap until it was really cold, and mixed a foaming cocktail of Alka-Seltzer and lemon-flavoured Redoxon tablets. Agnes watched, fascinated; George's stomach must be a constant series of coups and counter-coups.

Then he sat down with a cup of coffee. "How's Corporal Blagg?"

Maxim took a handful of kitchen paper and began to dismantle and dry the revolver. "Coming along. It must have been only a 7.65 that got him. It nicked a lung and probably cracked a rib, but it didn't open the abdomen. The doc drained air and blood from his pleural cavity and . . ."

"*Harry!*" George held up a wavering hand. "For God's sake, I didn't ask for all *that*. Pleural cavities. At breakfast. *Jesus.*" He slopped coffee into his mouth.

"The important thing is, he didn't lose enough blood to need a transfusion, so no hospital."

"Good. I'm sure you'd have related it to me drop by drop. Did you get anything out of him about . . . about anything?"

"No. He was hardly conscious most of the time, and I didn't want to put any more strain on him. I'll try him this evening."

George got up and put bits of breakfast onto a plate. "Is that his gun you're field-stripping? – and if so, hadn't it better really be thrown away now? They've already got at least one bullet from Rotherhithe they could match to it."

Maxim looked at the clutter of parts in front of him and realised how right he'd been in saying soldiers hate to throw away guns, even cheap Spanish ones. "I suppose . . . but half that stuff about matching bullets to guns is scientific malarkey. Juries only believe it because it always happens in TV cop shows. Anyway, you could scratch up the rifling with a file and steel wool so that it would never give the same markings on a bullet again."

"It's still an unlicensed weapon," George said, sitting

125

down. "And while you're still working at Number 10, a touch of Caesar's wife might be appropriate."

Agnes gave a snort of laughter. "After all he's been up to? You have to be joking."

"He could get stopped and searched for some quite other reason. It would still be a scandal even if it was quite a separate scandal."

Maxim had been reassembling the cleaned and dried gun. He stopped and thought for a moment. "Okay. Should I leave it here with you?"

"All right." George nodded amiably. "Nobody'll search this place."

"Get some sewing-machine oil off Annette to –"

"You're *both* just little boys!" Agnes wailed.

Chapter 14

Maxim woke slowly, sweaty and dry-mouthed and with no idea of what day or time it was. Then fragments of memory floated slowly to the surface like debris from a sunken ship, and along with them the aches and twinges of a busy night. By the time he climbed stiffly out of bed he knew it was just past noon and had the events of Rotherhithe roughed out in his mind like a draft report. It had also occurred to him that if he wrote that report it would be the last thing he ever did in the Army.

The day was cooler and still fresh after the night of rain. He cobbled together a brunch of cold remains from the fridge, with lemon tea. Living by himself, he had stopped taking milk: he never got through half a bottle before it went sour, since he drank coffee black and seldom ate cereals. But he'd have to drop the lemon tea lark when he went back to the Battalion; it would be like turning up wearing a frock. Or maybe he'd deliberately keep it on, as the endearing eccentricity of a senior major. But then he knew he wouldn't, because he would be doing it for just that reason even if he really preferred tea with lemon.

Why do I have to think like that? he wondered. I know dozens of officers with their own quirks of taste, dress and behaviour and they're just real people who'd be incomplete without such little fads. Why do I have to conform, to feel real only when I'm being normal? *You conforming?* he could hear George and Agnes shout in disbelief. But that's not what I mean, he would reply; why can't I just be myself?

But who am I? I used to be Harry Maxim, then I was me and Jenny, and now I just don't know and it'll take more than lemon tea and a pink silk handkerchief in my sleeve and reading Goethe over breakfast to tell me.

George rang. "Get your conscience clean, bright and slightly oiled: it's when–did–you–last–see–your–father time."

"Them?"

"Them. It had to happen."

They met in an undistinguished office block just off the Euston Road, two floors of which were used as secure neutral territory for committees and meetings between Government departments who would lose face by visiting the other fellow's wigwam. George didn't bother to explain the process by which he had deflected the first demand – that Maxim go round to Century House by himself – by a counter-offer of Number 10 ("As it's a Saturday, we could use the Cabinet Room; think how that would look in your memoirs") – or one of his clubs, naming the one that had been effectively the HQ of the Intelligence Service in the heady days of World War II, and finally agreeing on this no-man's-land. Somewhere in the hassle he had got what he really wanted: to go along himself.

"You took your time," he grumped at Maxim.

"I stopped to make a phone call, and I thought I'd better drop off some clothes at the dry-cleaner's." He was wearing his green blazer again.

George, usually a sloppy dresser at weekends – in an expensive sort of way – had on a weekday suit in his usual Prince-of-Wales check and a Dragoon Guards tie. That meant he was expecting trouble. "Any news of our patient?"

"Had a good night, barely any temperature, eating a drop of soup."

They began filling in forms for security passes at the little reception desk while a faded old man in a messenger's uniform rang number after number to find out where the meeting was being held. He couldn't.

"It's because it's Saturday, see," he said. "They could have fixed it while I was out at lunch and they never tell you, not if it's Saturday."

"Perhaps it's secret," Maxim suggested.

"Oh yes, sir, it's all secret, but the trouble is they don't tell you about it."

"Where does the Intelligence Service usually meet?" George demanded.

"The gentlemen attached to the Foreign Office," the old man corrected him, "usually use interview rooms 23C or 23D. But they haven't got phones, see."

They found them in 23C.

It was a square plain room, painted pale green below the cream above, in gloss, which showed up every unevenness in the plaster. The lower half of the window was frosted glass, and the furniture could have been hauled out of store five minutes before. A small gravy-coloured carpet, a trestle table in front of the window and five folding chairs, three of them behind the table and occupied. It was all very deliberate, keeping the interrogators' faces dark against the bright window, and it made Maxim grin.

George kicked one of the spare chairs across against the wall and sat heavily on it. "I thought we were only playing two a side, but never mind. Do you all know Major Maxim?"

Maxim had met Guy Husband before, once. The younger man smoking a cigarette, and whose ashtray was already half full, turned out to be Dieter Sims. The woman with a wide face and carefully frizzed hair was Miss Milward from the Foreign Office. Nobody shook hands.

Husband shot his crisp pink cuffs and laid his forearms fastidiously on the scarred tabletop, bracketing a small heap of files. This time, all the home team had paperwork with them. "We are agreed that there shall be no minutes, that this is all off the record?" he asked, just for the record.

"Oh, I can't promise that," George said. "If the Headmaster wants to know what's going on, it's my job to tell him. I don't necessarily have to get him over-excited, mind, but the decision has to be mine."

Husband and Miss Milward swapped what might, in that light, have been surprised looks. The very idea of being 'off the record' was nonsense, since the room was almost certainly wired, but George should still have stuck to protocol and said something polite like Oh yes, of course.

Maxim stopped trying to peer at the shadowed faces in front

of him and put on a pair of sunglasses.

"Is the light troubling you, Major?" Husband asked. "Perhaps you had a late night?"

Maxim just kept on smiling deferentially.

"I believe," Husband went on, "that Rotherhithe is particularly beautiful at this time of year. Especially when viewed in a midnight rainstorm. You were *seen* down there, Major, has the cat got your tongue? – or was it the Private Office?"

"Yes," Maxim said. "It was, but not now."

"What?"

"The light. Troubling me."

Husband paused, then said in a silky tone: "Thank you, Major. I'm so glad we've got that point cleared up."

"Mr Harbinger," Miss Milward cut in smoothly, "could you help us in this matter? I'm sure you know how vital The Office considers this whole business. Can you prevail on Major Maxim to give us some straight answers?" She had a musical voice, deep and patient.

"My prevailing power with Harry seems to be rather limited, but perhaps you could try him with some straight questions."

"All right," Husband said, "where's Corporal Blagg?"

Straight enough, Maxim thought ruefully. He kept his face polite. "Why should I know?"

"The man is a *deserter*. Last night he killed somebody; you might call it murder. More important to *all* of us, he has information of national importance. Now where is he?"

"If I knew where a deserter was it would be my duty, not as a military man but as a citizen, to report him if I couldn't persuade him to give himself up. Your duty's exactly the same. Did you report him when you spotted him at Rotherhithe?"

"This is just playing with bent paperclips. Are we going to get Blagg or do we go over your head? *And* yours," Husband snapped a look at George.

"And explain why you sent armed men down to pick up Blagg yesterday?" Maxim asked.

"We? We didn't send them. Are you trying to make out that we started that shooting?"

"Why else? You were covering Rotherhithe last night. You knew Blagg could be armed."

"We called off the surveillance after we knew Blagg had spotted us." Husband glanced at Sims, who nodded. "We put men in there again last night when we heard about the shooting. It was obvious Blagg could have been involved."

George asked pleasantly: "Did you clear *that* through the Co-ordinator?"

"And have his decision delayed for weeks by Agnes Algar's mob screaming Rape because we're trespassing on their territory? Blagg would have been dead of old age before we got clearance."

"He might have preferred that to a bullet wound," Maxim said.

Miss Milward pounced. "So you do know where he is?"

Bugger it, Maxim thought. Oh well, they were certain I did anyway.

Sims asked: "Will he live?"

"Yes."

"How are you sure?"

"I've seen bullet wounds before."

There was a short silence. George cleared his throat and asked: "Then just who was Blagg shooting it out with?"

"I would have thought that was obvious," Husband said. "One of the Sovbloc services. The dead man was German, wasn't he?" He glanced the question at Sims, who kept his appreciative smile fixed on Maxim.

"He had West German papers, but they are not real, we understand. Perhaps he was HVA, one of a travelling circus." The *Hauptvertwaltung Abwehr* was the espionage arm of the East German SSD.

Maxim asked: "How did they know Blagg was involved at all?"

Husband leant back, realised how uncomfortable that was on the wooden chair and rather self-consciously unleaned himself. "We've been doing some serious thinking about that. But in the end, there are just too many possibilities."

"I knew," Maxim said, "and you knew, and Blagg himself and your Mrs Howard, only she's dead."

"Blagg himself told you," Sims pointed out politely. "Can you be sure he did not tell anybody else as well?"

There was Jim Caswell, of course, but Jim wouldn't chatter . . . Blagg wasn't fool enough to tell Tanner, but just how much he'd told Billy Dann . . .

"I knew," George said. "And I told Agnes Algar after the meeting."

"In my Department," Miss Milward put in, "at least three people know the basic facts – if they are facts – behind Plainsong."

Maxim felt as if he had baked (if that was what you did) a perfect soufflé of evidence, all crisp and firm, and then *floop*: it was swimming off the plate and dripping on his shoes.

Husband said sympathetically: "Security, Major, *security*. So often interpreted in this country as merely not telling anybody who's actually got a hammer and sickle embroidered on his tie. But don't think I'm being complacent about this. I'm quite willing to accept the possibility of a leak within my own service, and I'm sure Dieter accepts that also." Sims did, nodding gently. "It would be foolish to forget that it's happened before. *But* that only adds a new dimension of urgency to the business. If the Other Side knows enough to be looking for Blagg, it could know enough to destroy or neutralise the information, whatever it may be, in his possession."

It was difficult to argue back. Maxim knew that George was looking across at him, on the brink of surrender.

"It was your people who got him into this," he persisted.

Husband took off his blue-tinted glasses and polished them on a silk handkerchief chosen to pick up the colours of both his suit and his tie. "When Mrs Howard asked for an escort, I naturally assumed we would assign her one of our own people. Apparently she said she'd prefer somebody she had worked with before, and she knew Blagg's battalion was in Germany, and Dieter – rashly, we now agree – left the decision to her. I think the German end was indeed mishandled."

"That's very reassuring," Maxim said coldly. "That boy could have been in my company or squadron. He was lied to, conned into believing that the Bad Schwarzendorn operation had been approved by the Army. He thought your freelance

Mrs Howard represented the same thing that he thinks he represents himself: the defence of this country. He could have wound up dead. Okay, that's something a soldier has to accept, in an abstract sort of way. But instead, he ended up a deserter and being chased by the police for a killing that was forced on him, and that's something he does *not* have to accept – and neither do I."

Miss Milward said "You're getting emotional, Major."

"Good. I didn't think I was getting anywhere."

Husband said: "I have agreed that Dieter was at fault in that, gravely at fault. But . . ." Sims's smile had gone a little rueful and he was looking down at his hands, turning a gold-tipped cigarette in his small fingers. Momentarily, Maxim felt sorry for him. Whatever his sins, he was being forced to pay for them in public – well, as public as the Secret Service ever wanted to get.

"But," Husband went on, "we have to deal with matters as they now stand. And with Corporal Blagg."

"What are you offering?" And when the three figures stiffened in surprise, Maxim added: "What are you offering him?"

"You mean money?" asked Husband.

Miss Milward was quicker, or more sensitive. "Can we put Humpty Dumpty together again as a Corporal with a clean record? – I assume that's what he wants. Well, we certainly ought to try, and if we can't then there'll be a very good case for generous compensation out of the secret funds."

"Quite," Husband nodded. "Quite so. Does that satisfy you, Major?"

"It's the best you can do at the moment. I'll talk to him."

There was a moment of shocked silence, then Husband said: "*You* will talk to him? Our whole agreement was that *we* should do –"

"We've got no agreement worth a damn to Blagg. I'll talk to him and see what he knows, if anything."

"Mr Harbinger," Miss Milward turned to him, "do you think you should intervene now?"

George shrugged and nearly slid himself off the chair in which he was slumped. "You can see what I'm up against.

Though I speak with the tongues of men and of angels, as I often do, Harry still goes and does whatever he wants. Perhaps I lack charity. Why don't you wait a few hours and see if he gets what you need from Blagg?"

The three of them looked at each other, and Husband said cautiously: "If you say a matter of hours, you do mean tonight?"

"I'll do my best," Maxim said. "Is there anything I should know in order to ask the right questions?"

They went into a huddle, with Miss Milward murmuring behind her hand at Husband and Sims shaking his head in a jittery movement. Finally Husband said: "I assume, security being what it is, that you know our ultimate target is Gustav Eismark? Quite. Well, according to the late Mrs Howard, we got this much from her at least, there is some doubt about the validity of his second marriage. His first wife was supposed to have died at the end of the war. There is, it seems, a strong possibility that he abandoned her in the West and took their baby son over to the Russian zone. In the confusion of 1945 and '46, there would have been no means for her to trace him. Once there, he could claim she was dead; in the West, she might build a new life. *But* if she were still alive at the time of his second marriage, nearly twenty years later, then it was bigamous."

"Is that bad?" Maxim asked, a little surprised.

"Perhaps not in every Sovbloc country. But the GDR, as Dieter will confirm, I'm sure, happens still to have the morality of Salem when they are putting little old ladies to the torch – at least at the highest political level. And bear in mind that's what we're talking about, Major: the highest level. Nothing to do with public morality; the public doesn't come into this. Somehow a Sovbloc politician can corner ninety-nine per cent of the vote without everybody having to know the name of his dog and which football team he supports." Husband smiled contentedly at his own wit. "It does keep things tidy: you don't suddenly lose your best men because of an unexpected scandal. I'm sure George would be delighted to see it introduced over here."

George ignored the sly threat and just grunted. Miss Milward chipped in: "Of course, if the first wife turned out to be still alive and willing to testify, that would be even better."

"And somewhere," Husband said, "Mrs Howard must have been keeping a file on Gustav Eismark. She reported very little to us, I mean to Dieter. I believe that's right?"

Ever-smiling, Sims acknowledged that it was.

Maxim said: "Her luggage got dumped in the river. There weren't any papers among it. I was told."

The three behind the table exchanged looks. Sims said: "It would not be likely to be just in her cases, like clothes. Perhaps in the lining . . ."

Maxim doubted Blagg had bothered to rip open the suitcase linings; he just wouldn't be thinking in those terms.

"It sounds," Husband said, "as if our soldier friend has probably destroyed anything that we might have to show for months of expensive —"

"Then get expensive enough to hire people who can put one foot in front of another without the Army having to tell them how!"

Husband was on his feet shouting, George saying: "Harry!" and Miss Milward: "Gentlemen, now *please* —" Sims just sat there, but momentarily without his smile.

Maxim said: "Your mother's moustache."

Everybody took a deep breath. Miss Milward said calmly: "I think the only other thing you may need to know, Major, is the first Frau Eismark's name. It was Brigitte Krone. So if you *do* happen across any documents relating to her . . ."

"You don't know where Mrs Howard got the first clue about this?"

"Major, we are not asking you to start the investigation again from scratch. *Please*. If you'd confine yourself to finding out what Corporal Blagg knows, we'd be very grateful."

George said: "Surprised, too, I imagine." He stood up. "If that's it, then . . . are we fit?"

Maxim said: "I don't want to be followed again."

"Harry . . ."

"No, if there's somebody behind me, I want to be sure that it's One Of Theirs."

"What earthly difference would that make," Husband asked

in a voice that still trembled slightly, "to your normal standard of conduct?"

That effectively ended the meeting.

George drove, not going anywhere, and for a few minutes he said nothing, then: "Ecology. That's it. You're going to have to develop a more ecological outlook. Tell yourself that, like the dung beetle and the greater horned toad, secret intelligence personnel are also God's creatures. It'll make life less exciting, but easier on the blood pressure. Do you think you can get anything for them?"

"If Blagg's got anything. This time he's going to tell the whole truth and nothing but."

"Good. We're running out of time."

"I'd like to be able to convince him that it wasn't *that* mob that took a shot at him."

George shook his head emphatically. "Husband would never authorise gunplay in London. In fact, I don't know how he *could* authorise it – he hasn't got the men. They just don't exist, not here. The Firm uses a few muscle-brains in the Middle East and so on, but they're employed at several removes and a lot's done to make sure they *stay* overseas. You can spend your whole life in The Firm without once meeting a pistol by way of business – in fact, you'd better, if you ever hope to be considered for Best of Breed."

Maxim made what might have been an agreeing noise. "All right, but what about Sims?"

"He's more vulnerable than Husband. If he makes a cock-up of this, anything approaching a scandal, he's finished in a very final way."

"Where did they get him from?"

"East Germany, via West Germany. He Saw The Light seven or eight years ago, and went to work for the *Verfassungschutz* at Ehrenfeld. Counter-espionage. Given his background, he built up a very effective little unit, then he offered the whole thing to us after the Flying Doctor business. Did you hear anything about that? – probably you were out of the country."

"I know the one you mean." Maxim had picked up the story from friends in the Intelligence Corps. A youngish doctor employed full-time to look after the health of the *Verfassungschutz*'s agents had been caught, by pure chance, passing on the details of those agents' medical histories and personal problems to the Other Side. He had, of course, been security checked and re-checked, and every time found to be clean. He was faithful to his wife – except for an occasional nurse, which she had to agree didn't count – and wasn't into drugs or gambling or politics. The security men had missed only one thing: the doctor didn't want to be a doctor, he wanted to be an airline pilot. They knew he spent his weekends at the flying club, but hadn't got around to totting up how many hours of blind flying instruction in a twin-engined Cessna he was buying, nor how much each such hour cost. And since the good doctor was a lousy pilot, it was a lot of hours and a lot of money, nearly half his government salary, and almost all paid for by sympathetic friends in East Berlin.

"It just goes to show," Maxim's confidant from Int Corps had summed up, "that sex and drugs and gambling aren't everything. One shouldn't be *narrow-minded* when looking for a man's weakness."

The doctor wasn't the only security failure in West German intelligence, but he had been the last straw for Sims. Rather than see his unit rotted away by the disillusionment of constant betrayal, he had approached MI6 with an offer they didn't want to refuse.

"Of course, it isn't the Done Thing to poach people – let alone a whole unit – from an Ally," George went on, "but our East German operations had completely fallen apart, the place had become a total black hole as far as The Firm knew, and they were desperate. Anyway, we weren't feeling too chuffed towards West Germany at that point: something to do with Common Market fishing policy, they kept sending their trawlers into the Hampstead Ponds or somewhere. So the Foreign Office turned a bland eye – nobody was exactly complaining out loud – and we took on the whole Sims organisation as a going concern. From desk bods right down to people in the field. Mrs Howard was one of his."

"Her? I thought she was supposed to be a sort of part-timer, an amateur."

"That's the story when something goes wrong: 'Not our normal standard, just somebody we picked off the street, don't judge us by her blah blah.' But she was one of his, all right. And overall, they seem to be doing pretty well. If Plainsong actually comes off it'll be a big boost for the whole Sovbloc desk. Then they can go back to asking each other where they got their blow-drys and leave the rest of us in peace."

After a minute or so, Maxim said: "Mrs Howard had a gun. Two, in fact."

"And look what a power of good *that* did us all."

Chapter 15

The doctor had been and gone by the time Maxim reached the little cottage on the hillside above Caswell's father-in-law's garage. Maxim suspected that the cottage belonged to the old man, too, and went with the job. He wondered how long Jim would stand that.

"Said he's doing very well," Caswell reported. "Gave him some more shots, his temperature's well down. Told me to keep him *still* for a couple of days."

"Is he awake now?"

"Yes, he's listening to the radio. I'll shift the telly in there for him tomorrow, that might keep him quiet."

"Has he heard about the one in the hospital?"

"Yes. It doesn't seem to bother him."

"Well . . ." But did they want it to bother him? Blagg's touching faith that Maxim would save him from murder charges in two countries might at least mean that he would stay where he was and do nothing – for once. Caswell led the way.

Blagg was lying flat on his back but bulging out of a small single bed that itself crowded the tiny room. It was all very cottagey, the uneven walls papered with a tiny flower pattern and all filled with an odd green light reflected in from the hillside that sloped up just outside the window. Blagg pulled out the radio earpiece and struggled to sit up.

"Lie still, you stupid little man!" Caswell thundered, all sergeant again. Blagg relaxed sheepishly.

For a couple of minutes they made sickbed small talk while Maxim tried to decide just how Blagg was. The right side of his face was a mass of scratches, there was a sticking plaster on his ear, and his chest was heavily bandaged, but even in that sickly light he seemed bright-eyed and calm. Best of all, he was talking long sentences without a hint of breathlessness. Maxim was fit enough himself but, he thought wistfully, there's no medicine like being only twenty-five.

"Is this the first time you've copped one?" he asked.

"Nah, I got one in Armagh. Smack in the arse, but it was probably just about spent. Bloody funny that was, for everybody else. Have you, sir?"

"Years back, out in the Gulf." Maxim touched the outside of his right thigh; through the thin cotton trousers he could trace the hard-edged crater that had come close to killing him, out in the desert hours from real medical aid. Instead, it had only taken away six months of his life – at a critical point that just might have foreclosed on his promotion hopes. If, of course, he still had any. Well, as they said, why did you join the Army if you can't take a joke?

"One thing," Blagg said; "I'm lucky I don't smoke." He grinned slyly at Caswell, who had already twice taken out and then put away his cigarettes.

"Right, then," Maxim called the meeting to order. "I've talked to Six, and somebody in the Foreign Office. I'm sorry it took all this to get them out into the open – as far as they've come. They've said they'll do what they can for you, and I believe them. That wound might help with some fairy story . . . But you've got to tell me everything now. You hadn't remembered you had that gun, last time."

"Lucky I had, though, wasn't it?" Blagg said aggressively. "Who was they, those two at Dave's place?"

"Supposed to be East German. They're involved, anyway."

"How did they know where I was?"

Maxim thought for a moment. "My guess – it's no more than that – is that somebody came around earlier and told Mrs Tanner that there'd be a couple of hundred quid in it for her if you showed up. She's out of work, and I don't suppose Dave makes a fortune . . ."

"That little *scrubber*," Blagg breathed. "I didn't think she liked me much, but I'm one of Dave's oldest mates and . . . when I get up, I'll bloody –"

"You'll do nothing. She can still tell the police you were in that shooting and once *they* get you, you can forget you ever had any friends or were ever in the Army. All right? Why did you go back to London in the first place? – why didn't you stay here?"

"Dave rang me, see, and he said there'd been some blokes asking around about me and he didn't think they were coppers at all, and I thought well, that could be The Firm –"

"It was."

" – and I wanted to get in touch with them, anyway, and . . . well . . ."

"And I didn't seem to be doing much that was any use. Go on."

"I thought I might get just to chat to one of them, but instead I suddenly found a whole bleeding pack of them behind me. Just following, but still . . ."

Sadly, Maxim remembered how long – and how much luck – it had taken for him to spot his own pack.

"So I thought bugger this for a lark and got rid of them, and the next couple of days I tried to ring you, but . . ."

The two days Maxim spent ambushing his own followers and then kicked into exile by George.

"All right," he said. "Problems all round us. But *now* let's hear the rest about Bad Schwarzendorn." He sat down on a tiny painted nursery chair beside the bed.

Blagg hesitated, or perhaps was trying to remember, and Caswell said in a firm voice: "The shooting was just after ten, you said. You left the car at Dortmund and caught an early morning train for Ostend – you said. Dortmund's less than a hundred miles, mostly by *Autobahn*, so you could have been there by midnight. And the first boat train's at half past six. Now don't tell me you spent the night sitting on the station, because they wouldn't let you, or parked in a stolen car, because you're not that stupid, not quite. Now . . ."

Caswell hadn't only been doing some thinking, he'd been looking up maps and timetables.

"Well," Blagg said slowly, "what it was, see . . ."

George belonged to things. He liked to boast that, in central London, he was never more than a couple of hundred yards from some club, institution or association of which he was a member and which could provide, at the very least, a roof in a rainstorm. "You can't *lose* a club, the way you can an umbrella," he once told Agnes. She had replied that it still seemed an expensive policy compared with even the dearest of umbrellas, and George had thought about that and said: "You can't piss into an umbrella, either. Not without attracting unfavourable comment anyway."

This particular club faced across Green Park, which on that evening looked very green and crisp, the trees standing tall and full against the restless sky. It was probably something to do with the view that had convinced George he ought to be drinking a very large glass of dry sherry from the wood. Agnes had taken a smaller one; she had just got back from her service's registry.

"You do appreciate," she was saying, "that all our material on Eismark is about thirty years out of date? We don't try to keep up with people like that. Really all we've got is what his sister told us when she came over."

"We're supposed to be interested in his first marriage and that's more than thirty years ago, isn't it? What did she have to say about that?"

"Well . . ." She was sitting in a very old overstuffed leather sofa and hiding a notebook behind her large handbag because she wasn't sure notebooks were allowed in the club; not much was. "Gustav's the younger by just over two years . . . he was nine when his father died . . . they moved away from Rostock, went to stay with relatives in the Harz mountains . . . mother married again and rather faded away, they were brought up mostly by grandparents and aunts. They don't seem to have been poor: she had all her piano lessons, Gustav had a racing bicycle when he was still at school. Did you know he had a glass eye?"

"Can't say I did. Why should – Ah, I see: no war service for young Gustav. Was that the bicycle?"

"Yes, he got his face mixed up with the spokes of –"

"*Please*: I get enough of that sort of thing from Harry. Go on with the non-bloody bits."

"He did well at school – Mina thought he was a genius – and actually got a year in college. At Bremen; he wanted to be a naval architect in those days. Then Hitler invaded Russia, everybody remembered old man Eismark had been a pinko, and Gustav was hove into the night."

"He was lucky not to be in a concentration camp or the Todt Organisation."

"He was lucky to have a talented sister. She'd already made a bit of a name for herself, only locally but you know what the Germans are about music, and the district party bosses liked romantic pieces so she became the star turn at their more respectable booze-ups. That was when she started using her mother's name, Linnarz, to get away from the Eismark stigma. And they tolerated Gustav – gave him a job on the land – as long as it kept Mina happy and she kept them happy. There must have been a lot of that sort of thing, when you come to think about it: tolerating ideological undesirables as long as it suited your own book – not that National Socialism had much ideology beyond being first at the trough. It couldn't last, of course."

"What went wrong?"

"The party got a new *Kreisleiter* who didn't dig music and wasn't going to have any damned Commie subverting his cabbages, so he blew the whistle. Mina got the tip-off just in time and they became U-boats, went underground. Just who did it for them she didn't seem to know, it was all contacts of Gustav's. Probably he made some useful friends in Bremen; Mina said he was always asking her if she'd heard any interesting gossip at her musical *soirées*. But one way or another, somebody came up with the full *table d'hôte*: safe havens, roadnames and the paperwork to back them up. Even money from time to time. This was November '43."

George made a long thinking, grumbling noise, then said, mostly to himself: "The paperwork must have been good . . . if they were living on it for eighteen months . . . they weren't escaped prisoners of war trying to reach Switzerland on a hand-copied *Fremdenpass* . . . Could they have been in with the real Communist underground?"

Agnes lifted her eyebrows in a facial shrug; George knew far more about that period of history than she did. "Could have been. I thought it was pretty badly penetrated, but . . ."

"Oh, it was. The Gestapo was just about running the Communist party by 1944, but to do that they'd have to let some small fry run free, and from their point of view the Eismarks would be very small indeed. They didn't actually go in for sabotage or anything, did they?"

"No, according to her they just stayed undercover – separately – in small villages and so on until the end of the war.

George grunted and finished his sherry. "Thank God: now I can have a *real* drink. What about you? Same again?" He pressed a bellpush. "Come along, young Algar: what about this marriage? – when do we get to that?"

"Very soon," Agnes said patiently. "Brigitte Krone: she was living with one of the families Gustav hid up with that winter. Parents had been killed in the Hamburg bombing, so perhaps she was feeling lonely. Anyway, all the other young men were away at the war, Gustav must have been spending just about all his time indoors, young love wove its spell and . . . 'ow's yer father?" Agnes lapsed into stage cockney.

George frowned, absent-mindedly gave their order to the servant who had appeared, and said: "I don't know . . . marriage seems a public sort of affair. I'd've thought that would be adding enormously to the risk . . ."

"There was a growing need for marriage lines."

He looked puzzled.

"Oh, for heaven's sake. The girl was in the club, knocked up, a bun in the oven – 'ow's yer father?"

George stiffened into the Compleat Civil Servant. "If you intend me to infer that she was pregnant, then for the life of me I can see no reason why you don't actually say so. I don't find all two-syllable words either incomprehensible or, when comprehended, necessarily shocking."

"She was pregnant," Agnes said, staring at the low coffee-table, not at George. "And marriage itself might have been a useful bit of insurance for Gustav: her relatives or guardians would have been less likely to inform on her husband than on some passing stranger who could get his trousers open in Olympic time."

"Is there something," George asked icily, "about the atmosphere of this place that causes you to come up with such

144

expressions? If so, we can easily adjourn to Fred's Caff in Brixton where you might react by trying to speak the Queen's English."

Agnes looked up. From over George's shoulder stared the portrait of a general whose handling of an attack in the South African war had caused so many casualties to his own brigade that he had immediately been promoted away to see if he could do the same thing with divisions and corps. In 1915 and '16 he had proved he hadn't lost his old touch, and so died in bed at a great age, garnished with colourful honours, many of them from grateful countries whose soldiers he hadn't got killed even on purpose. He was looking at Agnes with exactly the expression he would have chosen had he lived to see a woman in his club.

"It must be something about the place," she agreed meekly. "Must try harder. Where were we?"

"Gustav was just getting married."

"Yes. That happened in May 1944. The boy, Manfred, was born in the October."

George did mental arithmetic on his fingers. "That means around January . . . Gustav didn't waste much time about . . ."

Agnes didn't say a word. She looked very much like somebody not saying a word.

"And the wife, Brigitte: when did she die, or was supposed to have died?"

"April 1945, just before the end of the war. Mina said Gustav said she'd been killed by Allied planes. She hadn't been around herself at the time and said Gustav didn't like talking about it much. Fair enough, I suppose."

"Where did this happen?"

"She didn't say."

"Isn't that odd?"

"She wasn't hiding anything. If our people had asked her, she'd have had to answer. It was her applying for asylum, not us inviting her. But they can't have asked: why should they? They weren't interested in her war story, they'd heard a million war stories. They just wanted to know what was going on in East Germany there and then. She only mentioned one place after they'd gone underground and that was where Gustav got married: Sangerhausen. In East Germany, now."

"So we can't get at the marriage certificate." George brooded. There was a burst of male laughter from the bar, which had suddenly filled up with men wearing MCC ties; the day's play at Lord's would have ended just about twenty minutes ago. The servant fought his way clear and delivered their drinks; George grunted, Agnes smiled and shifted carefully on the sofa. There was no way to be comfortable on it, and even movement was risky because the old leather was cracking like dry parchment.

"Mind you," George said abruptly, "that certificate must be sheer balls because he'd have to use his roadname on it. Not Eismark at all."

Agnes sipped and shrugged. "They did the best they could in the circumstances. It showed willing."

"It also showed the baby was started before the marriage. Is there any leverage in that?"

"No, not even in the GDR. It wasn't adultery, he Did The Right Thing by a girl who had only months to live, Hitler's hounds baying at their heels . . . They weep over muck like that on their side, too."

George nodded. "The baby was only five months, still in arms. Why didn't he get killed, too?"

"A good question, and one widely asked in East Germany, I imagine. Manfred's a big boy now and a full colonel in the SSD. Old Gustav may still have some old-time socialist ideals about the rights of man, but the general feeling is that Manfred would have done well on the faculty at Belsen."

"So I'd heard. But anyway, that's all she had to say?"

"That's only one *page* of what she said. There's at least another thirty about life in the GDR in the fifties, how they treat musicians, how she brought up baby Manfred while Gustav was off in Moscow learning to run a shipyard and getting booster shots of dialectical materialism. It read as if having to play auntie instead of Schumann first gave her the idea of coming over – Here's our hunter home from the hill."

The junior hall porter was guiding Maxim through the crowd by the bar. George waved and Maxim was released to make the last few yards by himself. He sat down beside Agnes, who said: "Don't wriggle or you'll collapse a hundred years of military history."

"How is he?" George demanded.

"Better than I expected. He's tough."

"And talkative, I trust?"

"I think I've got everything, at last."

"What is it?"

"I didn't say I'd got any *thing*, but –"

"Harry . . ."

"Let him say his piece," Agnes said.

"We know Blagg picked up the money and the car keys. Now he says he also took a batch of papers and a bit of film, negative film. He thought the papers were all death certificates or copies; he remembers a word like *Sterbeurkunde* –"

"That *is* death certificate," Agnes said.

"It was when I learned German, too."

"Children, children," George said warningly. "Go on, Harry."

"About thirty or forty of them, all from April 1945. Seems a bit odd, but . . . All this was mixed up with the newspapers and the money. Something that *wasn't* there was a magazine she'd asked him to get: a back copy of a thing called *Focus on Germany*. It's a sort of goodwill thing that Bonn puts out for the Allied forces; it doesn't outsell *Playboy*. He just pinched it from the Services Liaison Officer's files in Soltau. I've got the date."

"Fine, fine," George said. "But you've got all the rest?"

"No, it's –"

"For God's *sake* –"

"He left it with a woman in Germany."

After a time, Agnes said thoughtfully: "That boy's no fool, keeping a nice big ace in the hole in case Six won't play ball. No fool at all."

"His mother abandoned him before he could crawl," Maxim said. "He didn't quite grow up with a happy trusting nature like you and George."

"Quite," George said. "But is he prepared to trust you now?"

"I've got her name and address."

"Good. Well, we give her to Six. It's all we can do, and perhaps we'll really finally be out of it."

"Hold on," Agnes warned; she had been watching Maxim's expression. "Something tells me it isn't going to be that easy."

Maxim flashed his quick defensive smile. "Blagg told her not to hand them over to anybody but himself or somebody with a letter from him. I've got the letter. It names me as the messenger boy."

There was a moment of silence, then George erupted. "You *arranged* that. We had our chance to get Number 10 clear of this whole . . . whole *catastrophe*, but not you, no, you want a front seat for the opening night of Arma*geddon*, you do . . ."

"I didn't arrange it, but I didn't dodge it," Maxim said doggedly. "Blagg just doesn't trust Six any more. They screwed him at least once and he knows it. And so do you."

A member, passing with both hands full of glasses, stopped suddenly. "George! We hardly ever see you. Do tell, how's the Prime Minister *really*?"

"Dead, if he's got any sense," George snapped.

The member stiffened, then edged away in a fading mumble: "Well, I suppose things must be rather trying for you, what with . . ."

George's short tempers were at least short. Suddenly he was Organisation Man, and Agnes could see why politicians liked having him around. "All right, you be in Germany tomorrow some time. You'll need some money. I'll ask Sir Bruce to send a signal to Rhine Army and then you tell him what you want: a room somewhere, I'll leave that to you. *Don't* go armed, for God's sake. And I'll have to tell Six. They'll probably get somebody to contact you over there and you just hand over the material and come quietly home without blowing any bridges behind you. If you think you can manage that, we'll get over to Number 10 and start the wheels turning."

Chapter 16

Hannover station was like a greenhouse and bustling with tanned young men and women hunchbacked by huge colourful rucksacks. Maxim had an hour and a half to wait for a train to Osnabrück, and half changed his mind about hiring a car, but that meant lots of signatures, and might be difficult to hand back if he flew home on a trooping flight from RAF Gütersloh. So he made a couple of phone calls to Osnabrück – he found he'd been given a room with an Engineer regiment – then sipped a lager until train time.

With the flat, disciplined North German plain rattling past, he suddenly remembered when he had first been posted to Germany how surprised and even unnerved he had been to find that all the buildings seemed familiar. It had been a couple of days before it dawned on him: they were the full-size versions of the houses and station buildings he and his father had made up for their never-quite-finished model railway layout. Like the locos and the rolling stock, the best plastic building kits – Arnolds and Heljans and Rikos – all came from West Germany and were based on West German originals. But for Maxim it was still the other way around: the landscape beyond the train window was just for show; secretly he knew those buildings were mere façades, without interior floors, furniture or live people.

The only person he'd told about his odd vision had been Jenny, and she had laughed delightedly and understood.

From the station he took a taxi straight to Blumenthalstrasse. He knew Osnabrück fairly well, as he knew most towns in 1st British Corps area, although he'd never been stationed there. It had taken a bad beating from the RAF and been widely rebuilt, much of it as copies of the original high-pitched medieval buildings. They looked phoney, but only because they looked new; once they had cracked and weathered and slumped a little, nobody would ever credit that they might just as well have been built as concrete and glass shoe-boxes.

The Blumenthalstrasse address turned out to be one of the shoeboxes, a five-storey block of flats with the staircase and lift-shaft stuck on at the side of a column of frosted-glass bricks. Maxim pressed the entryphone bell for Winkelmann and waited until a man's voice rasped: "*Bitte?*"

Speaking rather rusty German, Maxim said carefully: "I am Harry Maxim. I rang Fraulein Winkelmann from Hannover. I have a message from Corporal Ron Blagg."

"*Ja, ja.* I remember. It is the third floor."

Maxim looked round at his taxi-driver, who had parked two wheels on the pavement with the usual German disregard for the tyres, and got a nod and a rather strange smile in return. Then the driver hunched down with a magazine, the door buzzed open and Maxim went in.

A man was waiting in the doorway of the Winkelmann flat; he was shortish, stubby, strong-looking and probably around forty. He had a face that was both sensuous and battered – his nose had been broken at some time – with deep pouches under his dark eyes. He smiled widely and held out a hand, but the way he looked Maxim over gave him a little pang of disquiet. He felt that if he'd been wearing a gun, this man would have known.

"I am Bruno. Please come in."

The scent was the first thing: it was like walking into a peach-canning factory. The furniture came with the smell: soft, shiny, billowy and over-decorated like great banks of flowers; the little lampshades around the walls were all tassels and fringes, the ornaments were fiddly coloured glass and the not-quite-velvet curtains draped artistically and bound with golden cords. It was a very feminine room if you happened to like your femininity in ton lots.

Oh damn it, Maxim thought. I know what profession *she*'s in, and no wonder that taxi driver was giving me the big smirk. But I should have guessed: what other sort of woman with a permanent address would Blagg know?

Bruno was offering him a sticky-looking liqueur from a tall thin bottle. Maxim smiled and shook his head. *I know what business you're in, too, mate, and I shouldn't wonder if the conversation came around to money before long.*

After the room, Fraulein Winkelmann herself was hardly a surprise. Built like one of her own sofas, topped with crisp golden curls, she had big blue eyes, a vivid red mouth and three chins to do the work of one. The unexpected thing was that she made no attempt to hide her age, which was around sixty. Instead, she made up to it, becoming a perfectly painted and exquisitely detailed matron in a fur-trimmed green satin housecoat. She let Maxim hold her hand for a moment, then swept regally past and merged herself carefully with one of the big chairs.

"It is very warm," she said in English, fluttering at the air with a Japanese fan. Bruno handed her a glass. "You are not drinking?"

"Not at the moment."

"Have you come all the way from England? How is dear Ronald?"

"He's fine." Maxim sat carefully on the least-soft chair he could find. Bruno stayed standing, watching him with a small fixed smile.

"And you have a letter from him?" Her English had an unmistakable accent, but flowed easily. And why not? – the British Army had been in Osnabrück since 1945.

Maxim offered the sealed envelope, Bruno took it, broke it open and passed it to her. She blinked at it, said: "Ah yes," and gave it to Bruno to read properly.

Halfway through the letter, Bruno said in German: "Ah, he is a major in their Army," and then smiled hastily at Maxim because he had forgotten they had been speaking German earlier. Fraulein Winkelmann just nodded pleasantly.

Bruno read the letter twice, then folded it up, licking his lips as if uncertain how to begin. "Corporal Blagg is . . . quite all right?"

"Oh yes."

"But you have come instead."

"He can't get away at the moment."

"He is not . . . in trouble?"

Maxim shrugged and waved at the letter. "What does he say?"

"Yes, yes. What did he say to you?"

"Just that Fraulein Winkelmann was keeping some papers for him."

"Has he said what papers?"

Maxim looked curiously at Bruno, using the time to mask his own indecision. He didn't want to sound too eager and knowledgeable, but Bruno wouldn't believe him as a country bumpkin. "Some photographic negatives and a collection of certificates." When Bruno didn't say anything, Maxim turned to Fraulein Winkelmann. "Do you still have these things?"

"I let Bruno do all my business work." She surged upright.

"Business?"

"I will leave you." She touched Maxim's hand and went away.

Bruno indicated the bottle. "You are sure you do not . . . ?"

Maxim just looked stolid. Bruno squared his shoulders inside his tight-fitting shirt. "What photographs were those?"

"Some very small ones." Maxim hoped it sounded as if he were hiding something more than the fact that Blagg hadn't been able to tell what they were.

Bruno licked his lips. "There is a problem with the certificates."

"Really?"

"They are *Sterbeurkunden*, certificates of death, and they are from the *Standesamt* of Bad Schwarzendorn."

Maxim went on looking stolid.

"The night that Corporal Blagg brought them here, the *Standesbeamte* at Bad Schwarzendorn – he was killed." Maxim still didn't react. Bruno licked his lips again. "There was also a woman killed."

"Really? Can I have the negatives and the certificates now, please?"

"I think you do not see the problem –"

"Just get them, please."

"They are, naturally, in the bank. But –"

"I see." Maxim got up and walked through the inner door.

Beyond, the muttering of a TV set led him to another door. Fraulein Winkelmann was sitting at one end of a small kitchen table, separated from a big colour set at the other end by a cup of coffee and a plate of cream cakes. She snatched off a pair of gold-rimmed glasses and looked up at Maxim with myopic surprise.

When in doubt, à l'outrance – and a good lie or two, as well. "Fraulein, I understand from Bruno that you are prepared to swear to a document that Corporal Blagg brought you some death certificates on the night when Herr Hochhauser –" (thank God he had remembered the name) "– the Standesbeamte from Bad Schwarzendorn was murdered. I am sorry that I had to deceive you just now; I am from the Military Police Special Investigation Branch." He held out his ID; it showed nothing of what unit or corps he belonged to. "The Staatsenwalt at Paderborn would like to have those death certificates. If I can give them to him, then perhaps he will leave you out of all this. I cannot promise, of course; we are dealing with a murder. And Corporal Blagg is in a lot of trouble. But if he cannot show you have the papers any longer, then he cannot prove he was here on the night of the murder. But I have no authority here; I have to go through the police."

She stood up slowly, taking time to understand – if she ever did understand it, which was more than he did himself. He was just firing a smokescreen of emotive words and phrases. But she was just about to say something when her eyes moved and something touched the middle of his back. It didn't feel particularly like a gun, but with Bruno it would have to be.

Maxim lifted his arms carefully and sighed. "Bruno?" A hand began feeling at him in the places he might carry a gun, so Maxim said to Fraulein Winkelmann: "It would be complicated if he shoots me. I have come from London to see you, a lot of people know that, and I have a taxi waiting outside with my luggage in it." Bruno had taken his wallet; now he snorted. Maxim went on: "Take a look outside. A grey Mercedes, parked on the pavement about twenty metres up the road. He won't go away until he's been paid. And what are you going to do with my body, Fraulein? Cut it up in the bath – that's the best place – and then what? – eat me? It would take a long –"

She suddenly started screeching at Bruno, so abruptly that Maxim felt a jab in his spine and knew he'd come very close to being shot. But then the pressure from the gun went away, and very carefully he twisted his head around and saw Bruno clutching a worn old Luger by his waist, shaking it with impatience as he waited for Fraulein Winkelmann to stop yelling.

Maxim couldn't catch half of what she was saying, but it seemed mostly on his side. Bruno turned and stalked out of the room, then came back and pointed the Luger at Maxim once more and said Yes, there was a taxi waiting. Fraulein Winkelmann told him for the Good God's sake to get the papers *fast*, and Bruno went away and came back and pointed the Luger yet again. It was a farce, a terrible play, but still a real play because these two were acting out a charade of fright and face-saving and if he did anything to break the illusion that they were still taking decisions for themselves then he was going to get himself shot.

But finally he had an envelope of papers in one hand and his wallet in the other and Bruno was clutching a wad of Deutschmarks and challenging Maxim with a twisted leer to say something about *that*. That was part of the play, too, to give Bruno a final victory but not an easy or total victory because that would be unrealistic. He tried.

"Blagg said he'd promised the *Fraulein* some money. But you can't take all of it."

"How much money?"

"He said 300 marks." Blagg had said 250.

"Then I take 400." Maxim knew he'd had about 650 in the wallet. Bruno handed him the difference, note by note, grinning. Then he swatted himself across the nose with the 400, and walked out jauntily. They waited until the front door of the flat slammed.

Fraulein Winkelmann sat down again, staring at the TV. There was a zooming motor race on and Maxim simply hadn't even heard it until then.

"You are not very brave," she said.

"I paid 400 marks not to get shot. It seemed worth it to me. Did he give me all the papers?"

"I expect so. Now he will drink your money and come back and beat me."

"Do you know where he hides the gun? I could . . . make it so that it will not shoot, but he won't know until he tries."

"I don't care. Now he sniffs cocaine, too. Let him shoot somebody and the police can have him." She started eating a cream cake.

Maxim fingered the envelope of certificates: there seemed to be a lot of them. "Did he do anything with these? Copy them? – anything?"

"I don't know. He could have done anything."

Maxim put 100 marks on the table; it was all he could afford, with the taxi meter ticking over. "I don't want anybody to get into trouble. So if you remember anything, call me at the Allenby barracks. I shall have some more money when I've changed some travellers' cheques."

"I take them," she said, startling him. But why not? And why not credit cards? – no, he couldn't quite see American Express listing her.

"Major Maxim," he reminded her.

"At the Engineers barracks." She scooped in the money and he let himself out.

Chapter 17

The barracks known as Allenby – though not to the locals – were pre-1939 *Wehrmacht* buildings, very solid and spacious but a little worn by now. Looking round his room, Maxim realised how spoiled he had become by married quarters and flats. Here there was no soap, no towel, no water-glass or coat-hangers, not even the traditional ashtray made out of a tin lid. Just the plain furniture from Accommodation Stores and a prominent list of what that should comprise. Somebody had pinched the 'Bin, Waste Paper, Metal . . .1'

He unpacked what little he needed and changed his shirt, then reopened the envelope from the Blumenthalstrasse. It seemed to hold just what Blagg had described: a wad of old death certificates, or *Sterbeurkunden*, and two minute strips of colour negative film in a transparent packet. These were really tiny, the special film made for Minox 'spy' cameras, and Maxim was a little surprised that real spies actually used it. But the negatives, each no bigger than his little fingernail, were totally meaningless to the naked eye.

Altogether there were thirty-eight certificates, each for somebody who had died in the parish of Bad Schwarzendorn on April 15 1945. The times of death seemed to span the whole day, but he couldn't be sure the thirty-eight covered everybody who died that day because the numbers of each certificate didn't add up to a complete sequence. Some had been signed as much as three days later. But that was less surprising than that somebody had still been issuing such certificates in the chaos that had been Germany, just three weeks before the final surrender.

The results weren't impressive: Maxim had collected parking fines that looked far grander. Each was on cheap, discoloured A5 paper, about the size of pages from a novel, the individual details clumpingly typed into the spaces provided in the print, and attested by the totally illegible signature of the then *Standesbeamte*. Each had a 30-*Pfennig* stamp cancelled by the eagle-and-swastika symbol, but with the swastika roughly scraped away. Perhaps Bad Schwarzendorn had been in Allied hands by then.

He settled down to sort through them.

Half an hour later, he was back downstairs asking for the duty officer. The mess was almost empty except for an Education Corps captain who was also using the place as an hotel, and three unmarried young officers who'd been playing tennis and shouldn't have been in the ante-room dressed like that. When found, the duty officer obviously knew enough about Maxim's sponsors not to ask for more. He showed him the mess library and the official telephone, then discreetly vanished.

"All quiet on the Western Front?" George was civil servant enough not to ask a simple question if a fancy one would do. "Did you get the paperwork?"

"I think I got it all." He gave George the details. "There's one for a Brigitte Schickert, née Krone, who was living in Dornhausen. That's a small farming village a few kilometres out of Bad Schwarzendorn. She died there at 11.30. Husband's name Rainer Schickert: I'm assuming that's Gustav Eismark."

"Sounds like it. What was the cause of death?"

"It doesn't give one. None of them do, there's no space for it, but there were twelve other people who died at that same time at Dornhausen, and four more from Dornhausen who died in the Karls Hospital at Bad Schwarzendorn at times later in the day."

Over the telephone, George's grunt became an electronic honk. "Thirteen deaths at the same time, four later – that sounds like a bomb. She was supposed to have died from Allied bombing, so that ties up. Doesn't it?"

"The only odd thing is that according to the military history, the place had been overrun by American First Army, either the 3rd or 9th Division, I can't quite make out their boundary line, nearly two weeks before." George enjoyed military detail and Maxim had got lucky with the library.

"Well . . . Gustav needn't have been telling the truth about the Allies – though it sounds as if he might have been telling it about his wife. You say you can't make anything of the photographs?"

"I could ask if anybody in the barracks has an enlarger. There might be a camera club –"

"Better not. You've got a new thrill on the way: Sims himself is coming over. You remember *him*? You're at Allenby barracks? Good, he'll contact you there, it might even be tonight."

"Isn't he taking a bit of a risk coming to Germany? I thought he'd be in strife with the *Verfassungschutz*."

"That's his problem. I don't suppose he's travelling under his own name. He just wants to keep it all within his own unit. Anyway, you simply hand over everything you've got and try to be polite with it, by which I mean don't tell him how to do his own job. Buy him *eine kleine Knackwurst* and toddle home without a stain on your character. Is there any chance of your doing that?"

When George had rung off, Maxim reached for the First British Corps telephone directory which sat just beside the phone. He hadn't, after all, promised *not* to look up the name and home number of the divisional security officer, and one small stain wouldn't really count and might not even show.

Captain Brian Apgood was a slight, very young-looking man with pale skin and wispy blonde hair. In his Sunday dress of jeans and a fresh white shirt, he looked as if he'd get mugged the moment he set foot in a town with more cars than horses. He sat on the foot of Maxim's bed and lit a small cigar. "I'm not being inhospitable," he explained, "but we have to assume the chance of *them* having my house and office both wired, and I imagine Number 10 wouldn't like that. I know I shouldn't ask this, but –"

"That's right, you shouldn't," Maxim said politely. On the phone he had mentioned nothing but his name and rank.

Apgood smiled back. "Okay. Let's see what we've got." He held up the packet of film against the light and made non-committal noises. "It's infra-red, funny colours like this.

Doesn't look like much, but I can print them up for you. Only black-and-white if you want them tonight . . . ?''

"Please."

Apgood pocketed the film and sat down to browse through the stack of fragile old certificates.

After that, he said: "I suppose it would be a silly question to ask how you got these?"

"A . . . *roundabout* way. Am I right in thinking I shouldn't have them?"

"They're not secret, nothing like that. But they shouldn't be floating around loose. They aren't copies, they're the originals. They should still be in the files at the *Standesamt.* Unless they've microfilmed them, of course, and these are just waste paper. They *are* microfilming a lot of old stuff now . . . Does any particular one mean anything to you?"

"The top one."

Apgood skimmed through Brigitte Schickert's certificate, her husband's name, parents' names, place and date of birth, and the address of the Leistritz farmhouse, Dornhausen.

"I hope some of these names mean something to you; they don't ring any bells with me."

"That's all right. I just wondered what else you could tell me."

"Like what?"

"Well . . ." by now Maxim was far from sure himself; ". . . perhaps why so many of them?"

"Did these get pinched from the *Standesamt?*"

"Ah . . . in a sort of way, yes."

"The simplest explanation would be that by pinching a whole day's deaths you help conceal an interest in just one of them. And you couldn't ask for copies of all these, you'd have to ask for just one, and that would give away your interest, too. Still, it seems a bit drastic to go and start looting the place."

"But these can't be the only versions?"

Apgood looked up at him curiously. "As a matter of fact, they most probably are. How much did you get taught about German documents at Ashford? – or Hereford?" The Army grapevine hadn't lost its bloom in the early heatwave: Apgood had a very good rundown on Maxim's background.

"Assume it's nothing."

"Fair enough. Well . . . the thing to cling to is that everything like this is still decentralised. Births, marriages, deaths – all the routine stuff is still kept at the local *Standesamt* where it was first registered, and *only* there. No copies to central government or anywhere like that. And since there's something like seven thousand *Standesamter* in West Germany alone, you can have quite a job looking somebody up if you don't know where to start. I imagine it's a legacy of the war: centralised personal data sounds too much like the Gestapo – though mind you, it would be a hell of a storage problem if you *did* start collecting copies of all these. We'll see how long the libertarian principles last once everything's on microfilm."

"If you destroyed these, would it destroy evidence of the deaths?"

"No-o . . . these things are numbered and they'll be cross-indexed to some sort of register of names. But you'd destroy the detail: time of day, exact place and so on. Unless, as I say, it's all been microfilmed and these are just garbage. You could easily find out: just ring up the *Standesamt* at . . . ah, Bad Schwarzendorn, and – *Hold* on a minute! The *Standesbeamte* there got killed the other day. *Shot.*"

"I was in the UK at the time," Maxim reassured him.

Apgood pinched his nose like an airline passenger trying to clear his eardrums, and looked Maxim over carefully. Then he let out his breath in a puff. "We-ell . . . Has all that been cleared up? I seem to recall some mystery woman . . ."

"I think the police are treating the case as closed."

"Look – my first responsibility is to Division –"

"Of course. I just wanted an opinion. And I won't quote you."

Still looking wary, Apgood walked over to the washbasin, tapped the ash from his cigar and washed it away. "I can see why you might not want to go near Bad Schwarzendorn. Shall I ring up?"

"If you can do it without . . ." then Maxim remembered that Apgood's whole life was devoted to doing things 'without'. He changed tack. "So you don't think there's any chance

160

of anybody having put a fake certificate into the files? – years after the event?"

Apgood instinctively picked up a certificate and glanced through it, then shook his head. "No. I don't mean just the forgery, and that's a hell of a job, trying to fake something that's aged as badly as these – it's the numbering. It wouldn't fit into the sequence, it wouldn't match up with the ledger. Anyway, why should somebody want to do that?"

He really looked so absurdly young and guileless, so like a starry-eyed subaltern about to go over the top into the machine-guns of the Somme, that Maxim almost answered. Just in time, he remembered he was talking to a thirty-year-old Captain from Int Corps who was deeply interested in anything that might be happening on his patch.

"I really wouldn't know," he said carefully.

"Okay. But I can take some of these back to the office and have a look at them under the funny lights – ultra-violet, infra-red – to see if anything shows up. Having a whole batch together should make an odd one stick out like a sore thumb. That's another reason why you wouldn't try forging one."

"Thanks, but . . . if you could just print up the photos for me . . ."

"Will do. And you aren't asking for help to get the other stuff back into the files at Bad Schwarzendorn."

Thankfully, Maxim reflected that that was entirely Sims's problem. "I suppose they do belong there."

"If anybody wants them to prove anything, they do. Floating about loose, all they prove is that whoever's got them is more or less of a crook. Present company excepted, of course."

"Thank you. Do you want me to come and hold the stopwatch?"

"No need. You stay and have lovely din-dins with the Sappers and I'll be back before lights-out."

Maxim didn't argue. In barracks he was where Sims could find him and while he didn't expect much from Sunday dinner in a near-deserted mess, just being back with the Army was sauce enough for the moment.

The dinner, Maxim decided, would be best remembered as 'nourishing', and he went back to the ante-room to do something about the taste of it. A few more officers were drifting in from their various weekends, and the chatter turned to the likelihood of their being called out on an 'Agile Blade' exercise in the next few days. This was a test of how fast the regiment could pack up and move out to its battle positions, and was supposed to come as a big surprise, but Maxim knew how easy it was to predict. Most units were usually too busy to go to war: dispersed on training schemes, preparing for some grand parade, absorbing new equipment, training for a tour of Northern Ireland or retraining back from it. So on the rare occasions they did report themselves in a State of Readiness they knew an Agile Blade was likely. To the younger officers, Maxim's presence proved that tomorrow would be The Day and – by reverse logic – that he must be a spy from Allied Command Europe come to report on their morale and even sobriety. It became a joke to ply him with half-pints of beer and fantasies about each other's unfitness for battle.

The mess sergeant arrived with a brief respite: Captain Apgood was at the back door.

They sat on stubby pillars at the bottom of a short flight of steps leading to the parade square. The security officer handed over a bunch of small prints and lit a cigar. "Not very exciting, I'm afraid. Looks like just a test strip. It's flash, you can tell by the shadows. Must be infra-red, the thing you don't notice unless you're looking straight at it."

The pictures showed various angles of a small room that was furnished with little more than a big couch, a hi-fi and a table of drinks.

"Like going to the pictures, isn't it?" Apgood said. "Always seems there's something better coming next week. Oh, by the way, I ran off copies for myself, I hope you don't mind. It's just conceivable that room might pop up in some other picture some day."

Maxim didn't mind, although he had a vague sense Apgood was seeing something he'd missed himself. Then he remembered the magazine, *Focus on Germany*.

"If you could dig up a back copy –" he gave the date, nine

years before; " – If the worst comes to the worst, just lift one from the Liaison Officer's back room."

"Dear *me*. What strange morality one learns in high places."

Chapter 18

Maxim woke with a slightly tender head – those blasted lieutenants and their silly jokes – and the sombre feeling that he must be getting truly old if he could no longer sleep through a normal wakey-wakey in barracks. He lay for some minutes listening to the clatter of boots, slamming of doors and distant shouts before the snorts and squeals of armoured personnel carriers below his window made him realise this was far from normal and was, in fact, an Agile Blade.

He was just wrapping himself in a garish Hong Kong dressing-gown when the door burst open and a hulking first lieutenant in combat dress, his helmet stuffed with leaves and his face already smeared with camouflage cream, stood staring at him. Maxim was about to explain when the lieutenant obviously came to a snap judgment on his military value and slammed out again. So he stood for ten minutes at the window watching soldiers tossing bundles of equipment into the gurgling FV 432s parked around the parade ground and feeling the deep contentment of seeing other people working very hard very early in the day. Then he dressed and went down for what would now be a vulture's breakfast.

At nine o'clock he and the transient education officer were still sitting in the ante-room reading old copies of *Country Life* when the mess sergeant came in to say Mr Sims was on the phone.

He was all business. "I think you have all the papers? – good. Can you meet me at the parking place outside the cathedral in half an hour? I will come past in a dark blue Audi 100. Is that all right?"

"Make it a quarter to ten. I don't know how quickly I can get into town."

"Okay then, 0945."

Maxim got the film and certificates from his room, then stood for a moment at the top of the front steps, looking across the parade ground. It was another hot windless day, and they were living in a bowl of milky haze and smog, so that the blue only began perhaps twenty degrees above the horizon. It would be murder out in the field, digging in, and the soldiers knew it. They were all slumped in the shade of the vehicles, blurred by patches of cigarette smoke.

Then whistles started blowing and the scene shattered into movement. The mess sergeant appeared at Maxim's elbow, offering a key. "I don't know how long we'll be out, sir, but this is for the drinks cupboard. Write out a chit for whatever you use, as usual. And there'll be a sort of lunch in the cookhouse, nothing here."

"Thank you, Sergeant."

The sergeant saluted and then, because Maxim wasn't wearing uniform, couldn't resist asking: "Are you really from Command, sir?"

Slightly surprised at a mess sergeant who didn't know all about every officer, Maxim was about to deny it when he realised that, by chance, he had found a great cover story. So he just smiled as enigmatically as he knew how, and pocketed the drinks key. The first personnel carriers rumbled out of the main gate, blocking the workday traffic, and he watched them now with envy because they were off to play soldiers and he hadn't been invited.

Sims stopped the car on a wooded road just across the A64 *Autobahn*, lit one of his menthol cigarettes and opened the envelope. "Is this everything?"

"Everything I got. It's what Blagg said."

"Please tell me how you got it."

Maxim ran through a brief version of the Blumenthalstrasse meeting while Sims counted the death certificates.

"You are sure the man Bruno gave you everything? He could perhaps have changed something." Sims took out a jeweller's eyeglass and peered at the tiny negatives.

"He could have. But he only had about a couple of hours to do it in – after I'd rung from Hannover. Until then he'd been

expecting Blagg, and he might know exactly what he'd left."
Maxim had decided to play this bland and straight – well,
fairly straight. Captain Apgood and the prints he had made
weren't even going to get a mention-in-despatches.

"I understand. But perhaps you think he would have
changed something if he could?"

"Out of pure habit, yes."

Sims smiled at him. "Yes. Now, you have seen the certificates of death?" He had gone back to those.

"I had a look through."

"And it seems that something happened at Dornhausen at
11.30 hours on April 15 1945. A bomb, do you think?"

"Probably. The place had been occupied by the Americans
for ten days or more, but 9th Air Force was flying missions
down to the south and Czechoslovakia until the end of the
month. And not every bomb falls in the right place."

"That is very true, Major. But you have looked up some
history for me? I am very grateful."

Maxim shrugged. "The rest of the news doesn't look too
good. I mean, there's a death certificate for her and I don't see
how it could be faked. You'd have a problem trying to fit it
into the sequence, wouldn't you? There'd be a number in a
ledger – or something . . ."

"You are quite right, Major. You know something about
these matters."

"Not really."

"Oh yes." He brooded for a moment. "You know I have a
problem being in Germany. If I am recognised . . . I must be
careful. Please, will you come to Bad Schwarzendorn to help
me?"

"I can tell you want to go," George said. "And in the end I had
to say you could. Co-operation, that's the word. Show willing – but not too much. I just wish The Firm would find
somebody else to delegate to . . . and Harry, for God's *sake*
remember Number 10 when it comes to the crunch. And don't
let it *come* to the crunch, either."

He rang off and stared gloomily at the phone. He should
have been saying No, Never, Not Again. Yet while he didn't

much care about the outcome of Plainsong, except in a generally patriotic sense, he cared very much that it shouldn't fail in any way that would leave a vindictive Foreign Office with a load of blame to distribute. Anything to keep Plainsong alive and Scott-Scobie and co. quiet until the news from Scotland got better. Or perhaps much worse. Well, by tomorrow we should know . . .

But of course we won't, he told himself. We go through life saying Well, tomorrow we shall know, one way or the other. Whether we've passed the exam, got the job, if she's pregnant or not. And tomorrow comes and we don't know. Oh, it brings plenty of its own unique disappointment and despair, but nothing to solve the dilemma of today.

He picked up the phone again and asked for Agnes at the Mount Row number. She was out.

Chapter 19

The house was part of a terrace, narrow and rising four stories from the level of the semi-private road running alongside Kensington High Street. Victorian, of course, but if you spend sixty-four years on the throne then a lot of building styles are going to be named after you. There was no entryphone, just a column of assorted bellpushes and their faded name-cards. It would be a long walk down for whoever had the top flat. Agnes found a card lettered neatly PFAFFINGER and pushed the bell.

She had just pressed it a second time when she heard a faint voice above the High Street traffic. A small head was poking out of the topmost window.

"I'm Algar!" she yelled up. "I rang you!"

The head ducked back and out again, and a crumpled piece of paper fell fast to the pavement. It was a brown envelope with a Yale key inside. Certainly cheaper than an entryphone.

Leni was waiting at the foot of the last flight of stairs, which was partitioned off to give her a flimsy front door of her own. Despite the thick skirt and cardigan, Agnes was surprised at the delicate frailness of her, like one of those rather coy Parian ware figurines, and with much the same over-large blue eyes. They went on up.

"Would you like some coffee? It will only be a moment."

"Very much. Thank you." Agnes sat down gingerly on a worn green velvet wing chair. The room was low-ceilinged, comfortable, long-lived in. Sagging plank bookshelves covered most of the walls, with papers and magazines scattered over all the flat surfaces. From atop one pile on the desk under the window, a very fat long-haired black cat gazed impassively at Agnes.

Leni came back with the coffee and poured it into two

non-matching teacups. It was real and freshly made.

"Are you really from the Security Service? A young girl like you?"

"Of course." Agnes reached for her bag.

"No, no. I believe you. But why? Can you tell me why?"

"It's a living." No, that was too flip for this shrewd little old lady. "I like it and I'm good at it."

Leni smiled quickly, then just sat, very upright as if setting a good example, and seemed to be thinking something out. "Two other men came: were they from your service? They said they were attached to the Ministry of Defence – that's what you usually say, isn't it?"

"We have a card that says that. Do you want to . . ."

"No, they didn't show me their cards. But is it still true you only recruit people who are born British?"

Forty years of political broadcasting and handling refugees had probably given Leni as good a sense of how the twilight world worked as Agnes had herself.

"That's broadly true, yes."

"These men were German. At times we spoke German, it was easier for them."

"What did they want?"

"The same as you: to talk about Mina."

"Did they know she was alive, in this country?"

Leni hesitated. "Are you sure she is?"

"Oh yes. She came to visit you a week ago, at Bush House. She was issued with a security pass in the name of Linnarz." That was true, and if it suggested they had been alerted by the security pass and not by a friend in the underpaid BBC World Service, then so much the better.

"Look," Agnes went on, "these people were *not* from my service. I'd like you to be quite sure that I'm who I say I am. I can get anybody you name at the BBC to talk to my office and then vouch for me."

"I believe you. But who were the men?"

"I hope they were from our Intelligence Service, playing silly tricks. If not, then God help us. And Mina."

"You're saying that just to frighten me."

Agnes waited, sipping her coffee.

"I'm sorry," Leni said. "That was silly, like a radio play." For her, radio was too serious for plays.

"When did they come?"

"On . . . on Friday."

"What did you tell them?"

"They knew I had seen Mina, too. How did they know?"

Agnes shook her head helplessly, but knew that Guy Husband would also have his contacts at Bush House. Most likely the SSD had a friend in need, too. "Did you tell them where Mina lives now?"

"Oh no. She didn't tell me."

Agnes smiled and put her cup carefully down on an uneven surface of *Der Spiegels* and *Encounters*. "Good. Can you tell me something about Mina? – just talk about her. How you met her, how she got on when she first came over here . . ."

"You must have it all in your files."

"We have a lot of paper in our files. I rather prefer people."

They had met a few days after Mina had stood up at the end of a recital in the Usher Hall at Edinburgh to announce that she would very much like to stay here in England (a tiny mistake the Scots reporters had kindly ignored) rather than return to East Germany. In the early 1950s every defection by either side was exploited like a battle won. The Home Office granted her political asylum with uncharacteristic haste and from then on she was interviewed constantly by every newspaper and radio network represented in Britain – including, of course, the BBC's German language service, which was aimed directly at the East Zone.

Leni had taken pity – more than pity – on the young woman who was so grateful for a friendly German voice and so bemused by the political carnival she had unleashed. Leni soon realised that Mina had defected simply to join the Hollywood dream that the East Berlin loudspeakers were always denouncing. She merely wanted to be whisked from luxury hotel to draught-free concert hall in a big limousine, there to play to an attentive, elegant audience and be driven away again surrounded by *encores* and orchids. This wasn't selfishness or greed, just a feeling that it was due. She had no idea, Leni was certain, that she had even harmed her brother's career, let alone collapsed it. He had his ships and politics, she had her piano which she had practised for over twenty years, so now let the dream come true.

And for a few years it had just about done so. Looking back, nobody could now say how much of her success was due to her defection and how much to her playing. She had made only one recording for posterity to judge her by, and that was of Chopin, never her strongest point. She toured Britain and West Europe, she broadcast constantly – but she preferred recitals to the teamwork of symphonies, so never got taken up by one conductor, and in the long run that can be very important. Her agent – perhaps he wasn't the best in the world – never got her an American tour which, again, might have made all the difference. But probably the biggest shock, Leni thought, was the unexpected competitiveness of the top musicians in the West. In the East you worked, you were paid, there was no need to compete and no reward for it. In London, some of the stories about what pianists would do to secure a tour, a recording contract, a broadcast, had left Mina shattered. The Dream was real, but so were some of the things the Berlin loudspeakers had said about it.

Her career dwindled gently. She took to spending more time at Bush House, playing for very little except the chance to gossip in her native language. Oddly, she had never shown much interest in touring in West Germany – perhaps she was scared to go that close to the border – and had not even taken out a West German passport, to which she was automatically entitled. She lived day to day, as dear Mina always had – or rather, year to year, on a British Certificate of Identity renewed annually.

Agnes knew that already. "She never married?" She knew that, too, but preferred to imply that she hadn't seen the files.

"She went out with some men, yes, when she was here. She was not . . . not abnormal. But she talked about a boy she had loved in the war and who had been killed. That happened often enough, God knows. And then looking after Gustav's boy, I think after that she wanted a life for herself. Then she went to South Africa. No, she went on a Commonwealth tour, but it was in South Africa that she had her new success, and she stayed on there. She wrote to us about it, it was like the first days in Britain except the weather was much better. She sent us some notices of her recitals . . ." Leni smiled wistfully; " . . . and then we heard nothing. I thought . . . perhaps I thought she was dead."

"Did she marry out there?"

Leni didn't answer, didn't look at Agnes, just sat with her hands held primly in her lap. The big cat climbed stiffly down off the desk and squatted on a box of cat-sand under a corner table, staring straight ahead with a sublime conviction that it was invisible.

Agnes said: "She must have got some new identity. Her British certificate hasn't been renewed for twenty years."

Leni got up briskly and sprayed around the cat-box with an air-freshener. "Oh yes, she did get married."

That was all it took. Given a new name, she got a new nationality, new passport – a new life that was far more fundamental a change than she had managed just by defecting. It is much easier to vanish than most people realise, particularly if you're a woman and ready to cut yourself off from family and friends – most of which Mina had already done by coming West.

"She told you this last week?"

"Yes . . ." Leni hesitated; " . . . yes, she told me then."

"Was he British?"

"I . . . I suppose he must have been, to bring her back here."

That 'suppose' seemed a bit odd. "Can you tell me his name?"

The delicate face was lined with anguish. "But why do you want to know?"

"Because others want to know. I suppose that's the best answer. And merely because you didn't tell them her new name and address doesn't mean to say they'll stop looking."

"She didn't tell me."

There was one last hope of invisibility, as dignified as the cat's, although this time for her friend. And maybe a little shame that Agnes had to dispel.

"I know that," she said gently. "But somebody who cares as much as you do, you'd want to know." She waited, but

Leni stayed obstinately silent. "She played the piano for you, one last time. The men who came to see you, they wouldn't think of somebody having to empty their pockets before they play the piano – but that's really what a woman does, isn't it? She puts her bag down, somewhere aside, not on top of a grand piano, with her new name and address inside . . ."

Chapter 20

Until they had got out of the car to phone, Maxim had never seen Sims standing up. He turned out to be a couple of inches shorter than Maxim himself, but slightly heavier in build, the figure of a boxer rather than a sprinter – except for those tiny hands.

Now it seemed as if his arms tapered all the way down to his fingertips where they lay lightly on the wheel of the Audi. The cuffs of his cream silk shirt were still linked, the discreet but expensive tie still knotted at his neck; his only concession to the sun was that his light blue blazer was carefully laid out along the back seat. Maxim wondered if he dressed that way only because he worked for The Firm, and decided probably not. As a nation, the Germans were far more formal dressers than the British: the only people around the centre of Osnabrück not wearing ties were obviously foreigners by the rest of their dress. Maxim had a tie with him, but at the moment it was in his pocket.

"Will you be able to get those photographs blown up?" he asked casually. Now that he was going to be with Sims for most of the day, knowing what was on the photographs was an uncomfortable burden.

"I will arrange it in Paderborn." It was just about a hundred kilometres to Bad Schwarzendorn, with Paderborn – another town with a British garrison – shortly before it.

"What are we going to do at Bad Schwarzendorn?"

"You will look. Go to the place, Dornhausen. On the map it is a very small place. Somebody will remember."

"Do the Germans – I mean in the West – know Gustav Eismark was Rainer Schickert?"

"No. It is what Guy told you: a politician in the GDR has no public past. The official history is that he was in the Communist resistance. That is all, the whole war, for him. And of course everybody was in the Communist resistance – now."

"Wouldn't somebody in West Germany recognise him?"

"He was Rainer Schickert for only a year and a few months – and mostly in hiding. How many saw him then? And then he was, I think, twenty-three. By the time he is becoming a politician, his picture in the paper, he is fifty. It is a long time, a lot of change."

"How did *you* know?"

Sims took a long time to think about answering that. He was driving well, perhaps too well, as if there was one perfect speed for every individual metre of road and he had to slow down or speed up to reach it. It wasn't jerky, just a little unsettling, and Maxim might not have been asking so many questions if he'd been able to sit back and watch the countryside flow past.

At last Sims said: "It was Mrs Howard who came to know that. It was the first thing we had . . . Do you know the island of Hiddensee, near to Rügen? Ah – of course you must know Rügen."

And 'of course' Maxim did, because it was the island – little more than a peninsula really – in the Baltic where the East German version of the Special Air Service did its training. He had studied the snatched photos of their Jeeps and Land-Rovers, their NATO uniforms, that proved their wartime mission was just the same as the SAS's. It could have been Sims's unit who supplied those photos.

"I don't know Hiddensee."

"It is a place for *Freikultur*, not what you call nudism but . . . a liberation of the body, a going back to natural things . . . It was very strong with the old Weimar Republic. People go there to holiday, to lose all their problems, and also their ranks. The Democratic Republic is very bureaucratic, very much full of class distinctions. But at Hiddensee, you become anybody . . . or nobody. Somebody will sit down beside you on the sandhills and just talk. They will tell you anything, things they would never say to anybody anywhere else. Things they would get arrested for."

"Sounds a good place to plant a few informers."

"It is not easy to be diguised without clothes," Sims said dryly. "The Republic needs that place, places like that. It is a safety valve, you might say a brothel of the mind. But yes – there are some informers, too. There was one who was sitting beside Gustav Eismark, many years ago, just when he was about to be married the second time. He talked about getting married – of course he did not know the man recognised him, although it is not far from Rostock, where he lived then. Eismark said he felt guilty because his first marriage had never ended, he said it could never end – *das wird nie vorüber sein* – and it would always be a secret he must keep from his new wife.

"So of course the informer – he worked for himself, not the state – tried to find some proof of this. But all he could discover was that Gustav's roadname had been Schickert, and the marriage certificate at Sangerhausen."

"It wasn't the marriage that was in question."

"No, but all the other proof was in West Germany so he could not do anything more. Then one time when he was doing some other business with the woman we called Mrs Howard, he sold her the story for a few marks. She did nothing much about it – Eismark was still just somebody in shipping, not a politician – and it was only when he came onto the Secretariat that she asked for money to do some more work about it."

"It doesn't seem much, just a few remarks made at a *Freikultur* camp twenty years ago."

Sims glanced a smile at him. "In our work we live on whispers. In your work perhaps you control a thousand tanks. In one way – please understand me – that is easy: they are *there*. They can do many things, but they cannot destroy a man's reputation. One whisper may do that. Our work is to find that whisper, to control it."

Maxim had been long enough in Whitehall to know what Sims was talking about.

They cruised in silence for a while, then Sims asked abruptly: "Have you got a camera?"

"No."

"You should buy one at Paderborn, there may be something to photograph. And hire a car also; I must take the photographs for printing. We will meet late in the afternoon."

So in the end it would be Maxim's name on the pieces of paper, not whatever Sims was calling himself on this trip. And it must be a nice life to be able to decide *I need a camera* and buy a camera, just like that. He wished . . . Oh, come off it, Harry, he told himself. You've said 'Fire!' and seen the price of a dozen cameras blow away in a few seconds' worth of flash and bang, with nothing left at the end to stick in the family album. Every profession has its own little extravagances.

The village of Dornhausen lay about eight kilometres out of Bad Schwarzendorn itself, and the final road to it was a narrow concrete track that even in June was still covered in flaking mud and cow dung. It ran straight up a wide shallow valley, with tilled fields on both sides, to a huddle of buildings. Beyond, a slightly steeper slope of pasture rose to a low skyline with a toupee of trees. Maxim drove it slowly, enjoying the first real countryside he had been in since the hot weather began.

When he reached it, the village was little more than six huge farm buildings in the classic German style: each wall a grid of brown-painted timbers, filled in with rough-plastered brickwork. And each building could be a farm in itself, housing animals and machinery on the ground floor, humans above that, wine and vegetables in the cellar and hay in the loft under the steep-pitched tile roof. You could never believe just how big such places were until you got up close. Beside them, the modern tractor sheds and dairies looked ready to collapse in the first breeze.

And the villagers would have the same massive unity as their houses. Maxim had run into that before, on exercises, when he wanted to dig his troops in among the growing vegetables, and probably Hitler's soldiers had been no more welcome. A small farming community would be a good place to hide out a war.

The tap-room of the tiny inn was down a deep step and he nearly sprawled on the tiled floor, coming abruptly into the cool darkness. When he had got his balance back, a woman in a dowdy black dress was looking at him with tired amusement. There was nobody else in the room.

"Are you open?" he asked.

"We are never closed. Did you want to eat?"

"No, thank you. Just a Pils."

It came in a stone mug, deliciously cold and wiping out in one mouthful the heat of the morning and the traces of last night's headache (he wondered briefly how the Engineer regiment was getting on in its battle positions; by now they should be dug in and pausing for sips of lukewarm water or barely warmer tea. Even war games are hell).

He finished the beer and asked for another. The woman was probably in her middle forties, with a body that looked strong rather than fat under the shapeless clothes, and a long lined face that had already done all the ageing it was likely to.

"Were you here in the war?" Maxim asked; he'd never feel comfortable trying to start conversations like this.

"Yes."

"Can you help me? It's about somebody who was killed here. I think there was a bomb . . ."

"Yes. The Bomber. There's a memorial, up by the church."

"The church?" He hadn't seen anything that could be a church.

"The old one. Up the road." Her expression hadn't changed by a fraction throughout.

A little perplexed, he left the second mug of Pils on the table.

Not noticing the church hadn't been quite as crass as he'd feared, because whatever else the bomb had done, it had blown the church apart. Hardly any part of it stood more than waist high now, much was covered in grass or blackthorn bushes, and it could never have been more than a chapel anyway. The road ended just there, in a long concrete hardstand where a cart and some rusting old farm machinery were parked. Beyond, the pastureland sloped up to the skyline.

Beside the ruin, the grass had been scythed to rough ankle-length around a handful of old gravestones and an incongruously clean slab of veined grey marble that lay glinting in the sun. It was carved with very competent lettering, but all it said was 15 April 1945 and a list of names. There were seventeen in all, three recurring – Scholz, Leistritz and Brenner; probably the main families in the village. The Schickerts' address had been the Leistritz farmhouse. Brigitte Schickert's name was there, too.

Maxim wrote down the names, then took out the new camera and fiddled with it; presumably the gravestone was evidence of a sort.

"Are you looking for something?" The old man must have moved very softly to get within twenty yards of him unheard, although the quiet afternoon was in fact a steady rumble and distant clatter of farm machinery.

"Er . . . I was interested in a name."

"One of those?" The old man jabbed his stick towards the marble. He had a face like a leather potato, all bumps and creases, and wore a thick cloth jacket over-shirt buttoned to the neck, all grey and brown and far too hot for the day. But he was well past seventy, when the blood runs thin even in June.

"Brigitte Schickert."

"Oh, her. Did he send you?"

He? Which *he*? Of course, the presumably-still-alive Rainer Schickert. Now we find out if they really don't know what became of him. "No, not her husband. Just a London lawyer wanting to know where she's buried. They don't tell you what it's all about, but they pay you for it." He took a second picture and pocketed the camera. "I have an unfinished beer at the *Wirtshaus*. Would you like to join me?"

The solid old barrel of a body moved stiffly but not very carefully, like a heavy vehicle in low gear. Seeing the village again, from a new angle, Maxim could see other scars of the blast and its debris. The great linden tree, the traditional place for a village parliament, was lopsided even now from missing branches, and the nearest farmhouse was patched with unmatching brickwork and some of the window frames were too square to be old. But the signs of prosperity far outweighed those of damage: the new BMWs and Mercedes, freshly painted woodwork and the constant noise of machinery from the outhouses.

"A nice village," Maxim commented. "How many farms is it?"

"It used to be three, now it's two. The Leistritz family packed up and sold out, just after the war. Two of the boys were killed in Russia, then their father was killed by The Bomber. The last boy couldn't keep it going."

"You lost more in the war than we did," Maxim said, and instantly felt he'd pitched it too strong.

But the old man nodded emphatically. "Yes, we did that. You're right. War is a terrible thing."

"What happened about the Leistritz farm?"

"That's it." The stick waggled at a great building nesting among its outhouses at the bottom of the village. "Karl Scholz bought most of the land and my father bought the house and the rest and gave it to me to run. It was a terrible business."

Maxim said nothing more until they were back at the inn.

The old man's name was Brenner and he chose a Dunkel and a Korn – a very dark beer plus a chaser of the local heart-stopper that tasted somewhere between very young whisky and vodka. Purely out of tact, Maxim braced his brain cells for a kamikaze mission and opted to drink in parallel.

For a quarter of an hour, Brenner talked about the weather, the Common Market and taxes. When he had finished the first beer, Maxim asked: "Did you know the Schickerts well?"

"Not well, no. They only came in the last winter of the war, just a few months. Old Leistritz took them in – he got paid, naturally. Everybody was taking in women and children from the cities, away from the bombing, or storing their furniture for them. My father said he'd never known a season before when chairs and commodes were the best crops." He chuckled, and finished his Korn as well. "After 1941 the village was full of strangers. They even sent us some French and Belgians, people like that, to work the land. Our own lads were getting killed in Russia, so they sent us Belgians to play with their widows. War isn't just terrible, it's ridiculous."

"But you did know them?" Maxim persisted.

Brenner looked at him. "Him, yes, a bit. He had a glass eye.

Something of a scholar, and Leistritz said he'd done farm work before. He liked him."

"And her?"

"Ach." Brenner banged his right hand on the head of his stick as if to knock some feeling back into it. "I hardly saw her. It was winter, she stayed indoors with the baby."

"Of course. Would you like another drink?"

While the woman was bringing more beer and the bottle of Korn, three other men came in. One wore a city suit but was carrying the jacket; the other two were in farm clothes. Brenner called the one in the suit over and introduced him as Rolf Scholz.

"This young Englishman wants to know something about Frau Schickert – do you remember her? What was her first name?"

"Brigitte," Scholz said.

"That's right."

Maxim asked what Scholz would drink. He was a hulk of a man in his middle fifties, inches taller than Maxim and instinctively stooping under the low beams of the tap-room. He moved with a delicacy that emphasised his power, and he had a slow smile and a gentle handshake.

They drank and Scholz asked bluntly: "What did you want to know about her?"

"Nothing much . . . just that she was killed by the bomb."

"The Bomber." It was said just the way the woman and Brenner had said it, *Das Kampflugzeug*, like The Event, and Scholz saw Maxim's puzzlement. "It wasn't just a bomb, but a whole bomber. An American, a B-26. I don't know what was wrong with it, but it still had all its bombs on board when it came down there, behind the church."

Maxim had wondered about that: the blast effect had seemed pretty widespread for just a bomb. Now they were talking about perhaps four tons of bombs toppling out of the sky one morning when Dornhausen thought the war had passed it by. And not even an air raid warning to send them into the cellars.

Maxim thought of asking if the bomber's crew had bailed out, but decided it might be tactless.

181

"She didn't actually get killed by The Bomber," Scholz went on. "She died later. Oh, there would be seven or eight who died later, in hospital."

Maxim sat for a while, absorbing that thought. "She didn't die here then?"

"That's what he said." Brenner sounded testy.

"You didn't help take her to hospital, or anything?"

Scholz took out a meerschaum pipe that was burned to a dark orange and blew through it. "The Americans did that. They were quick with it, too. Their medical service was probably the best thing about their Army."

Maxim glanced at him sharply and Scholz smiled a slow smile back. "I was in the Army then. Field engineers. But I picked up glandular fever and liver trouble in Italy that winter and I was still at home on sick leave when the whole thing finished. So . . . I just privately discharged myself and let the Americans think I'd been here all along." Maxim instinctively smiled at him, then despised himself for the silly band-of-brother-soldiers stuff. Anyway, they didn't know he was a soldier.

"Do you know how badly she was hurt?"

Brenner burst out: "No, we don't! D'you think when The Bomber came down it just killed twenty people and left the rest of us drinking Korn and singing fal-lal-lal? It blew the whole village upside down. They took another twenty people to hospital and I had the dairy roof down on my back and it took them two hours to dig me out. I was in bed for a week with concussion and the doctor said at first he thought I'd got a broken pelvis. And my leg's never been properly better since. No, I don't know how badly she was hurt. Just badly enough to die, I imagine."

Scholz listened gravely, taking pinches of tobacco and pressing each gently into the pipe with his thumb, then sucking noisily to make sure it wasn't too tight. "I think I remember seeing her. She got it in the back of the neck. With neck wounds you can't tell, it could be nothing or everything. Her husband, Rainer, he wasn't hit but he went in with them. He spoke the best English. Then he came back the next day – I think it was the next day – and told us who'd died. Then he came again a couple of days after and took the baby."

"He just took it away?" Maxim was surprised. "It was only five months, wasn't it?"

Scholz lit his pipe and puffed quickly. "What else should he do? We couldn't look after it forever. He said he was going off to find his sister. It wasn't easy, travelling, in those days, but it wasn't as if he belonged here anyway."

"Who arranged things like the death certificates?"

Brenner said: "How should we remember who arranged them? I was in bed the whole week. You may say the Americans were wonderful with their ambulances but they didn't pay for the dairy and half the animals were dead already or had to be slaughtered. It was an American bomber. But the English would have been worse."

"It was Rainer who did that," Scholz said unperturbed, as if Brenner had never spoken. "I remember him going about the village, collecting the details, the birth certificates and things. He was good with forms, dealing with the bureaucrats."

"He was a scholar," Brenner said, banging his hand on the stick again.

"And you never saw him after that?"

"Why should we?" Brenner wanted to know. "He wasn't one of the village."

Scholz was wearing that wise, reflective look that pipe-smokers get or act on the few occasions their pipes are working well. "There was somebody else asking about him, or her. A few weeks ago."

"I didn't meet them." Brenner sounded offended.

"Neither did I. I forget who told me; probably somebody in town. Would you know who it was?"

Maxim tried for an expression of indifference – tried desperately. *Of course* Mrs Howard must have been asking around. You know, the one whose driving-licence picture was in the paper, she'd been shot, wasn't she asking about the Schickerts? And now there's this Englishman asking about them: will you ring the police or shall I?

He should have thought of that risk; he wondered if Sims *had* thought of it.

"I haven't heard of anybody," he said casually, "but if the

lawyers asked me they might have asked somebody else before . . . You said a few weeks ago?"

"About a month, I think it was."

"I've got to get back to town," Maxim said, "but can I get you another drink?"

Brenner was willing; Scholz had to go into town himself. Maxim waited nervously while the woman brought one more Dunkel and Korn. Trying to change the subject, he asked: "And nobody did anything about the church? I mean rebuild it."

"It's still church land," Scholz said. "Nobody's stopping them building it up. But the pastor only came for one service every two weeks even then, in the war."

"It wasn't much good as a sanctuary, either," Brenner said with an odd cackle.

"It was a Sunday," Scholz explained. "April 15. The Bomber came down in the middle of morning service."

Outside, the sun lashed him across the forehead with a warning of another headache to come, and he wished he hadn't had a drink with lunch at Paderborn. No wonder plainclothes coppers ended up able to conduct surveillances from behind the cover of their own stomachs.

The easiest way to turn the car was to drive on up to the hardstand by the church, and as he swung about he realised it was in fact the old foundations of small cottages, completely gone with The Bomber. He paused, working out that a shallow dent in the pasture was the remnant of a huge crater, and then got out to take another look at the marble. Seventeen names. Seven or eight had died in hospital, yes, and some of those would have lingered for a day or two; fair enough or even *blond genug*, as the Army usually put it. But the death certificates had shown thirteen people dying in Dornhausen itself. Thirteen plus seven or eight . . .

The woman came out of the inn and saw him, hesitated, then walked up. He waited.

"Did they tell you what you wanted to know?" she asked.

"I think so. Did you know Frau Schickert?"

"Yes. I was young at the time, a little girl. Sometimes I'd go in and she'd let me give the baby his bottle." A smile rippled across her wrinkled face and was gone. "A hussy from the city who peroxided her hair to look like a good Aryan."

"Did she?"

"I suppose so. It was something my mother said. To me, she just seemed kind. But sad."

"What about?"

"Nobody was happy, that winter. The Americans were coming. I thought that must be a good thing. I didn't understand."

"Were you here when The Bomber came down?"

"Down in the cellar, getting some vegetables for lunch. The whole earth went *schunk* and all the dust and bits fell out of the ceiling. I thought I was going to be buried."

"Did you see her? – after she was hurt?"

She folded her arms and frowned briefly at the memory. "There was blood all over her shoulders. He – Herr Schickert – was holding a towel to her neck. Why do you want to know?"

"Some lawyer wanted to know where she was buried. I don't know why. But now I've got a photograph . . ."

She gave a little snort of laughter. "She isn't buried here."

Maxim looked from her to the marble and back. "Not? – not there?"

"Not all the ones named are buried here, and some are here who aren't named. It's just a memorial, really."

"Some are buried here who aren't named?"

"Three Belgians, labourers. They were in the cottages." She nodded at the hardstand. "By the time they put this up, nobody could remember their names, and they didn't belong here, of course."

Death, the great leveller. Except in Dornhausen. But it explained the numbers that didn't add up – though not why Brigitte Schickert was shown on her certificate as having died in Dornhausen when everybody seemed to know she had been taken to hospital.

"Do you know where she *is* buried?"

"No. It isn't in the Evangelical cemetery, with the others who died in hospital. None of them came back, you see: the

Americans couldn't spare the trucks and the farms weren't allowed to use their petrol for anything but getting food to market. Later, months later when I was taken into town for the first time since The Bomber, I wanted to put some flowers on her grave. I couldn't find it. Nobody seemed to know. They just said she didn't belong here really."

For strangers, death in Dornhausen seemed to be oblivion of a peculiarly total sort.

Chapter 21

He had half an hour left before meeting Sims, so he took a cup of coffee at the café where Mrs Howard had set up her last rendezvous, then walked her route along the great *Gradierwerk* in the park outside. He had never seen it or anything like it before: a solid wall of blackthorn twigs a good forty feet high, smeared in long rusty streaks by the gypsum and salt in the trickling water that had changed the wood into coral branches. The spa season was at its height and the park was full of elderly couples strolling or filling the benches, the café tables and the chairs in front of the bandstand and staring down at their paunches from grey faces. It made Maxim feel not just young but uncomfortably young, and to walk at his usual pace would have been hooliganism. But the trimmed grass, the bright flowerbeds and the constant whisper of water from the wall and the many fountains gave the park a sedate gaiety – and made it a very odd place to get shot. *Two* murders must have been the talk of the sanatorium for . . . well, it still would be. He began to feel too conspicuous and walked without pausing through the archway where Hochhauser and Mrs Howard had died.

The Korn was now clenching his forehead with an iron glove, and he was trying to doze it away while the orchestra on the bandstand played Rossini – at least it sounded like Rossini to him, though so did a lot of other composers – when Sims dropped onto the chair beside him. Maxim struggled awake.

"Good afternoon." Sims's smile flashed under the blue sunglasses. "Thank you for being punctual. Did you discover anything interesting?"

"Something, I think. How did you manage with the photographs?"

"I have them, but there is nothing of importance there.

Nothing I understand. Tell me your news."

"They remember the Schickerts, all right: glass eye, spoke English well, good at form-filling, had worked on the land before – that's Gustav, isn't it?"

Sims nodded.

"Well, the incident was a loaded bomber crashing there. They lost about twenty-three dead, but that includes three Belgians, who don't really count. But I think we've got the certificates for them. The odd thing is, the certificate for Brigitte said she died there at 11.30, the time the bomber hit. But two people there remember her being taken into town – here – with a neck wound. Still alive. Along with about six others who died later."

Sims thought about that. "And who arranged about the certificates?"

"That's right: Our Gustav. Rainer. He went in with the wounded."

Sims took out his cigarettes, then glanced around. Other members of the audience were already glaring feebly at them. Sims stood up again. "Come. Tell me everything, carefully."

There was a monument to Bad Schwarzendorn's war dead of 1914–18 at the corner of the park closest to the shopping streets, and the two of them drifted inevitably towards it. Perhaps because they were talking about a memorial to another war, perhaps even more because a symbol of the dead young was more cheerful than the sight of the dying old.

"I walked round the Evangelical cemetery myself," Maxim finished up; "and I couldn't find any Brigitte Schickert. Not that that proves a thing. She could be planted anywhere."

"It helps. It is strange that she is not there, with the others. It . . . *suggests* . . ."

"But if he was filling in the forms himself, why fill in something that can be proven wrong so easily? It took me just one trip out to Dornhausen."

"Because you know what was on the certificate. But at Dornhausen they do not know *yet*, after more than thirty-five years, what is on that certificate. Why should they know? – people do not go looking up death certificates unless there is something they have to prove for a lawyer. Have you ever looked one up? No. And perhaps it would have been much more difficult to say she died in the hospital here, where the American doctors are making up records and signing things for all the others who die, but not for her because she is *not* dead."

"Yes . . ."

"Now, it would be perfect if the Karls Hospital still had the records to show that Frau Schickert was treated for a neck injury and was cured after two days."

"That's pretty hopeful, finding the records of an American Army surgical unit after these many years."

Sims's smile widened. "I know: I am dreaming. But some proof, I would like *some* proof."

"A whisper won't do?"

On top of the stone monument there perched a bronze eagle, blackened and streaked with green oxidisation. It looked sullen and hunched, with its wings half spread as if to dry. To look at it, Sims had his head well back, showing that his light tan was completely even right under his chin and down his throat.

"In the end," he said slowly, "we are looking for what Eismark will believe is proof. We do not want to destroy him, only to control him by the threat to destroy him."

"Blackmail."

Sims brought his head down to a cocked, quizzical position, and for once his smile looked as if it went deep back inside. "Do you disapprove?"

"There's a war on."

"At first it is blackmail. It does not go on that way. It becomes a secret that the two people share, something that brings them more and more together, something that pushes the world further away, outside. You can be closer to a man than his own wife, because she does not share the secret. And that man can come to love you, because every day is another day when you did not destroy him, one more day you have given him. And when at last they catch him, when he goes to confessional with the Electric Priest, you feel that a good friend has died."

189

He sighed rather melodramatically and looked at his watch. "Do you want to take your car back to Paderborn?"

"I suppose so. If you can take me on to Osnabrück."

North of Sennestadt, Sims skimmed the Audi in and out of a wide-spaced convoy of Army trucks, their headlights glowing feebly against the late afternoon sun. Soldiers with shining patches of sweat betraying the camouflage cream on their faces stared down at them with dead eyes.

"There's a load of instant pacifists," Maxim remarked.

"Not a good day for a war," Sims agreed.

"It's usually too hot or too cold, or too wet."

"Do you ever think you are getting too old for it?"

"It has to happen." And when it does, the Army politely pulls out the chair for you, the way it taught you to do for the lady on your left at a dinner party, and leaves you sitting down for the rest of your career. For Maxim, that was nearly another twenty years: the Army had promised him a career until he was fifty-five – but it had never promised he would rise above major. Majors aged fifty-five are seated a long long way from where the action is.

"Are you offering me a job?" he asked.

"You know I cannot. But I think you would get it."

It happened, Maxim knew. The Intelligence Service did recruit occasional officers in their thirties. It could always use a new face that was trained in military matters, security-minded and presumably a patriot, though the face was probably most important of all.

"Yes, I can just see Guy Husband laying out the red carpet for me."

"Guy is not the whole service, Major. He is not the most loved man in the service. And he will not always be head of the Sovbloc section."

Maxim glanced at Sims, who shook his head. "No, it will never be me, Major. The service has some rules it does not break. My work will always be with my unit, my own people. No promotion. So I have to care, perhaps more than most, about who is to be promoted."

Maxim wondered how much Sims knew about his own

promotion chances, and despite himself couldn't help feeling slightly pleased that somebody thought he could get, and do, a different job. No matter what that person's motives were in mentioning it.

He eased the seat-belt that was pressing his sweat-soaked shirt against his chest and changed the subject. "How long had Mrs Howard been working on this?"

"Some time. There was no reason to hurry. Not until the shooting."

"Why had she only just got round to getting hold of the death certificate? I should have thought that would be the first thing – once she knew it was there. And she'd know that once she knew about The Bomber at Dornhausen."

"It would take time, to know the *Standesbeamte*, to be sure he will take money. You cannot just walk in and say Hello, I wish to bribe you."

No, Maxim supposed you couldn't. "Well, what happens now?"

Sims patted his hands on the wheel. "I think I might like to talk to this Bruno. About the photographs . . . Mrs Howard was not a fool. To be carrying photographs that mean nothing . . ."

"He's a tricky bastard. Or tries to be. He's got an old Luger."

"Do you have a pistol?"

"No."

"I have one . . . but we will wait until it is dark."

Maxim seemed to have been recruited again. There must have been something about the quality of his silence, because Sims glanced across and asked: "Or would you want to ring Mr Harbinger again?"

But Maxim had trouble enough without that.

He stopped off at the barracks to change, especially his shirt, and pick up any messages. There was nothing from London, but Captain Apgood had left a large envelope. Maxim opened it in the privacy of his room. Along with a nine-year-old copy of *Focus on Germany* there was a note:

I tried ringing you. Herewith the magazine. Page 12 looks like your meat. Bad Schwarzendorn has not been microfilmed yet, but due to start next month. Anything missing will be noticed then, so you have been warned.

The magazine was a thin, staid but professionally produced affair intended to interest the American and British forces in aspects of Germany outside their normal military round, but not too far out. It gave their wives recipes for German cooking, news of cycle clubs and stamp collecting, articles on places with vague military connections. This one featured Dornhausen, recalling the first days of the occupation in 1945, and spread across the width of the page was a photograph of all the inhabitants in front of the unbombed church.

"It's very much an Army way of doing it," Maxim explained. "Line everybody up and photograph them, put a caption underneath and just hang it in your office – or under glass on your desk – and look at it. You know what armies are like about Must Know Your Men's Names." He assumed Sims had been in some army, most likely the East German NVA. "Then after The Bomber the American Civil Affairs people just crossed out the ones that had got killed. That's explained in the text."

"It says also that this picture is hanging in the *Wirtshaus* at Dornhausen."

"Not in the main room. And nobody mentioned it. That's nine years old." It didn't much matter what he said: he still knew who would be going back to have a look the next morning.

Sims had his jeweller's eyeglass out again. But there were around fifty people in the picture, which was reproduced hardly bigger than a postcard, and no glass could see through the Civil Affairs' officer's bold wax-pencil strokes. "That is him, is Gustav." But that wasn't difficult to guess, because he and a Goliath who must be Field Engineer Scholz were the only two young men in the scene. Next to Gustav and crossed out they could just make out a blonde woman, a few inches shorter, who held a baby.

"Is the baby the right age?" Sims demanded, shuffling a small pack of head-and-shoulders photographs.

It was a long time since Chris had been of a size to hold in your arms . . . until three months you had to support the head, didn't you? This one was older than that but didn't look of crawling age.

"About five months, yes, it could be."

Sims put down one of his photographs. "I am sure it is him, see?"

The stern, confident young man could easily be the one in the village picture, but the clothes seemed too neat and recent.

"Is that Eismark?"

Sims chuckled. "Yes – but the baby, Manfred. You can see he is his father's son, no? The most early one we have of Gustav is this." The bones of the face were the same, but this was a forty-year-old shipping manager, balding in front and wearing a moustache and glasses.

Maxim put the photographs and magazine down on the low table. They were sitting in Sims's motel room, part of a low modern block behind an all-night café just off the *Autobahn*. It was quiet, comfortable and cool – and instantly forgettable because it didn't belong to a place, but in between places. Sims hadn't even bothered to make it more his own by scattering things around: only the litre bottle of Scotch on the table and a portable sun-tan lamp on the dressing table, with a reflecting aluminium collar that fitted around your neck. His under-chin tan was explained now.

"Did you know the Eismarks – either of them?" It was the first time he had given any hint that he knew of Sims's origins, but no bad thing after Sims had shown what he knew about Maxim.

"Gustav, I did not know him. He was still mainly in Rostock, he came to Berlin only for meetings. But Manfred, yes, I knew him. He was crazy. Then he was only a captain, but crazy already. There was a story – I believe it – that once he beat a man in his office so much that he died. It was called something else, he hanged himself in his cell or jumped from the windows . . . probably he jumped from the windows, it would fit better. But do you know what that man had done?

Nothing – only his brother had escaped to the West. Manfred believed he should have known it would happen, that the man should have stopped his brother. Do you understand that?" He cocked his head with a sly smile.

"Did Mina Eismark's defection hurt Manfred?"

"He was only a schoolchild, and she was just his aunt. But it leaves a smell. I think he believed he must try harder, in the SSD, because of it. And perhaps a psychiatrist would say it was beating his father in that office."

"Perhaps a psychiatrist would say anything that would get his name in the papers, or am I being cynical?"

Sims laughed cheerfully. "I think you have psychiatrists in your Army, too. Would you like a proper drink now?" He waved the whisky bottle.

"Not just yet. But how would Manfred take the idea that his father had deserted his mother, then committed bigamy?"

"I think he would like it – if it was only he who knew it. Then he would have control of his father, his father who is on the Secretariat. One day, Colonel Manfred thinks also he would like to be on the Secretariat."

"Everybody a contender." Sims looked at him, puzzled. "Sorry, go on."

"It would not be strange for a father to help his son. And who will know *why* he is helping him? Also, Uncle Bear likes Manfred. They want strong men, since the strike. The Democratic Republic will have many years of paying for that, now . . ." His smile blurred for a moment and he poured himself another Scotch.

Maxim said slowly: "Somehow . . . compared with the strike and defection and getting beaten to death . . . I don't know, but somebody just walking out on his wife a long time ago – doesn't it sound a bit thin to you?"

Sims smiled. "Ring your friend Bruno. He won't let you go there right away, he will want time to be ready. We can have time for dinner, then."

Reluctantly, Maxim reached for his notebook and Fraulein Winkelmann's phone number.

★

Guy Husband came into Number 10 through the connecting door with the Cabinet Office, the usual route for anybody from Intelligence or Security since it bypassed the tourist-haunted front door in Downing Street. He was wearing a midnight blue dinner jacket and ruffled shirt since he was supposed, at that moment, to be boarding a helicopter at the City Helistop to fly down to *Don Giovanni* at Glyndebourne. He didn't look in a very good mood.

"*Very* kind of you to drop in at such short notice," George told him. "You do know Agnes, of course? Do you feel like a spot of something? – it's about that time, I think."

Husband refused the drink and glanced suspiciously at Agnes. She took a postcard-sized picture out of her handbag and offered it. "Do you recognise this man?"

Husband put on his tinted glasses and studied it. "Yes. Yes, it's one of Dieter's team. I can't recall his name right now."

George gave a long contented rumble and sat back in his desk chair. Husband switched his suspicion to him, then back to the photograph. "He looks a bit odd, mind you, but –"

"Oh, he's odd, all right," Agnes said. "He's in the mortuary at Guy's Hospital waiting for somebody to identify him, on account of a couple of gunshot wounds he received in Rotherhithe last Friday night." She let that sink in, smiling cheerfully, then added: "He was also identified by Leni Pfaffinger, more or less of the BBC World Service, as one of two men who came around posing as *our* agents and trying to get Mina Linnarz's new address."

Husband cleared his throat. "Well, I'm not absolutely certain it's the same chap . . ."

"But you can *be* certain just by stepping round to the hospital and having a look-see."

"I suppose it does make more sense," George said, "it being one of your people on the Rotherhithe business. If it *had* been the SSD it would imply that Gustav Eismark had called them in, and since it's evidence about his own bigamy that we're chasing, that really isn't too likely."

"I assure you," Husband said stiffly, "that I had absolutely no knowledge of this. Dieter Sims was acting entirely off his own bat."

"Whatever you say." George agreed. "But somebody's going to have to step across the road and tell Scottie. Would you prefer the honour?"

At first, Maxim was surprised that they didn't go to the all-night café itself, but then he realised it would be the very opposite of the anonymous motel room. It was open, public, almost part of the *Autobahn* itself with travellers flowing through, and the people who would remember Sims would be busy, travelling people. So they ate in a small, candle-lit Italian restaurant and Maxim chose escalope *al marsala*.

"Now what were you saying?" Sims prompted. He was on whisky again, that and *fegato Veneziana*.

"I've only been involved in this, in Plainsong, sort of step by step," Maxim said carefully. "I didn't get any real briefing on it until a couple of days ago, and you heard how much that was. I assumed your people had got a lot more data . . . I hadn't started thinking about what Brigitte Schickert was doing. And I'm damn sure she wasn't just sitting there while Gustav hauled her baby off to the Russian Zone. She'd go completely spare. And apart from anything else she'd go back to Dornhausen to see what they knew."

Sims shrugged. "When he took the baby from Dornhausen he could give it to her, while she got better from the wound, then leave her later."

"She'd still go back to Dornhausen. She'd go everywhere she could think of. Somebody had stolen her *baby*. Are you taking this seriously?"

"Perhaps not so much."

Maxim put down his knife and fork with a clang. "All right, Mister bloody Mystery, find yourself a new errand boy for the next —"

"Yes, we believe Gustav left her. But not alive."

Maxim peered at him through the flickering gloom. "And you don't mean The Bomber now?"

"No. Then the certificate would say she died in hospital, and she would be in the cemetery. We believe she died later, somewhere else. Because when he had got the certificate accepted, and in the file of the *Standesamt*, then it would be a licence to murder her, no? And he must hurry, to kill her before somebody who thinks she is dead will see her. All he must wait for is to get the papers so he may become Eismark again, who is suspected of nothing. It is a good murder, I think, to wait until you have proof of the death by accident first."

Maxim began chewing again, slowly. "The death certificate must have been pure opportunism. She really did get hurt by The Bomber." He remembered Agnes advising: "Keep your eye on the opportunists . . ."

"Oh yes. He was waiting for opportunities. He had his plans."

"It can't have been only because she didn't want to go over to the Russians with him . . . Christ, he must have *hated* her."

"Perhaps we should forget all the war, the politics. It is not the first time a man kills his wife. It is not the first time he hates her because she got pregnant and he must marry her. And for Gustav – perhaps she would denounce him to the Gestapo if he did not marry her. But about that we cannot know."

Maxim pushed the last stringy bit of the escalope to the side of his plate and sat back, sipping a glass of thin red wine.

"How long have you had this idea?"

"It never was probable that Brigitte would do nothing when he took the baby away."

"But Guy Husband was still talking about bigamy on Saturday. You heard him."

Sims shrugged again. "We had no proof. And I cannot decide what Guy will say when he tells everybody what his department is doing." The contempt in his voice was quite blatant.

So there was Husband all set to take the credit for proving Gustav Eismark a bigamist and when it suddenly turned out that he was a murderer instead, it would be horribly clear that Guy had had nothing to do with it at all.

"I'll *think* about taking that job at Six," Maxim said.

"Please do." Sims grinned and canted his wristwatch to catch the candle-light. "We have time for coffee before we visit your good friend Bruno."

Chapter 22

Bruno again had the flat door open and wore a smile, but he kept his right hand behind his back and beyond him Maxim saw the silhouette of a second man in the dark hallway. He walked in well past Bruno, keeping his hands unmistakably high so that when Sims rushed the door behind him he was close to the second man and already had his hand raised to smash him across the bridge of the nose. He heard the clatter of Bruno's Luger hitting the floor and shuddered as he recalled the likely condition of the gun's springs. Then they all hustled through into the fragrance of Fraulein Winkelmann's reception room.

"Is the Fraulein here?" Sims demanded. He was holding a small automatic near Bruno's chest.

"No. No. She is out." Bruno was white and his lips were trembling, and he was clutching the point of his right shoulder where Sims had whacked it with the automatic.

"Good. Sit down. Do you want this?" Sims offered Maxim the Luger and he took it, rather the way a vet might take an ailing tarantula, and cleared the cartridge from the breech. He wasn't going to need it as a gun; the second man was sitting back in a chair trying to stifle a nose-bleed diluted by streaming tears. He had a narrow face, big ears and a flick-knife in his jacket pocket.

Sims smiled at Bruno. "We've been here all this time and you haven't offered us a drink, yet."

"What would you like to drink?" He had trouble getting the words out.

"What would we like to drink? What have you got to drink?"

Bruno stumbled through a list; the flat was surprisingly well

198

stocked until you remembered what it was stocked for.

"I'll have a Scotch. What about you?" Maxim shook his head. He was having trouble enough keeping up with Sims's quick-fire German. Sims let Bruno make the drink for him, giving him a freedom of movement to rub in the realisation that he daren't exploit it, that he was completely subservient to the little gun and the constant smile.

"Cheers. You live well, for a procurer. Do you ever get a nibble at the old lady in between acts? Or do you just live out of her handbag? You should have stuck to that, not tried to make money out of my good friend here."

"I haven't got the money now. But I can get it for you."

"*You* can get it? Oh no, you mean *she* can get it. Roll on her back a few more times to save your little investment schemes. How soon can *she* get it?"

Bruno's eyes flickered side-to-side but he found no help in sight. "I could . . . at the end of the day after tomorrow."

"And how many times . . . ach, never mind. We can wait. Now let's talk about the papers you gave my friend. I think there was something missing. Find me that and we might not worry too much about the money."

"But I gave him everything."

Sims nodded, still smiling. "No trouble. Just find it."

"But truly, I —"

Sims moved so suddenly that Maxim could never have stopped him even if he'd tried. Bruno went staggering back with Sims slashing his head with the pistol. He collapsed on a sofa, wrapping his arms around his face. Blood seeped out between his fingers.

Sims sat down again, his smile unchanged. "I do wish people would listen to what one says. It saves so much trouble."

Maxim went over to look at Bruno. He had a cut on his left cheekbone and a graze on his temple. "I do recommend you to give my colleague what he wants." Bruno spaced his fingers and one anguished eye rolled at Maxim.

"Shall I take a look around?" he asked, hoping Sims got the real message, Can I Trust You Alone With Him? The first thing he found was a bathroom and brought back a hand-towel for the man with the nose-bleed. Then he went looking for Bruno's room.

It was as obviously masculine as the rest of the flat was feminine. Not just untidy but quite unplanned, with stacks of suitcases and old newspapers, a small refrigerator full of bottled beer and a freestanding old wardrobe too small for the number of clothes – rather expensive clothes – that Bruno had come by. There was no desk, just a table with an ultra-violet sun-tan lamp sitting among the mess. Maxim started opening drawers and suitcases at random.

He had been doing that for five minutes when Bruno screamed again.

This time he was huddled in an overstuffed chair and Sims was still beating at his head as if he really meant to destroy him. This was no act; the other man was staring horrified over his bloodstained towel.

"For Christ's sake –" Maxim grabbed Sims's arm and then with both hands as Sims turned, wild-eyed, trying to ram the pistol against Maxim's stomach. They stood for a moment in a weird pose that might have looked good in a self-defence manual, then the anger clouded over in Sims's eyes.

Maxim pushed the pistol hand carefully away. "He's not much alive but he could be a problem dead. We haven't got a certificate for him, remember?"

Sims's smile flashed on. "I don't like being cheated."

"Sure. Go and have a snoop. His room's the one with the light on."

Sims stepped into the hallway and Maxim took another look at Bruno. His head was bleeding from another cut, but Sims had been lucky or careful enough to stay clear of the thin pterion area of the temples; most of the new damage was to Bruno's hands.

"I'm sorry about him," he said. "He gets these crazy rages. I can't do much about them. Give me something, anything, before he comes back."

The tough, stocky Bruno of yesterday had shrunk and melted so that he was part of the flabby lines of the chair.

"Just anything," Maxim said earnestly. "Any old thing, to keep him happy. Then I can get him away from here."

Bruno's mouth opened and shut stickily. "I told him . . . I didn't do it . . . it was done already. I just noticed it by chance . . ."

"What are you talking about?"

"The certificate, one of the certificates . . . it must have been that Corporal Blagg . . ."

There was a muffled crash as Sims 'searched' something heavy.

"Never mind the certificates: the photographs. Tell me something about the photographs. He didn't like the ones you gave me."

"They are in the bank."

"Oh dear life, dear life. He won't like that. I'm sure it's true, but he so much wants something *now*. Let's say you keep the *negatives* in the bank. That would be sensible." There was another clatter from some other room. "But the prints – you'd take the trouble to print them up. Can you think of any prints, *any* prints that would look right?

"Of course," he added, "they'd have to be off infra-red film. He'd know the difference . . ."

"In the door of my refrigerator," Bruno croaked. "Inside it."

Outside the door, Sims said: "I heard that. You were good. I really could work with you."

"You really are working with me, if you hadn't noticed." Even with only Sims, he kept speaking German. To change to English would have broken the flow of the action. "Get on with it."

He watched as Sims unscrewed the moulded plastic lining from inside the door and took out a plain envelope. Inside was a second strip of Minox film – so Bruno had been lying about the bank, as usual – and four black-and-white prints of about half-plate size. It was easy to see why Bruno hadn't taken them in for colour-printing at a shop.

"Well, what do you think?" Sims asked.

Maxim's cheeks felt a little warm. "She looks a little young for what he's doing to her."

"Yes, but she doesn't seem to mind. And I'm sure she was well paid for it."

"By your Mrs Howard. I'm assuming he's the *Standes-beamte*, Hochhauser."

"It must be. I'd say he wasn't doing badly for a man close to his pension."

"If those got about, he'd've been a long long way from his pension."

"That would be the point." Sims slid the prints back into the envelope.

"You'd been expecting something like that."

"Something." Sims was looking at him with tolerant amusement. "Are you shocked, Major?"

"No . . . but I see why she wanted Blagg and the gun and all, going to show Hochhauser these. Why didn't she stick to bribery?"

"It is usual to combine bribery and blackmail. Sugar-bread and the whip. With bribery alone, he could have reported her to the police."

"Why don't you dig her up and ask her if she wouldn't have preferred that?"

"She was a good agent. And a good friend." Sims was no longer amused.

"All right, all right. Can we go now? I hope it was all worth the trouble."

"Major: it could have been Mrs Howard in the pictures; I did not know what Hochhauser's taste was. And either way, they were skilled pictures taken on specialised film. It shrieks of the trade. A dangerous loose end to leave about – particularly with a man like Bruno."

Maxim nodded. "You're right. Perhaps I was a bit shocked."

The front door suddenly opened and Fraulein Winkelmann was surging down the hallway and coming to a quivering stop as she saw Bruno and the man with the nose-bleed. Between them there was quite a lot of blood on display.

"*Wass hat sie . . .* ?" She hit a soaring operatic note until both Sims and Maxim instinctively held up their pistols. She recognised Maxim. "Oh yes, the English Herr Major. I think we might talk to the police about *this*."

Maxim shrugged. "Happy to. You were right about him

sniffing cocaine, by the way. If the police come . . . well, it isn't where he hid it. It's where I hid it."

There was a long pause and her carefully preserved expression collapsed into rouged meat. Maxim said soothingly: "He only got a bit knocked about. He's got money for the doctor. I do know that."

"*That* money, that was yesterday." She looked around the room. "You animals. You rotten animals."

Sims had edged past her to the hallway, smiling hard. "We're on our way, gracious lady."

She followed them to the door. Maxim said: "I've taken his gun."

"Oh yes. First you take his balls, why not take his cock? You know who he'll beat up for all this, after a sniff and a few drinks."

He didn't know what to say to that.

"Leave the gun with me," she suggested. "Show me how it works. Just for protection. He won't know I've got it."

Maxim hesitated. "You don't want to shoot him."

"How do you know what I want to do? You beat him, he beats me, who do I beat?"

Sims said: "Try poisoning him. You could get away with it."

She looked at him, gathered her face into a gracious smile and spat in the middle of his chest. "Animals." She slammed the door.

As they clattered down the stairs, Sims asked: "Was it true, about the cocaine?"

"No. But I think she believed it."

"I think she did. It was a good idea. But for a moment there, I thought you were going to stand out on the landing and teach her to fire that Luger! Bang! You know what she would have done then? Shot you in the back – bang! They hate their men and they protect them like she-bears. And she called us animals. My God, why did your Corporal Blagg go to her? Does he have fantasies about fornicating with his own mother?"

God alone knew what fantasies Blagg's childhood had left him with, and Fraulein Winkelmann had fulfilled; Maxim wasn't going to play psychiatrist, least of all in front of Sims. Anyway, whatever Blagg did in that perfumed garden of an apartment was less risk to world peace than when Sims's mob persuaded him to 'help out'.

"I don't know. Drive me across the river, would you? I want to lose this thing permanently." The old Luger with its weak return spring and chancy sear was one gun even a soldier was happy to throw away.

The air conditioning in Sims's room worked at nothing less than full power, and there was no turning it off until Sims had stopped chain-smoking so Maxim was deliberately drinking whisky and luke-warm water against the chill.

Sims was slumped in a chair, turning the pages of the old *Focus on Germany.* "Will you go back to Dornhausen to-morrow?" They spoke English again; Maxim's German was out of practice and blurred easily late in the evening.

"It's a bit risky, and I don't know what we'll learn, even if the picture's still there, and I swear it wasn't . . ." His sentence structure was crumbling, too. "How about the Karls Hospital? I could get somebody from the Army to find out if the 1945 records still exist. Asking about that wouldn't give anything away. But it's a bit too neat to expect proof of her discharge, all alive-o . . . And we haven't got any real evidence except for a false statement on the certificate . . ." Something flickered in his memory like a movement seen from the corner of an eye, but when he tried to concentrate, it blurred with his weariness. He shook his head. "And it's a bit late to find her body . . . do you really think you can find something?"

"A witness."

"To the *murder*?"

"That she was alive after April 15."

Maxim picked up the bottle and gently toppled more Scotch into his glass. "That might do it . . . but who?"

"The sister. Mina Eismark. Or Linnarz."

"Isn't she dead?"

"No. She is in England, now."

"When did you learn that?"

"Just now. And we know that after The Bomber Gustav went to find her – perhaps she would have the papers to make him Eismark again – so she could have seen Brigitte."

"Will she tell you, though? You can't hit her on the head with a pistol."

Sims smiled. "Perhaps you will come and help, like with Bruno."

"Sure . . . How are you going to get the certificates back into the *Standesamt*?" The flicker of memory came again, escaped again.

"Somehow. There is no rush. They have been gone for three weeks now, and who looks for death certificates of thirty-five years ago?"

"There's a rush now. They're all supposed to be microfilmed next month."

"How do you know that?"

Blast. That was tiredness making him careless. Blast *and* damn.

"An Army friend rang up for me. That wouldn't make anybody suspicious."

"How can you be sure?" Sims was suddenly all bristles, up on his feet and prowling, stabbing out one cigarette and lighting another.

"It was less risk than me going out to Dornhausen again."

"It is my job to decide the risks. Always you must tell me, if we are to work together properly. I thought I was getting you trained."

That was either quite an insult or quite a compliment, and probably Sims was giving him the choice.

"All right," Maxim said mildly. "I'm sorry. But your Mrs Howard got in just in time. Next month she wouldn't have had any choice but to ask for a copy."

"Yes." Sims was still prowling, instinctively suspicious of all the hiding places in the room. He picked up the wad of certificates and put them down again.

Maxim remembered. "Something Bruno said – before the photographs; were you listening? Something he hadn't done to the certificate, something Blagg must have done . . . what the hell was he talking about? Something he'd noticed . . ."

He got up and went to the certificates and picked up the Schickert one. It looked just as it had before.

Sims said: "He could have meant another one."

"We don't care about the other ones." Maxim held the old paper up against the light, but that did nothing. He put it down, quite near Sims's ultra-violet lamp. There had been one of those in Bruno's room, too.

Now he *did* remember something from the Ashford course. "Turn off the lights, will you?" He fumbled around with the sun-tan lamp's lead.

The lamp came on with its searing brilliance as the last of the room lights went out. Sims held up a hand to shade his face. "There are some glasses to use . . ."

Maxim ignored him, tilting the certificate at the edge of the glare, so that it glowed faintly, fluorescing as almost anything does under ultra-violet. Two lines of the certificate glowed more brightly than the rest. Maxim held it down so that Sims could see the lines:

ist am . . . 15. April 1945 . . . um . . . ll . . . Uhr . . . 30 . . . Minuten in . . . Dornhausen . . . verstorben.

"That was the only part we were interested in." He gave the certificate to Sims and went to switch on the room lights again. "Bruno would know something about altered documents, looking for signs of chemical eraser under ultra-violet. With a mind like his, the first thing he'd think about an official document is to see if somebody's faked it. And for once he was right."

Sims was still twisting the certificate under the lamp; Maxim turned it off. "Only it wasn't Blagg who did it: it was Mrs Howard. We thought she was collecting those certificates, that night. No: she was giving them back. And in a month they would have been microfilmed and thrown away, the forgery would never show on the film and Gustav would be immortalised as a liar. Neat. That was really why she wanted the whole batch: so that Hochhauser wouldn't notice she'd been fiddling just one of them."

"What do you believe it said?" Sims's voice was toneless.

"The same as you do: that she died in the Karls Hospital some time in the afternoon or evening, just like the others who *did* die. And it means the hospital records can't matter even if they're still around. He'd never have named the hospital if there'd been anything to show she *didn't* die there."

Very slowly, Sims put the certificate down on top of the rest. At the last moment his hand trembled and almost clenched, as if he were about to crumple the thin paper. But he didn't. He walked back and sipped his whisky.

"I suppose," he said, "she had decided she could not find any true proof, so she decided to make some. Perhaps I was pushing her too hard. We needed Plainsong. All of us."

All of us. The unit Sims had created, had rescued from the whirlpool of the *Verfassungschutz* only to land it in Guy Husband's uncertain hands. They needed one big success to make themselves secure, but in her desperation to achieve it, Mrs Howard had turned to methods which could destroy the unit itself – just as her forgery had effectively destroyed Brigitte Schickert's death certificate.

Maxim finished his whisky and put the glass down. "She's still not buried in that cemetery."

"The sister," Sims said softly. "Mina. She must know. She *must* know."

"I'll go to Dornhausen tomorrow morning," Maxim promised, but he wasn't sure Sims heard him.

Chapter 23

In the morning, Sims was gone.

Maxim hauled his hangover back from the telephone box by the barracks gate through a barrage of stamping feet and troops answering their names in ringing shouts. There was an atmosphere of rich self-satisfaction around; whatever ACE thought, the regiment was convinced it had done very well on its Agile Blade call-out and was flaunting it noisily. Maxim found himself having Civilian Thoughts as he escaped back into the officer's mess.

There was, he told himself, no point in ringing George at Army dawn – particularly by German time, an hour ahead of Britain. The politest thing he'd get told would be to come home immediately, and however much he wanted to, he had promised Sims that second visit to Dornhausen. He went to ask advice on hiring another car.

Just on eleven, he parked in the shade of Dornhausen's great linden tree and walked back to the little inn. The woman was sitting in there alone, drinking coffee and reading a newspaper. She instinctively got up as he went in, recognised him, and smiled perfunctorily.

"Do you want coffee, or beer?"

"Coffee, please."

The floor was still damp from her mop and a cool evaporating smell contrasted with the sudden bitter tang of the coffee she put down in front of him. She wore the same dress as the day before, the same lined, tired expression.

"Did you find out any more about Frau Schickert?"

"I don't think so. Except for this . . ." He spread the *Focus on Germany*. "Is that picture still here?"

"That old thing. I haven't seen it in ages."

"It says it used to hang in here . . ."

"I remember. On the wall, there." She pointed to a faded nude from a tyre calendar, tacked up just to the right of the front door. "But the glass got broken and somebody took it to be repaired and they lost it."

"Lost it?"

"Yes." She met his look boldly. Too boldly?

"Oh." He sipped the coffee; somewhere outside, a tractor worked in erratic surges of power. "When did that happen?"

"Soon after they printed the picture there. A few people came in to see, because of that article. I think one of them took it down, dropped it."

"Oh," Maxim said again.

She wiped the table, an unnecessary but instinctive movement. "Does it matter where she's buried?"

"Not to me."

"Do you know what happened to the baby, little Manfred?"

He looked up. Little Manfred, the one you gave the bottle to? Oh yes, I heard something about him. He hasn't quite grown up yet – some childish game he played with a chap in his office. Just boyish high spirits.

"No," he said. "I don't know what happened to him." He put too much money on the table. "Thank you for the coffee."

First he had to ring George, then probably catch the Gütersloh flight. He paused at the door, taking the last sniff at the country air: the rest would be busy roads, airports, Whitehall. Agnes had been right about needing to get out into the countryside, and it didn't matter much whose country.

Behind him, she asked: "Are you going back to England?"

"Yes."

She paused. "The glass didn't get broken. It was borrowed, somebody wanted to make a copy of it, just like the people from the magazine had done. He didn't give it back."

"*He* came back. Gu– Rainer Schickert. He came back."

"Yes." She put the empty cup on the bar. "I was a fool to lend it him, he said it was the only picture of her at that time. He didn't even have one from the wedding. He said he was in shipping, I think, in Hamburg, but I couldn't find him in the directory."

209

"It was really him?"

"He looked different, but it was him. He knew everything; you can't be wrong about that. It takes only a few words. He came early one morning, before anybody else who might know him – I don't know why. But if you see him, you might mention the picture. He did promise."

"Oh yes, it can be done," Captain Apgood said. "Happens all the time. If you know the right people, or you've got the right money, any East German can get a doctor's chit saying he needs a couple of weeks at some West German spa. It's one of the accepted perks of office, over there. Of course, they want to be sure you'll come back. You've got to own property or leave your wife and family behind. Does your chap fit into that category?"

"I think he would." Nine years back Gustav – soundly remarried, sister's defection forgotten, back in political favour but not yet important enough to make a trip West into an Event – would fit perfectly. And he could be using his SSD connection to tip him off to any mention of wartime Dornhausen. Any magazine written for the Allied forces would be on the SSD's reading list.

So Gustav had come back.

"I can get somebody to check around the hotels in Bad Schwarzendorn," Apgood offered. "They've probably still got their old records. What name would your man be using?"

"I wouldn't know . . . You wouldn't have any idea when the Gütersloh flight goes?"

"Ah, you've missed that already."

At the start of the holiday season, commercial flights and even train/ferry tickets were difficult to come by, or so Maxim told George on the phone. He would spend another night with the Army and be on the next trooping flight for certain sure, honour bright, cross his heart.

"Stay there a couple of days," George said, surprisingly. "Enjoy yourself. Talk about Pay And Emoluments, discuss SA80 and PJRAD and why the Headmaster always chooses such clunks as defence advisers. As long as that so-and-so Sims

210

has got what he wants, there's no rush. I don't think you've heard about Rotherhithe?" He told about Sims's unit being involved in the shooting, and Maxim saw why he was being offered a short exile in Germany. George feared he might want to have words with Mr Sims. And George, Maxim reflected, could be right.

"How's the Prime Minister?"

"Birds of a feather, mostly carrion coloured, are flocking to his bedside." George sounded suddenly tired. "His chest doesn't appear to be good. I think he'll resign next week and then God help us all. But I don't want him going out in a cloud of cow-shit."

"All right, I promise I'll stay in Germany."

"I didn't mean that . . . I don't think I did, anyway. Just make sure we know where you are."

"If he goes, will you stay on at Number 10?"

But George had already rung off.

The summer days were too long. While the light lasted she couldn't really feel sleepy, so she sat by the window and watched the slow shadows pooling in the valley. Lights glowed on in other houses down there, but she just waited, soaking in the darkness as if it were drowsiness itself. Soon it would be time for the last of the yellow pills, then the sleeping pills and then perhaps two hours of total oblivion, sleep without pain, before the terrible long process of waking, remembering and hurting all over again.

For the moment, there was the brandy which she was trying to make last until the weekend, and little nibbles of cheese or chocolate and of course the flask of soup. Like most touring musicians she had learned to take a flask of soup to a recital, since wheedling even a plate of sandwiches out of a provincial hotel at ten or eleven at night was a virtuoso performance in itself. Now she clung to the habit as one last reminder of having been Mina Linnarz.

A little crowd of people spilled out of the chapel down the street, swirled gently for a moment in final conversation and then drifted away in twos and threes. It couldn't have been a film show, they would have asked her to that, but they didn't seem to have them any more. Probably everybody in the village had television by now. Most likely it had just been some committee meeting to organise or object to something. They'd tried to get her involved in that sort of thing, but she was past trying to reform the world. No, she'd never really cared enough; that sort of thing she always left to Gustav.

But she liked the villagers, with their slow speech and equal slowness to interfere. They were farmers, like her mother's people in the Harz mountains. They knew about frost and hailstorms, and crippled hands too; these things happened. There was no peace, but there at least there was silence, silence that she would never find in a city. She had been a fool to go to London, even to see Leni . . .

She took the pills with the last of the soup, saving the final half-inch of brandy in her glass for when she was in bed. Now the drowsiness was real, the pain dulled to another brief defeat. This was the best time of the day and she stood up slowly, luxuriating in the silence within her own body. At first, she barely heard the tap on the front door.

Oh dear Lord, not somebody come to say little Rosemary won't be at her piano lesson because . . . it could wait until tomorrow. What did they think she'd do if little Rosemary simply didn't arrive? Perhaps make the greatest-ever recording of the Romance in F Sharp? Or merely dash down and give a sell-out Wigmore Hall recital? Or maybe drink a little more brandy, a little earlier than usual.

When she opened the door she didn't know them, but she knew what they were. For thirty years they had been visiting her in nightmares; at last they had come when she was awake.

"Get Major Maxim back from Osnabrück," George told the Number 10 switchboard.

Chapter 24

Although it was the middle of a normal working day, the corridors of the Foreign Office seemed almost deserted, and Miss Milward's high-heeled footsteps echoed between the cracked mosaic floors and the high arched ceilings. The walls were lined with central heating pipes, pneumatic message tubes, drooping power cables and clumps of odd-lot filing cabinets and cupboards secured, if that was the word, by an extraordinary variety of padlocks. Everything had a dusty look, although that was probably the faded colours and the lighting.

"You haven't been in here before, have you?" she asked. "First they plan to tart it all up and then they say No, we're having a whole new office built, so they scrap the paint job, and then they find there isn't any money for the new office anyway . . . and so it goes. They keep the one corner up to snuff to impress visiting Arabs . . . Scottie's using the Foreign Sec's room. He's up in Scotland consulting the PM . . . It's just up here . . ."

After two flights of stairs and a near-miss with an old lady pushing a trolley of file boxes, the fresh paint suddenly appeared and they were in Arab territory.

Nobody actually explained why Scott-Scobie was colonising Lord Purslane's room, since his own could hardly have been insecure, although it might have been too secret for a mere major. Looking back, Maxim decided it was probably a move to impress him, which the room did. High ceilinged, it was built on a corner overlooking both the Horse Guards and St James's Park, and furnished like the Committee Room of a well-off but moderately progressive London club. The walls were papered in dark green and gold, with a tall cabinet of bound Hansards; the furniture was made of rich wood and red leather and – except for the leather-topped desk – not too antique; the quiet pinky-blue shade of the thick carpet could have been taken directly from the faces of the hunting aristocracy. In the evening, lit only in patches over the pictures on the walls and from the desk lamps in their green glass shades, it would have been a place for considered opinions and memorable phrases; at midday it was still impressive but dominated by the familiar babble of a television set by the empty fireplace.

George was sitting in front of it, the usual glass in his hand. "Morning, Harry. You haven't met Scottie, have you?"

Scott-Scobie was chubby but quick, striding across to shake hands and smile one-two-*off* like a fast salute. "Very kind of you to come in, Major. You know Agnes already."

She was sitting at one end of the long overstuffed sofa; she lifted a hand.

"A nice little place Milord's got here, don't you think?" Scott-Scobie went on. "George, do turn that blasted thing off. What would you care to drink?"

George leaned forward and switched off the TV. "If they'd got it, they'd be flaunting it. More Scotch, please."

"I didn't mean you. Major?"

"Nothing for me."

"You can change your mind at any time. George, how much more background does the Major need?"

"My impression all along has been that he knew more of what was going on than any of the rest of us, but I may be wronging the honest fellow."

Scott-Scobie coughed and looked at Maxim. "Sit down, Major, sit down." Maxim sat carefully in a horseshoe-back chair; Scott-Scobie paced abruptly away, turned and asked: "When you last saw Dieter Sims, in Germany, what conclusions had you come to about Plainsong?"

Maxim said carefully: "*He* reckoned that Gustav Eismark had killed his first wife."

"Did you think so?"

"Yes, I think I think so."

"But he didn't have any proof?"

Maxim blinked at him.

"I'm sorry, Major, but the only really silly question is the one you don't ask."

"He had no proof that I knew of. He said he was going to get hold of the sister — Mina."

"He got hold of her," Agnes said in a flat voice; Scott-Scobie shot her a look, ran a hand quickly through his dark curls then had to reach for his pocket to hoist up his trousers. His figure really needed braces but he liked taking off his jacket — as he had now — and showing one's braces was no part of British foreign policy under Lord Purslane.

"Do you think she would be able to supply proof?"

"I don't know. Gustav said he was going off to find his sister; we know he found her, but I couldn't guess whether he killed his wife in front of her or even told her he'd done it."

"I'm not joking, Major!"

"What other sort of proof could she have?"

Scott-Scobie ignored that. "Can you think of any other proof that might exist?"

George said: "It's a serious question, Harry."

Maxim tried to think. "Germany must have been a mess at the time, but even then you'd take *some* care about murdering somebody. And he was pretty cool about arranging the death certificate; that wasn't an impulse . . . I'm sorry: I suppose you could scratch around asking anybody and everybody if —"

"Which we do *not* wish to be caught doing," Scott-Scobie said.

"Yes . . . The only answer is that it was a hell of a long time ago."

Scott-Scobie looked across at George, who was holding out his glass hopefully in the direction of Miss Milward, and gave a brief sigh. "So it appears to be Mina Linnarz or nothing. At least *they* seem to accept that she might know something."

"What's happened to her?" Maxim asked.

There was a sudden silence. Scott-Scobie walked a quick little circle and stopped. "Major — I want you to realise that this is above and beyond Top Secret. Do you appreciate that? I'm sure Agnes will back me on this. This is one where there's nothing on paper at all."

Maxim didn't know enough about the Diplomatic Service

to realise that Nothing On Paper was not just the ultimate in security but also the supreme sacrifice. Still, he got the general idea and tried to look impressed.

Agnes said: "Our Harry may have his little failings, but telling people what's going on isn't usually one of them. I thought your people would have told you that much." She was sitting with her legs primly together, the skirt of her pale greenish suit arching just across the middle of her knees. She smiled wanly at Maxim, who was looking at her legs.

"Very well." Scott-Scobie sat abruptly on the edge of the conference table. "What Sims and his brotherhood have done is to kidnap Wilhelmina Linnarz – or Eismark – and are preparing to hand her over to her brother Gustav from East Germany. How does *that* grab you?"

"Do you mean they haven't actually done it?" Maxim asked.
"No . . ."
"Then how do you know about this?"
"Agnes's service – no, Agnes herself, I understand – managed to locate her a couple of days ago. Until then nobody even knew she was alive. Then she suddenly vanished. Am I right?"

"They got the address," Agnes said grimly, "from a routine report I had put in to *my* service's registry. All in the spirit of inter-service co-operation."

"You mustn't blame your own people," Scott-Scobie said, deliberately missing the point. "Sims was exceeding his authority – of which he appears to have been given far too much in any case – and your registry wasn't to know his allegiance had changed."

Agnes didn't even glance at him. "We weren't keeping a watch on her, just being aware. Yesterday morning the neighbours reported to the police that she'd gone missing, her bed not slept in, and she couldn't really get around by herself much. There was a story of a strange van late the night before . . ."

"Are the police involved, then?" Maxim asked.
"Not very much. They don't know who she really is, for a start, and there's no proof of abduction. She was a bit of a loner

in her village, so she wouldn't necessarily have told anybody if she was going away. They're not actually *doing* anything yet."

"Then how are we sure that – ?"

"Ah yes." Scott-Scobie took command again. "One of Sims's little friends had the . . . you can't call it patriotism . . ."

"A strong sense of pension," George suggested, taking a fresh Scotch from Miss Milward.

"Anyway, he got cold feet and Told All, which wasn't very much since he was still in London and supposed to be maintaining a façade of Business As Usual. So he doesn't know where they're keeping her except that they *did* have that 'strange van' and the handover point hadn't been fixed, only that it's tomorrow some time."

"We're pretty sure it has to be to an East German ship," Agnes said. "I don't see how it can be any other way, not if Eismark's going to keep the whole deal in his own hands. He still must have a very big influence in *Deutfracht*, their freight line."

"That's the whole point." Scott-Scobie stood up, then hoisted his trousers after him. "Sims is bypassing all the *apparat*, giving Eismark a chance to buy back the only witness to his guilty secret. To that extent Plainsong's still *virgo intacta*, as one might say."

"So she's still worth something in the market place." George cruised down behind the desk to stare out of a window at the lunchtime traffic and the trees of St James's Park beyond. "I've always thought this room was particularly splendid for forming British foreign policy: all the windows look firmly inland and you only see the sun when it's setting."

"George, will you please stop trying to drink us out of Arab's Ruin and concentrate on the fact that we are faced with a whole unit of the Intelligence Service trying to defect?"

"The kidnapped lady apart, how much of the family jewels did he actually get away with?"

"Just about nothing, thank God. Guy at least had the sense to keep the unit in quarantine, gave them their own house but had his own people to handle their communications and requests for filed info. But it isn't just what they're taking, not even kidnapping a British citizen, it's a whole part of the service going over to the Other Side. It'll make us a laughing stock with the Big Friends, and ruin morale inside the rest of the service for *years*."

"Could they have been planning this all along?" Agnes asked.

Maxim found himself instinctively shaking his head, agreeing with Scott-Scobie before he even spoke. "No, no, snatching the sister like that was just an act of desperation. When Sims came back from Germany empty-handed and Guy confronted him with having sent armed men after your runaway Corporal *and* getting one of them killed, well, I gather they had a bit of a barney and I suppose Sims saw his whole unit being wound up. So he grabbed the petty cash and ran. Guy's handling of the whole thing seems to have been consistent right down the line."

"Where *is* Husband?" George asked.

"In bed with the vapours." Scott-Scobie showed a certain relish. "He's having a little trouble adjusting to the new reality."

Mutineers get shot, Maxim reflected, but when that's all over, their commander is quietly posted to run a carrier-pigeon loft on Rockall. "Sims certainly felt the heat was on out in Germany. He came near to killing a man who was holding out on us."

"*That* you did not tell me," George said sternly.

"I didn't think it would improve your day. But if we're sure it'll be a ship, there can't be that many East German ships coming in: can't Agnes's mob and the local Special Branches watch them all?"

"Major," Scott-Scobie said, "if we arrest them we have to try them and have the whole thing come out in court. If I could be sure they'd keep quiet about it, I'd far rather they got clean away with it and we wrote Sims and Plainsong off to experience. But you know perfectly well they can't keep quiet. They'd have to make a big song and dance just to explain why they're accepting Sims back to the fold. Normally they'd just shoot him."

George sat heavily in the Foreign Secretary's chair and

swivelled himself from side to side. "You're quite sure there isn't some gamy piece of blackmail we can pull to buy their silence? – in exchange for letting the whole boatload go over?"

"George, the cupboard is completely bare of British sporting spirit as far as East Germany's concerned. That was why we needed Sims and his blasted gang in the first place. And we've got no hold on them personally; one of them's left his wife here, but there's nothing we could do to her, not even illegally, with them pointing the spotlight from the Magdalenenstrasse. Anyway, you know what people like that are about wives. Of course, if Plainsong had actually come *off* . . ." he waved a hand and strode the length of the conference table and back.

"Very well," George said. "I have to accept all that."

Agnes turned on the sofa to look at him suspiciously.

"Major –" Scott-Scobie jingled coins in his pocket "– so what do you think you can do for us?"

"You mean the SAS? I can tell you who you'll be talking to there, but you still –"

"No, I don't mean them. I mean you. You've displayed a certain *initiative* ever since you got involved in this business, so perhaps you can keep it up by solving this little problem for us."

Agnes stood up slowly and faced Scott-Scobie. "You cannot do that," she said in a flat voice. "You can *not* let Harry go out and take on Sims and his mates by himself and –"

"No no *no*. He can recruit whatever help he likes. It just mustn't be official, that's all. It isn't as if your own service is prepared to take it on."

"A thing like this, you know perfectly well we can't act except through the police. But why can't The Firm mop up after its own puppies?"

"Agnes my dear, you know they just don't have these sort of people. Your own service has done as much as anybody – far more, indeed – to *stop* The Firm building up a rugger club of its own. The only musclemen they've got in this country turn out to be in Sims's unit and that was only because we got them sight unseen as a going concern." He looked back at Maxim. "So, Major?"

Maxim stood up, too. "I'm working to Number 10."

George cleared his throat. "I can't possibly give you orders on this one, Harry. I've told Scottie you could be asked and that the Number 10 connection can be severed in good enough time. But you don't have to go."

Agnes stared at Maxim, willing him ferociously to smile and say No.

"Don't I?" Maxim said. "The Army's always the last resort. It's what we're for."

"This most definitely is not an Army matter," Scott-Scobie said.

"You call it what you like. I wouldn't be any use to you if I wasn't Army. How many people are we talking about?"

"Sims and two others is all we know about. What comes in with the boat we don't know at all."

"Except that one of them has to be Gustav Eismark in person."

"Quite. If he's buying back his Shameful Secret he can't do that by proxy. And I wouldn't have thought he'd risk bringing much of an entourage, but *I* won't get hurt by being wrong."

"Sims and co. are armed, I assume?"

"Sure to be. We can ask our drop-out friend what they've got, if he knows."

"I'd like that done."

George took a folded paper from his inside pocket and passed it across the desk to Maxim. "Harry, if you wouldn't mind . . . ?"

Maxim read it, smiled briefly, signed and passed it back. "How *is* the Prime Minister?"

Agnes demanded: "What was that?"

"My request to be relieved of my post at Number 10, dated two days ago."

"You *bastard*," Agnes told George.

George ignored her. "He's resigning as soon as he can see a clear patch, so that he doesn't seem to be going under pressure . . ."

"Also very much Top Secret, Major," Scott-Scobie put in.

"He *knows* that!" George spat, then controlled himself. "But I'm not asking because of him, it's more than . . ."

"That's all right. I wasn't looking for reasons." Maxim turned for the door, then back to Scott-Scobie. "One thing: the way I go about this, I don't see where any Top Secrecy comes in. A lot of people – certainly on their side – are going to know what's happened."

"Oh yes, they'll *know*. But they just won't know *out loud*."

Maxim said: "Oh."

Chapter 25

Jim Caswell was running the garage by himself when Maxim got there. Blagg sat in the tiny office listening to the radio and guarding the telephone; he grinned and made a joky salute through the window to Maxim.

"Did you find me some wheels?" Maxim asked.

"Yep: a Renault 16TX."

Maxim looked dubious. "Ouch. It's complicated . . ."

"It's in good nick. I've got it up on the lift now." He ushered Maxim through to the rear half of the garage, a gloomy and grimy workshop shut off by big sliding doors. A ragbag collection of cars sat around awaiting buyers or, for some, a generous scrap dealer.

Caswell caught Maxim's look. "Yes, the old man isn't going to get any Rolls-Royce dealership, he's let this end of the business go. But that one's all right."

The Renault up on the lift was dark green and several years old – indeed, the model had been out of production for several years – but looked reasonably clean and undented. Not that Maxim knew all that much about cars: he just thought Renaults were too complicated for most British garages to understand.

"I've checked it all over," Caswell went on, "your brakes, lights, exhaust, cooling, tyres. It's all *right*. They don't have all that much acceleration, but it cruises like a bird and you said you wanted to go a distance. And it's a family car, a thing like this: big boot, bags of comfort. It's not a tearaway's car; the law doesn't get suspicious about these things. I suppose you are going to break the law with it?"

Maxim nodded. "Oh yes. I'm going to break the law, all right."

"D'you want to tell me?"

"Yes, I want to tell you."

When Maxim had finished, Blagg was staring open-mouthed. Caswell ground out his cigarette, nodded to himself, and said: "I knew they had some real fruitcakes in The Firm, but they must've gone right to the back of the oven for that lot."

"They can't always be choosey; they have to take the people with the experience and the contacts, and they're competing with all the other intelligence services – the CIA, France, Israel. You can't run it like a security service, handpicking your people and training them up yourself." Perversely, Maxim found himself defending Six, though the words were George's.

"It was those buggers that shot me?" Blagg wanted to be certain.

"Yes, but you didn't do too badly yourself."

"All right if I come along?"

"Are you fit?"

"Let them worry about that."

Caswell said: "He's a bloody sight better than you'd expect. I suppose you're offering me a job, too?"

"Yes." Maxim forced himself to look Caswell in the eyes. "I've got no bullshit to spread on it. It's a good job to say No to. You're a married man."

"I've been a married man as long as you've known me. It didn't stop you trying to get me killed before."

Maxim smiled. "I'd still settle for the wheels and whatever you've got in your bottom drawer."

Blagg looked puzzled; Caswell moved very slowly to light a fresh cigarette, one-handed, and said with wide-eyed innocence: "I wouldn't know what you're talking about, Major."

"I don't either, but I'd still like to borrow it. I've heard you often enough about what the world's coming to and how when you left the service you were going to be damn sure you had something to defend your home and family with."

After a pause, Caswell said: "There's an automatic shotgun."

"Automatic?"

"I know, I know." Soldiers despise the automatic shotgun which is strictly speaking only semi-automatic, reloading itself after each shot, as being too complex and likely to go wrong. The SAS preferred a pump-action type for blowing away locked doors and sometimes softer targets. "But you try using a pump-action with a stiff elbow; take you a week. It's the usual Browning; holds five."

Blagg asked: "Aren't they *legal*?" That idea seemed to shock him as much as the automaticness.

"Oh yes," Caswell said, "if you've got a licence. I have."

"I'll take it," Maxim said, "if the shot's the right size."

"Special SG." That was a form of buckshot, quite big enough to kill a man at twenty metres. "But why are you scratching around for stuff like this?"

"Jim, you just don't know how unofficial we are. All I've got so far is two thirty-eights, mine and the one Ron was using."

Blagg's knobbly face cracked into a happy smile, showing very white but irregular teeth. "You hung onto it, then. I was beginning to like that one." What he meant, Maxim reflected, was that he'd killed two people with that pistol – though that was no bad reason to like a gun. "Mind," Blagg added, "I'd as soon use the Browning, if you don't want it, sir?"

"That's mine, lad," Caswell said. "You can use the grenades."

Maxim stared. "*What* grenades?"

"I was going to tell you about them."

Maxim took his own car down to the village to stock up on food and put together a first-aid kit from a chemist that stayed open late. When he got back the garage had CLOSED signs out and Blagg was checking the tyre pressures of the Renault on the forecourt. Caswell waved Maxim through the sliding door to the harbour of lost cars; both he and Blagg had changed into baggy trousers, drab shirts and jackets with lots of pockets. Agnes must have rung.

"We're all loaded up," Caswell reported crisply. "The young lady from Five rang to say they're as sure as they can be about the place. She didn't say where, just to meet her outside the old John Barnes building at Finchley Road station; she said you'd know it. I told her we'd be there at 2100." Half an hour ago, he'd have said nine o'clock.

Maxim parked his car among the drop-outs, a little saddened to see how well it fitted in, and carried the bag of first aid and his holdall out to the Renault. They helped him. The hatchback was open before he got there – the Browning and grenades had to be in there somewhere, but nicely and casually concealed – and they stowed his stuff for him, smiling cheerfully the while. Then Caswell held out the keys so that he could drive the first stretch, to get to know the car, the way a commander should.

God. damn it! – this isn't an exercise. It isn't even The Real Thing, a Widow's Pension or Glory. It's just an amateur-night effort to save something from somebody else's cock-up. And yet they're grinning like chimpanzees at their first tea-party, even Jim with those years of service, and they don't even know . . .

They know, he thought, oh they *know*. It might be a lot easier for me if they didn't know.

He took the keys. "All right, gents: we're off to war in the usual way and for the usual reasons."

Getting to Finchley Road station meant a diagonal grind right across south-east and central London, and Maxim hoped to hell there was some point in it and that they weren't going to have to turn back to Tilbury or out to Harwich. But it was certainly a chance to get to know the car, both on the brief snatches of motorway and in traffic. It was much as Caswell had said: a high-revving hot-running engine giving a very comfortable fast cruise but not much jump-off from traffic lights.

Every now and then Maxim caught himself feeling guilty about not watching the mirrors enough, or taking too direct a route. But this was one time he knew nobody was following. Sims was busy and nobody else wanted to know.

Agnes was waiting for them, wearing brown slacks and a worn but expensive suede jacket and carrying an airline bag.

Maxim looked at her suspiciously. "Now hold on, *you're* not joining the People's Private Army."

"I'm liaising, duckie. You get information out of my service only through me. Aren't you going to introduce me?"

Maxim did. Agnes smiled at Blagg and nodded. "Ah yes, we've heard quite a lot about you of late. How are you, now?"

"I'm fine, thanks, Miss." Blagg was suddenly all big feet and hands and a bashful grin. He simply wasn't at ease with women.

"A good car. Inconspicuous," Agnes commented, and Caswell chuckled. "Who's driving?"

"You can if you want to." Maxim didn't want either of the others tiring himself out. He slid into the passenger seat. "Where are we going?"

"Goole."

"Where's that?"

"Humberside. About forty miles upstream from Hull and Grimsby." She slid the car out into the Finchley Road again, heading north.

Maxim opened the AA Guide. "180 miles. About three hours or a bit more; it's mostly motorway. How sure are you about this?"

"It's only about fifty miles from where Mina Linnarz was living, up in the Dales beyond Harrogate. And just a few hours ago, *Deutfracht* changed the destination of a coaster they had coming in to Hull and booked a space in Goole instead."

"Is that so odd?"

"They haven't made a change like that for months; it means going another forty miles upstream, over some dicey sand-banks so you have to take on a pilot, and then pay God-knows-what to get the lock gates opened and watermen to push you into a berth. So you're losing time and money and all for slightly better road and rail links. Only for them there's another advantage: you know what most docks are like, all fences and high walls and gates with coppers on them? Well, Goole's wide open. You can walk in there day or night."

"That sounds bloody odd," Blagg said, remembering his own dockland childhood, then: "I'm sorry, Miss."

"It's bloody odd, all right: there's even a public right-of-way across the main lock gates. It could be that there isn't much worth pinching there; it started off as a coal port, now it's mostly importing wood."

"You've been swotting," Maxim said.

She grinned. "That's right. We aren't expected to know every British port by heart, though we do keep a fairly active eye on them."

"When does the ship get there?"

"Around midnight, it's the tide. They start unloading in the morning, so if they're going to push the old lady on board it has to be some time between them getting through the lock and tying up, and dawn."

"You mean like they work at night?" Caswell asked, not believing it of civilians.

"They get paid for it. Ships have to come up just about at high tide – it's those sandbanks – so they lose twelve hours if they wait for the next one."

"4.43," Caswell said.

"What?" Maxim twisted round to look; Caswell was consulting a diary.

"Sunrise. Be a bit earlier up there. Call it first light around four."

"It'd take about three-quarters of an hour to berth her," Blagg said. "So whatever happens, it'll be between one and four – I mean if it's the right ship. Begging your pardon, Miss."

"And if it isn't," Agnes said cheerfully, "we'll all have had a nice drive in the country anyway."

The abrupt silence startled her. Good God, they *want* to go through with this charade! she realised. Even Harry . . . she snatched a glance at him; he was squinting ahead against the sunset with a fixed smile on his face and his shortish fair hair snapping in the breeze from the half-open window.

Harry is a *silly* name, she thought, and Harold is even worse. But I just don't want him getting hurt.

They came onto the start of the M1 at Brent Cross just on sundown. Agnes kept the speed down to let the traffic sort itself out, then moved up smoothly to seventy in the middle lane. The traffic was light, most of the London-loaded trucks had left hours before.

"I did get some of the stuff you wanted," she said. It was the first thing anybody had said for twenty minutes or forty miles and she had been *so* determined that it wouldn't be she who spoke first. But they had retreated into a dreadful male/military communion of silence where a fart would be criticised only for its length.

"Like what?"

Oh, the *eloquence* of the man, she thought, and pushed her airline bag towards him with her left foot. Inside were a folder of photographs of Sims and his two colleagues, and two Citizen's Band walkie-talkies.

Maxim passed the photographs to the back seat and fiddled with the radios. They weren't in a class with the Army's Clansman sets, with 840 channels to pick from, but they were handier in size and when switched on close together they produced nerve-scraping howls. He turned them off, satisfied.

"Good. We're in communication, then."

"Are we?" Agnes asked.

"I beg your pardon?"

"Skip it. Oh – and somebody at The Firm had another word with the one who dropped out of Sims's scheme. He said they've got hand-guns, and he believes there's a silenced submachine gun."

"What sort?" All three spoke together.

"He didn't know."

"It could be just a Patchett/Sterling."

"I bet they've got hold of an Ingrams."

"Make a difference if it's a .32 or .45."

"You won't hear it anyway . . ."

At least they're talking, she thought. Maxim took a packet of sandwiches from his own bag and passed them around. They were strictly non-drip, cheese, ham or corned beef without mayonnaise or pickles. He gave out individual cartons of orange juice.

"I've got a hip flask of Scotch," she offered.

"Thanks. We'll have an issue later."

The car thrummed on the stretch of concrete that begins at

the Bedfordshire border, the northern sky turned gold and dark blue and Maxim collected up the photographs, then said: "Ron, give me Sims himself."

"Five-ten, well-built, about forty, dark brown hair neatly cut, clean-shaven, smokes heavily, usually well-dressed . . ."

"That's him. Jim, give me one of the others. Don't bother with the name: they're all phonies. Call the older one S2, the younger S3. I want S3."

"Five-eight, late twenties, fair-haired with moustache . . ."

This game was part of Agnes's profession and she had routinely memorised the photographs and descriptions when she first got them. Now she could catch them out on an occasional detail and felt they respected rather than resented it. As the night closed around them they were becoming more of a unit, as she knew Maxim intended. She had never thought to see the day – or night – when Harry Maxim would be giving her orders and she'd be taking them.

Chapter 26

On the straight stretches the wide road was a two-tone river of twinkling red and white lights, soothing and even hypnotic if you forgot it was two counter-flowing streams of metal at closing speeds of up to 140 mph. Or faster, for a brief period around Nottingham, when it was time for the local Jaguar owners to hurry home from an evening of scampi and Scotch.

Maxim was dozing, or pretending to doze, beside Agnes; in the back Blagg had gone fast asleep with his head on Caswell's shoulder, which at least stopped him leaning forward every few minutes to breathe tobacco into her ear while he checked the dashboard instruments. But the car ran very smoothly, apart from a rhythmic rise and fall in the engine temperature: probably a sticky thermostat.

They had been on the motorway just two hours when Maxim woke up and called for a stop at the Woodhall service area. That was still fifty miles short of Goole, but he didn't want to show their faces any closer; in a couple of hours their descriptions might be chart-toppers on police and all-night radio wavebands. Agnes made a phone call, Maxim paid for the petrol, everybody used the lavatories and they tested the radios across the width of the car park. In ten minutes they were on their way again, the sleepiness gone.

"His sister had been living in the Dales, you said?" Maxim asked.

"She's got a cottage there. It was her husband's."

"I don't think I knew she'd married."

"Out in Africa, twenty years ago. He was working in South Africa and Rhodesia and seems to have been one of the few who didn't make money at it, or else they spent it all. He got leukaemia and came home to die in his family village. She still lives there. She gives piano lessons."

230

She gives piano lessons. It was nothing to be despised, but what a leaden phrase it was for somebody who had toured the world.

"One of her hands is a bit of a mess, arthritis I think," Agnes said.

"That can't help," Maxim said uselessly.

Caswell leaned forward again. "D'you mean, Miss, that somebody can just marry a Brit and walk in without your people knowing?"

"Just about, unless we were asking for tabs to be kept on her. She'd pick up her passport from a consul out there, and that's all there is. Six thousand people do it every year, we can't check on every one, and we never thought we'd be interested in Mina Linnarz again until last week."

"And we grab her back," Blagg said. "I mean, that's the idea, and that's all, is it?"

"More or less." It was a tricky question for Maxim. They were used – indeed, entitled – to clear orders. "I'll try and tell you just what the score is at each step, but you're going to have to go by Sass rules." The SAS training at least meant that they were accustomed to making decisions for themselves.

"This Sims," Caswell said. "Is he good?"

Maxim hesitated, and Agnes chipped in: "You were with him in Germany; how did he come across?"

"He's a hard case. In his way, he's got a real grievance; everybody's been saying how important this Plainsong operation was, but leaving him to do all the work and take all the blame."

"That's our Guy Husband," Agnes said. "And swinging S-S besides. At our meeting they were using him like a glove puppet."

"At *my* meeting, Husband pissed all over him in front of me and he just had to take it. I think he's got a lot of loyalty to his people and he knows that if this caper doesn't come off, they're dead."

"Do you want them dead?" Caswell asked bluntly.

"It wouldn't hurt," Maxim said reluctantly. "I wouldn't give them the first shot." It was an important point, perhaps one that Agnes didn't quite notice being made, and it marked a whole world of difference between civil and military thinking.

"One of those buggers can shoot," Blagg said. It made Maxim feel a little better to remember why Blagg knew, and that he owed him the same order Sims must have given his people: shoot first.

They slid off the motorway and down into the bright silent streets of Goole just after midnight. It gave no immediate impression of being a port: it was just a collection of low, mismatched shopfronts and then a level crossing in the middle of town. Agnes pulled into the station carpark, and a man got out of a dark car and walked over.

They never got his name, he was just Our Man, stocky, old enough to be retired, wearing a cloth cap, blazer and a silk scarf against the evening chill. He spoke in a clipped telegraphic voice that suggested a service background – presumably Navy.

"She's in the Ocean Lock now. Things running a bit late. Be berthing in the Aldam Dock. West side – there." He held a street map of Goole out under the Renault's inside light, a single sheet where the complicated dock area was no more than a few inches square. But Blagg seemed interested, tracing a stubby finger around and saying: "Seems to be all corners."

Our Man grunted agreement. "A boatman's harbour, is Goole. If you're any tonnage at all, you need boatmen to haul you round all those right angles. Ship you're looking for is the *Seesperling*, fo'c'sle and poop job, grey hull, blue and white funnel, 650 ton." Seeing Maxim's blank look, he added: "That means small, about 180 feet end to end."

"Fine, but I hope we can stay away from the ship. How would somebody get up to where you said, with a van? How'd they get into the yard?"

"In Goole, if you want to walk in, walk in a thousand different places. To take a van, to that berth, you'd go in the gate by the church."

"Is it open?"

"Never closed as far as I know."

"So if we cover that gate, we'd catch anybody going in for the ship?"

"Should do. Mind, they could be there already. Some people are." They looked at him. "Dockers, somebody from the harbourmaster's office, pilot vans, Customs went on board at the lock most likely, somebody from the owners. Rush hour in Piccadilly every time a ship comes in."

"They won't try and push an old lady on board through that, not yet," Caswell said.

Blagg coughed politely and asked: "What about the dock police, sir?"

"Prowl around from time to time. Want to know who you are if you're off the beaten track. Nothing much to pinch except Renault cars and you've got one of those already." He gave an elderly cackle. "They deliver 'em here, a compound over beside the Ocean Lock. They say they've got guard dogs loose in there, but some kids got in the other night and scratched up a whole lot of cars and I never heard of anybody getting bitten."

There was a moment of silence, then Our Man said to Agnes: "Is that it, then? Where d'you want me?"

"Back by the phone. Just –" she said something quickly and quietly to him; Maxim realised there must be some fallback plan, to try and muffle any scandal he might stir up. Our Man grunted a good-night and drove away.

"All right," Maxim said. "Time to hand over all identifiable possessions."

Agnes watched, wondering, as Blagg and Caswell started turning out their pockets, putting wallets, keyholders, Caswell's cheque book and Blagg's necklet ID disc into the holdall. Maxim put in his own share; they all kept some money.

"You're sure your clothes aren't marked?" he asked, handing out packets of field dressings. "Not even laundry marks?"

They stood confidently silent, and with a shudder in her stomach Agnes realised they were trying to make their corpses unidentifiable. Maxim gave her the holdall and she said: "I'm glad you didn't ask me. I'd be starkers before I was sure I wasn't wearing anything marked."

They grinned with a wolfish politeness, then started distributing and loading weapons. The grenades, ten of them, were

233

American M26A1's, probably smuggled in by Caswell from Germany stowed somewhere in a military vehicle. The Customs would be looking for booze and drugs, not weaponry. They screwed the fuses into six of them, and were as ready as they could be.

Maxim said: "You mentioned a flask of Scotch . . . Anybody in the market?"

Blagg wasn't interested, but Caswell said casually: "I'll take a dram," and Agnes poured him a stiff one. Maxim took a taste, more to keep Caswell company than anything. Perhaps Jim had become more adjusted to civilian life than he cared to believe. They got back into the Renault, Maxim driving.

Goole was built entirely on one side of the river; there wasn't even a bridge in the town itself. The dock area began just south of the centre, where the streets suddenly became rows of boarded-up broken-roofed houses and shops, an abrupt reminder in space of how fast the British ports had collapsed in time. The Army could have moved in tomorrow to use those streets for training and hardly disturbed a private citizen.

At least it meant there was no one to see the creeping Renault as Maxim fixed the pattern of the area in their minds. The docks themselves were surprisingly bright, given an almost carnival air by tall street lamps throwing patches of blue-white, orange and yellowish light. The occasional ships – the berths were far from full – were also well lit, with floodlights boasting their funnel markings and harsh worklights glaring down from the masts. Each ship hummed to itself, living off its generators, so that when they stopped the car the dock was a basket of purring metal creatures, and very far from the stark silence and darkness Maxim had expected. He had been through ports at night before, but only as a passenger smugly assuming the place was staying alive for himself alone.

There was some distant shouting from the lock gates, and from where they had parked on a disused railway line sunk into the road, they could see a small bunch of figures on the far side of the dock waiting for the *Seesperling*. The ship itself came gliding in with the dignity that even the smallest vessel

...as when moving slowly through dead calm water, also bright and purring. The Goole boatmen were out of luck that night, since she was taking the simplest route in the harbour, with nothing more than a thirty degree turn out of the lock. Their turn would come when she had to back out again.

Maxim drove slowly back to the huge nineteenth-century church that stood right up against the low dock wall – or perhaps it was the churchyard wall; in any event it was no more than four feet high – and the ever-open gate down past the warehouses to the Aldam Dock.

"I don't know where we're going to set up here," Caswell said, and Maxim didn't know either. The lowness of the wall and the fact that the gate was on a corner of two streets, each quite wide, made it near impossible for an ambush.

"Somebody had better go in for a shufti," Maxim decided. "You, Jim. With a radio."

It had to be that way: if you split your force, you had to split your commanders. Caswell took Blagg's pistol; they set the radios at channel 3 and agreed to change to 5, 7, 9 and 11 in that order if they had to shift. Caswell walked quickly through the gate and was lost behind a stack of forklift truck pallets. He had about three hundred yards to go to the *Seesperling*'s berth.

On the other side of the church, the town centre side, there was a small car park. Maxim backed the Renault in there, behind a truck loaded with what looked like sections of oil pipeline, and they waited. The walkie-talkie was jammed in the driver's window so that its telescopic aerial stuck up outside, and it murmured to itself. Agnes doubled herself over to light a cigarette near the floor of the car, trying to hide the flare of her lighter. They went on waiting. There was no way to call Caswell: his own radio would be turned off, that close to the enemy.

He came in surprisingly strongly. "Jim."

"Go."

"Pilot van's just leaving. White job."

"Roj."

They got just a glimpse of the van beyond the church, thirty seconds later. They waited.

"Jim."

"Go."

"Customs just leaving. Blue Allegro. And two men on bikes."

They saw that, too, again just about on thirty seconds later. The bikes – probably dockers – came up Church Road past them, much more dangerous than a car driver surrounded by his own noise and light. Maxim snapped off the radio until they were gone.

Caswell was calling.

"Sorry. Go."

"One car left, a green Metro. I can't see anybody around."

"Roj."

The night went silent again. Blagg whispered: "Would they be using radio themselves, sir?"

"Likely enough." Now that CB radio was legal, they wouldn't even have had to pinch sets from the Intelligence Service's quartermasters. But there was nothing he could do about it.

The walkie-talkie suddenly squawked: "Hey, did I hear a good buddy out there ready to shoot the bull? This is the Dog in the Smog tooling down the rip strip and feeling kinda lonesome. Do you copy?" It was an adenoidal Birmingham voice trying to sound like a Tennessee truck driver.

Maxim glared at the radio as if it had bitten him, but the voice came back, jamming the waveband with more verbose CB garbage. Given a pause, Maxim snapped: "You fucking moron," which wasn't military radio procedure either, and switched to channel 5. It stayed silent.

Then at last: "Jim."

"Go."

"I've got Sims and S3 out on the deck. Two others with them. Nobody who looks like Eismark."

"Roj."

"Well, I'm damned," Agnes said. "We're in the right place."

"D'you think the old lady's there already?" Blagg asked.

Maxim and Agnes glanced at each other, then she said: "No. Sims and his bloke will have gone aboard to set up a deal. She's stored away somewhere."

Caswell's voice crackled: "Sims is using a walkie-talkie. S3's getting off the boat. Going for the Metro."

"Roj." Maxim started the engine. "We're going to have to stop him."

"He's most likely going for the old lady," Agnes said. "He could lead us there."

"He'll talk once I get at him."

"You and your trusty ammonia? It could take hours."

Caswell reported: "Metro's on its way."

Maxim pulled the radio back into the car. "We *have* to stop him. I can't tail him, not through an empty town, this time of night."

"Of course you can't, but *I* can. Shift your arse."

Maxim scrambled around to the passenger side as she slid across under the wheel. The green Metro slipped out of the gates and up past them; there was one person in it. Without turning on the lights, Agnes jumped the Renault forward to the edge of the park just as the Metro turned left at the end of the road.

"Stanhope Street," Maxim said, juggling the map, a torch and the radio. "He has to go either left or right in three hundred yards."

Still lightless, the Renault bounded forward and slewed into Stanhope Street; the Metro's tail-lights swung left.

"Bridge Street. Long and looks dead straight. Leads out of town southwards."

It was indeed dead straight – it was the main road feeding the west side of the docks – but became a series of humped-backed bridges over offshoots of those docks. Agnes let the Metro go over the first, out of sight, and then hurled the Renault down to it, jammed to a stop and crept up for a look. And so she went on, driving like a rifleman moving forward under fire, using the car with a skilled savagery that made Maxim and Blagg, men who lived with machinery, wince as they would have done had she used the walkie-talkie to hammer in a nail. But she kept a quarter of a mile back from the Metro yet out of its sight until it crossed the last bridge and turned down the Swinefleet Road along the south bank of the Humber. The soft-sprung Renault screamed around after it.

The radio said: "Jim," already noticeably fainter.

"Harry. We're behind him, going south out of town, by the river. *Shit!*"

The street lights had suddenly ended and they plunged into a moonless darkness and Agnes braked heavily to let the Metro's lights vanish beyond the next corner. Then she snapped on the headlights and tore forward.

"Jim – check in every ten minutes if you can."

"Roj."

One side of the road was a walled dike holding in the river; if the Metro turned, it could only be to the right. That was some consolation for moving in briefly lit rushes and suddenly dark stops as they rounded a bend. But at least the road would be dead flat as long as it clung to the river, and there were occasional tiny villages with lamps up on telephone poles to give them some respite.

Then, inevitably, came the bend which had no tail-lights showing beyond it. Agnes must have been prepared because the lights came on and she changed to an easy cruising drive. "Get your heads down. He may just be checking his back."

They kept going for another thirty seconds or so, and Agnes said: "He turned off. I've gone past, it should be far enough for him not to hear. D'you want to wait, or walk it?"

The car coasted to a stop and Maxim lifted his head off his knees. "I'll walk it. You follow up in a couple of minutes."

He ran – which he hadn't wanted Blagg to try and do – back the quarter mile to the corner, where a wooded lane led off beside a disused-looking wooden barn. The Metro, unlit, was parked just on the verge; the van, if it was there, would be up the track beside the barn. He waited a few seconds, recovering his breath. As a hiding place it made good sense, since they could have sat on top of the dike a few yards away and watched the *Seesperling* come chugging upstream and timed their trip into Goole itself precisely.

Gun in hand, and using the Metro as cover, he reached the corner of the barn and paused to listen. There was a mutter, a pause, another mutter. Of course: somebody was speaking German on a radio. He eased an eyebrow around the barn and there was the van, a windowless Bedford of some dark colour

238

he couldn't make out, with a man perched half on the driving seat under an interior light and using a long-lead microphone. There was no sign of any second man.

Behind, he heard the drone of the Renault heading back. The man with the microphone put it down and shut the door, putting out the light, and the second man came around the back of the van zipping up his trousers. Maxim leaned out around the corner pointing the little revolver and said: "If you move I'll *kill* you."

He was fairly sure he was starting a gunfight, although he wasn't worried about the outcome. They would be tensed up, almost certainly armed, reckoning on the darkness and a two-to-one superiority . . . But then the vital first milli-seconds flowed away, they felt the surge in their bowels and ideas of pain and death welled up inside them. Then he was herding them against the side of the van, spread your hands and feet, more, *more* I said, but staying back and waiting for Blagg and the shotgun. A part of his easy victory was ex-plained already: one man had his right wrist wrapped in a rigid plaster bandage right up to the palm.

Blagg noticed that, too. "It looks just like somebody shot you there, don't it? And on account of I'm a great detective, I'd say it happened in Rotherhithe, know where I mean? I'd even say it happened in back of Neptune Court, while you was trying to blow me away. Would you remember that?" He was rubbing the shotgun muzzle up the man's spine.

"Leave it, Ron," Maxim ordered. The man – S2 – hadn't even been armed. S3 had had a Czech Vz50 automatic in his pocket.

Agnes came from the back doors of the van, "She's in there; all right, I think, but . . ."

"Ron, you're in charge."

"Could I have your .38, Major? The noise of this thing . . ."

"You're in poaching country here; Lincolnshire starts about ten metres down that road. Nobody'll lose a drop of sleep over a shotgun going off; just stay well back so you don't get splattered." He wasn't talking to Blagg and nobody thought he was.

There was a dim interior light in the van, which was fitted

with a bunk bed on either side. Mina lay on the right one, her head on a grubby flower-pattern cushion and her left hand loosely shading her face. She wore a jumble of old clothes including a stretched woollen cardigan. The van smelt of habitation.

"She's pretty much sedated," Agnes said. She nodded at a box of Valium phials and disposable hypodermics on the other bed. Maxim sat beside them rather than stand in an awkward stoop.

"So here's the last chorus of Plainsong," he said, feeling a sudden weariness. "Did they try to get her to talk?" He picked up the drugs box and shook it. "There's no sign of sodium pentathol or anything like that."

"You don't need that," Agnes said, a little angry. "She's just an arthritic old lady with no training in how to resist. Fear's the best truth drug for people like her, and it comes cheap."

Maxim just nodded, reached across and lifted Mina's hand gently away from her face. Her eyes opened with drugged slowness, then a sudden spasm of revulsion.

"It's all right," he said soothingly. "We've come to take you back home. It's all over." He eased the other hand out from under her neck, so that he held each of them, stroking her knuckles reassuringly with his thumbs. "We'll get you back to the Dales. What was the name of the village?"

"Ramsley," Agnes said softly.

"Back to Ramsley. Just one thing: did they ask you questions?"

Mina moved her head fractionally.

"Did you tell them? Did you say you'd helped kill Brigitte Krone?"

"Harry," Agnes said warningly.

"We have to know what they know. Did you tell them?" He reached around and stroked the back of Mina's neck, as if to soothe a knot of muscles under her back hair. Her eyes widened and she said faintly: "Yes. I did tell them."

"Fine. You told them you and Gustav had killed Brigitte."

"Yes."

He put her hands back, but she took a moment to discover them, and rearrange herself in slow motion. Her eyes closed.

"I told you it was cheaper than drugs," Agnes said in a bitter voice.

"She's lucky: I saw the last person Sims started questioning. I want to say something."

But when they stepped down from the van, all he said was: "Did you bring out the radio?" and she showed it him, propped by the aerial against the barn. He put it on top of the van, for maximum range, then got a pair of handcuffs from the holdall and locked the two men together, wrist to wrist but around the front bumper of the Bedford so that they sprawled awkwardly on the grassy track ahead of it. But they said nothing, and neither did he or the watchful Blagg; it could have been standard moves in a game of chess where, Agnes recalled, you also stay silent and only win by the other side's mistake.

Blagg sat down against the barn, husbanding his strength. Maxim came back to Agnes.

"You were going to say something," she reminded him. "Or was that it?" (Why does this man always get me angry?)

"Yes. Mina — that isn't arthritis she's got. Not in her hands, anyway. The muscles in her left hand are flat, wasted, compared with the right."

"Arthritis was just what I heard. *I'm* not a doctor."

"No, you drive a car pretty well —" (now I remember why I get angry with this man, she thought) " — but you haven't spent six months in hospital or ten years married to an Army nurse. We got a lot of these cases, people applying for a disability award years after the event. A wound sort of hardens up and it can squeeze the nerves controlling a limb. They call it fibrositis when they can't think of a fancier name."

"So she's been wounded now, has she?"

Maxim glanced back, but Blagg was interested only in the two men and the radio. "Yes, high up in the neck, where the nerves for the hands come out. You can feel the scar. I think somebody tried operating there, too, probably when her hand started to go numb and seize up."

"All right, but what's this got to do with anything?"

"That was the wound the wife, Brigitte, was supposed to have got in Dornhausen, back in '45."

"D'you mean this isn't his sister but his *wife*?"

"Same person. He got his sister pregnant and married her to make it look better. There wouldn't be any problem – they were both using roadnames at the time. If that's the little secret he's been keeping all the time I'm not surprised how hard he's been working at it."

"God Almighty."

"He's seen worse in His time."

Chapter 27

Mina Linnarz — or Eismark or Krone or Schickert or her real name in the Dales — lay with her eyes half-closed under the dim light in the van, breathing with a slight rasp but steadily and deeply. The mousy sharpness of the little neat face was unfocused by wrinkles, the hair a thin grey tangle, no longer peroxided for a far more urgent reason than to look truly Aryan. Even if the American officer hadn't wax-pencilled out the young mother in the Dornhausen photograph, probably nobody could have recognised her now. And Gustav had stifled even that chance by coming back to steal the photograph.

But no matter. There would be other proof — now they knew what to prove. There would be, in some other *Standesamt*, the real death certificate of the real Brigitte Krone to prove she died young and not in the parish where her birth certificate was filed. That — and her being an orphan — had been why the Communist underground had picked her to create a new Brigitte. Just as they had created a new Rainer Schickert from the real one whose birth and death certificates were also in different *Standesamter*. That was standard technique, just as uncovering it would be. No need for truth drugs.

(But what if Sims had found the time for truth drugs? Agnes smiled as she thought how eagerly Mina must have confessed to the simple murder Sims's unit had invented for her and Gustav!)

Oh yes, we will prove it, Agnes thought. But we won't understand it. We shall never know what really happened. A brief lust, or compassion, or even real love between two parentless children? Or just loneliness? God must forgive much that stems from that most terrible of all troubles. There lies a little old lady whose story I would rather understand than any other in all the computers and files of our registry. But now nobody will understand it, because even Mina and Gustav

243

will have lost the understanding under the fibrosis of shame and deceit.

The radio crackled faintly and Maxim grabbed for it. "Go."

He thought he could hear Caswell muttering across a crackling infinity, but couldn't be sure.

"Jim, get out of there. Call me when you're clear of the docks."

The radio crackled back. Those things had very little power or range; even the Army's 350 set only went five kilometres reliably, and they must be that far from the docks at least.

Slowly and loudly, Maxim called: "*Get – out – of – there – Call – when – you – are – clear.*"

"HEY YOU BREAKERS, ARE YOU PLAYING COPS AND ROBBERS OR SOMETHING? AND CAN ANYBODY JOIN IN?"

Whoever it was must have had an illegally long aerial wrapped around his car or truck, and probably an illegal booster as well. His contribution came through like the chimes of Big Ben.

It merely infuriated Maxim. It made Jim grab for the *off* switch so suddenly – and he was using the radio right-handed, because of his stiff left elbow, which went against all his training – that he lost it. He had climbed onto a stack of timber some earlier ship had unloaded, perhaps eight feet high, and the walkie-talkie tumbled down the irregularly stacked planks like a staircase, lodged a few feet above the dock, and said: "DOES ANYBODY COPY?"

Caswell took out the revolver and began planning which way to move.

Maxim came around the van. "What do we do with these two now? I want to get moving."

"I don't think it matters, not any more. They can go to East Germany or stay or whatever. Eismark isn't going to cook up any scandal about our people defecting, not once he knows we've got Plainsong. We just have to get that word to him."

"We can use the van radio. They're probably listening out at that end."

The Bedford's radio was a bigger affair, roughly built-in, and using the private military 30–70 megahertz band. So perhaps Sims had robbed the Secret Service stores after all.

He picked up the microphone, then hesitated. "I don't know just how to put this. It'd be a sight easier on the telephone."

"Make a date to talk on the phone, then. In the morning. He can't sail until midday anyway."

"That's right." He pressed the transmit button on the microphone. "*Seesperling.*"

He had called several more times before a voice said: "*Ja. Erwin, bis Du das?*" It was distant, but much better than the CB walkie-talkies.

"No. I want to speak to Gustav Eismark, please."

The radio just hummed. Then Sims said: "Major Maxim, I think."

"Right. We've got the van and everything. None of your people got hurt. It's all over. Can I speak to Gustav Eismark, please?"

"Not quite all over, Major. We have a friend of yours. I do not know his name, but he had a radio and a pistol. He is being questioned."

Maxim and Agnes looked at each other. "They captured Jim. God *damn.*"

"Exchange him for the two goons."

"Yes." He picked up the microphone. "*Seesperling.*"

"Go ahead, Major."

"We'll do an exchange. Your two for my one."

"Stand by. I have to ask the Colonel."

"What? What Colonel?"

Sims seemed to pause fractionally. "Colonel Manfred Eismark," he said carefully. "Gustav Eismark is not here. Stand by."

Maxim let out a long breath. "Damn. I should have thought of Sims going for Manfred; I knew he knew him. Far easier for an SSD man to sneak out of East Germany than a top politician . . . and he'd be more used to deals like this. Sims said he wouldn't mind getting a bill of goods on his own father. A bit of a nutter."

"And now we know why. Those genetics aren't going to help him in his future career – if anybody knows about them. You realise we've got a bill of goods on both father and son? Plainsong's come off better than anybody even hoped."

"Not yet it hasn't. There's weeks of paperwork before we could prove a thing and we need it *now*. To get Jim back."

Blagg was waiting permission-to-speak. "Is that right, sir? They've got Jim?"

"Yes. I'm trying to work an exchange."

"We could just go and take him back."

"Stay cool. It's been a quiet night so far, and there's one thing we didn't find in the van."

"Yer . . ." Blagg had momentarily forgotten the silenced submachine gun. "What do we do?"

"Wait."

They waited, and Sims came on the air. "Major – we want also Mina Linnarz."

"No chance. No chance at all."

"Stand by."

Agnes found she had lit a cigarette, but only from the annoyed hisses of Maxim and Blagg, worried about the dazzle of her lighter on their night vision. She dropped it and trod it out.

Sims came in: "Major. All right. Just my two men. Come to the ship."

Maxim looked at Agnes. She said: "Somewhere public, middle of town, where he won't want to risk any shooting."

"The *ship*'s the place he won't want any shooting. Not with Colonel Eismark on board."

"Major?"

"Okay. The ship, twenty minutes. I don't want to see anybody but you and him."

"Twenty minutes. Okay. Out."

Agnes said: "He's going to try something. He didn't push for us giving him Mina, and she's his ticket to ride."

"He still doesn't want any shooting."

Blagg had the Goole street map. "That bridge we come over, the last one, and Bridge Street – I mean, it's the only way back into town. They could know that."

246

"But they don't know the Renault. We could be anybody."

"That's right . . ."

"Agnes – you take the old girl, probably in the Metro, I imagine you'd prefer that to the Bedford –"

"Harry, how are you two going to cope with that lot?"

"Look – apart from Mina and Gustav, you and me are the only two people who know about Plainsong, the truth of it . . ."

"I can change that the minute I get to a phone."

"Right, so do that. But what else do you suggest? – you're the little girl who skips pistol practice."

"We could quit while we're ahead. We've done ninety-nine per cent of the job and a lot more than Scott-Scobie deserves. Now we just go. They'll almost certainly let Sergeant Caswell go, whatever we do."

"I've heard things about Colonel Eismark . . . and Jim's the only card *they've* got now."

But it was still one of the oldest military problems in the world. You gain your objective by high morale, troops knowing they won't be let down, wasted or abandoned. You also gain your objective by being ready to accept casualties, sending out men who won't come back, abandoning some because to save one might mean losing three or four more. It might even be a good idea to stop all wars until that paradox was worked out. But this wasn't a war. It was just Jim Caswell being persuaded to help out and . . .

Maxim said: "Sims could play it straight. He wants these two back; he's very loyal to his own people."

"It isn't difficult being loyal to your own people," Agnes said pointedly. "The tricky bit is being loyal to an idea. Anyway, he isn't in charge on that ship."

"Colonel Eismark's got more to lose if he's caught here and identified."

"Harry – they just want to grab you or Blagg to give themselves a second card."

"We don't grab easy."

Under her breath Agnes said something that *sounded* like 'fucking supermen' but, given her upbringing, obviously couldn't have been.

Chapter 28

The two captives, S2 and S3, were in the back seat of the Renault, handcuffed together (for once a handcuff key had worked, letting them loose from the van) left hand to left hand. That way, they could only move fast by some sort of ballet routine which it seemed unlikely they had practised, although Blagg was taking no chances. He sat swivelled around in the passenger seat with Maxim's pistol – he despised the little Czech .32 automatic taken from S3 – pointed.

"How many people do you get on a boat like that?" Maxim asked.

"Could be just five or six," Blagg said. "That's what a British ship that size would have. It's all automatic, steering, the engine, you know. I don't know about East Germany, but it looked pretty modern. Mind, that doesn't tell you what they *have* got. There'd be room for more."

"We know they've got one extra, at least."

"Major – one thing: if we have to sort of go on board, remember a ship's all made of metal. Most, anyway. I mean, you can't just blow away a door lock, not in a metal door. And all the glass, that'll be pretty thick, too."

"Thanks. Did you pick this all up around the docks?"

"We used to . . . look around . . . some of the ships. Like, Dave Tanner and me and the others."

"Why didn't you go for the Navy instead?"

"Say a lot of things about the Army, at least it don't bleed-ing sink." From his tone, Blagg could be recalling the flooded shelter in Rotherhithe. Maxim just nodded.

The town was bright but utterly empty of movement. At the top of Bridge Street he kept on, so as to turn back near the station and come down to the docks by a broader and less obvious road. But he wasn't really expecting trouble. They

248

rove slowly in through the gate by the church, along behind a warehouse and its loading bays, then turned as the *Seesperling* came into view two hundred yards ahead and parked in among several other cars and vans left there overnight.

That part of the Aldam Dock was a small headland sticking out into the water, so that they could come up to the ship from only the one direction. She lay bows-on to them, still brightly lit by lights on the stumpy masts and the front of the wheelhouse. To look at, *Seesperling* was really nothing more than a big barge, a long metal box sharpened at one end and with all the living space and engines stacked at the other. They began walking.

There were no big cranes at that berth, but the broad dockside was littered with stacks of timber that filled the night air with a rich resin smell and left a road perhaps only ten yards wide alongside the ship. They went slowly, a very close foursome, passing the bows of the ship on their left, the timber on their right and Blagg watching that way with constant nervous twitches of his head and the shotgun. The irregular piles made little dark alleyways in the harsh dockside lights.

Nobody was in sight, and the only sound was the mumble of a generator somewhere in the fo'c'sle. Maxim halted the group about twenty yards before they came level with the wheelhouse.

Sims must have been watching from behind the superstructure, because he immediately stepped out into the light and raised his hand.

"Are you ready, Major?" he called in a voice that was half whisper, half shout.

Maxim waved his left hand. Somebody pushed Caswell out beside Sims. He was heavily blindfolded and his hands were tied in front of him. He limped as he walked.

"I am afraid your friend got a little hurt," Sims called down. "But he is all right." From the deck beside the wheelhouse they had to come down a steep flight of steps to the main deck level, which was about the same height as the dockside. Sims helped Caswell carefully down, step by step.

"All right, Major?"

Maxim looked carefully all round, but saw nothing. He

hadn't expected to. It was just the moment of decision . .

"Ron?" he asked.

"Go ahead."

Maxim unlocked the handcuffs from S2 and S3, but hel
one of them back, close. Sims let Caswell go forward, feelin
his way with his bound hands on the side of the ship tha
reached up perhaps four feet above the deck level. After a fev
paces he caught his foot on something, stumbled, but save
himself even though his face fell nearly into his hands.

"*That's not Jim!*" Blagg shouted, but Maxim had seen th
fully bent left elbow himself and was dropping and rollin:
aside. There was a vicious rattle on the hull and the docksid
went totally dark.

Perhaps not totally, but enough for a human eye striving t
adjust, and that moment was what Sims had planned on. A
Seesperling's lights and the nearest dockside lamps had gon
out while the silenced submachine gun, somewhere in th
timber stacks, had nearly taken Blagg out of contention fo
good.

The moment was gone. The shotgun boomed – Blagg ha
shifted a surprising distance – and the fake Caswell, hand
suddenly free, collapsed as he jumped the ship's side to reacl
Maxim. The two goons were galloping away somewhere, bu
unarmed so he ignored them and fired twice down the neares
alleys among the stacks. Then he ripped two grenades from hi
pocket and threw one into the ship, one over the nearest stack

"Grenade!" He flattened himself, hands over his ears an
hoping Blagg did the same.

A four-second delay can be infinity or the blink of an eye
depending on which you don't want. Then both explode
almost together, so either the fuses varied or he'd acted faste
than he realised.

He scrambled up. "Get the bastard with the SMG!" The
rushed the little village of timber-stack houses, moving as fas
as they could behind the dazing, deafening grenade. The
worked entirely by trained instinct, swapping sharp barks o
command, fire and move, fire and move.

Somebody staggered out from a cross-alley and Maxin
shot him in the face, but he had no gun with him. Perhaps he'c

en the one to turn off the lights. He jumped past the alley
mouth and the wood tore open behind him, slashing him with
splinters. The shotgun blasted. Blagg said: "Okay now,
Major."

Maxim took the silenced gun – it was a 9 mm. Patchett/
terling after all – and tried to test how many rounds were left
by the pressure of the magazine spring, but that was never
much help. Call it fifteen for certain. There couldn't have been
more than nineteen fired.

"Reload," he ordered, but of course Blagg was doing so
already. "And give me your grenades. I'm going for the ship."

"Sure, Major." Blagg sounded surprisingly breathless until
Maxim remembered the lung.

"Are you all right?"

"Course I am." But in the feeble glow from across the dock,
he saw Blagg smear away a trickle of blood from his lip.
Maxim hesitated, then there came a gabble of distant shouting.

"You're the light machine-gun. Give me the Go."

Blagg moved through the stacks to get a better angle on the
ship's superstructure. Maxim peered out at the *Seesperling* and
now his eyes were getting used to what was really only half
darkness. The fake Caswell lay sprawled, unmoving, on the
dockside. Where S2 and S3 had got to he couldn't tell;
probably still running.

Blagg called softly: "Go," and Maxim ran for the ship.

Behind him the shotgun boomed regularly, one . . . two
. . . three, spattering the wheelhouse and the portholes aft of it
with shot. Fire and move, always keeping one foot on the
ground – and as he ran he had a brief sharp vision of the
schoolboy sergeant on the bright Kent cricket field. Then he
had vaulted into the ship and came up in the narrow walkway
between the side and the hatch coaming. He moved towards
the wheelhouse, the muzzle-heavy submachine gun trying to
droop in his hands and still counting. *Five.* He froze as Blagg's
gun emptied.

"Major? Major, is it you?"

Sims's voice sounded tired, but Maxim tried to grovel
himself invisible among the deckplate rivets until he could just

make out the shape jammed in a space between the steep step
and the foot of the wheelhouse. Sims must have dived in the
when the grenade clattered aboard; the blast couldn't hav
slotted him in so neatly.

"Where's Jim? Where's my man?"

"A hand grenade . . . I should not get into fights wit
soldiers . . . What has happened to my men?"

"Where's Jim?"

"It is too late, Major . . . It was too late from very early o
. . . Colonel Eismark got angry with your man when h
would not talk . . . he is not very subtle, as I told you . . ."

Blagg called: "Okay."

"Hold it, Ron." Maxim dragged Sims from his corne
one-handed, finding surprising strength in anger. He had bee
within six or eight feet of the grenade when it exploded, an
the steps hadn't been enough protection: his face was nearl
blind with blood and he was limp, panting at every move
ment.

"How many more?" Maxim demanded. "How many mor
guns?"

"There is one . . . I think he is down there . . ."

Maxim rammed him against the steps and then up them
using him blatantly as a shield. Behind the cabin affair at th
back of the wheelhouse there was an open metal door leadin
into darkness.

"Say something," Maxim ordered. "Like: Don't Shoot Me."

"I say you do not have to go down. Your man, he i
already —"

"Tell them to put on a light."

"Einschalten das Licht!" It was a tired shout.

Nothing happened. Maxim reached around and fired th
Patchett/Sterling one-handed into the dark. It made only
pobbling noise, but bucked in his hand and the bullets clange
and crashed very convincingly.

"Tell them a grenade comes next."

Sims told them. A feeble yellow glow came on, from
somewhere down a stairwell directly in front of them. Maxin
called Blagg on board, waiting until he was beside them befor
moving. One foot on the ground, as they said.

Clutching Sims by the nape of the neck ahead of him, Maxim stumbled down the steep companionway. At the bottom was a tiny U-shaped lobby, its veneered panels ripped by his burst of fire. Doors led off each arm of the U; one was open, showing light. With his back to the wall, Maxim pushed Sims through.

The man sitting upright with his hands on the folding table must be Colonel Manfred Eismark. He looked like his photograph, anyway, which was just about all Maxim could remember for the debriefing team later; it didn't impress them. But he could have told them, only they didn't ask, exactly what Jim Caswell looked like, stripped to his underpants and socks to clothe the phoney Caswell on the dockside. There were bullet wounds, which must be from the silenced gun Maxim now held, but they weren't what had killed him.

Maxim pushed Sims down onto the bunk beside Caswell and lifted the submachine gun at Eismark.

"Major?" Blagg called down. "Things is moving up here."

All it needed was a little pressure on the trigger, let the gun lift with the recoil and Eismark would tear open from crotch to neck. So easy – and that was the trouble. It would be almost as easy for Eismark.

"Colonel – I could kill you. Instead, I'm going to own you. I know something about you that you don't even know yourself. We'll make sure you know, and we'll make sure you believe it. And then you'll belong to us, and begin to love us. Every day you'll love us a little bit more because it'll be one more day we didn't destroy you. All the rest of your life, Colonel, every second of it, you'll never be lonely again because there'll always be us. And your little secret. That's the way it goes, isn't it, Dieter?" But Sims was silent, perhaps dying. "That's the way it goes."

He wasn't even sure that Eismark understood English, but was happy to know that he would understand in the end. Indeed, quite soon.

"Major!"

"On my way. And Colonel – don't tell the police who you are and we won't tell either. That would spoil our little secret. And we don't want that, do we?"

In what Blagg called 'a real docks', meaning something that needed his childhood expertise to break in and out of, they could well have been caught, at least momentarily. In Goole they waited while a thin swarm of dock police and real ones buzzed into the area asking each other where to go, because the source of shooting is always difficult to establish, and when there was a brief lull they just got into the Renault and drove away. Caswell had been right: it didn't look like a getaway car.

The police never set roadblocks on motorways, and they could join the M62 just over a mile to the west. Agnes found them back in the car park at the Woodhall service area soon after three in the morning. She had somehow acquired a two-year-old Cortina.

He told her, briefly and efficiently, what had happened; she knew a lot of it already from Our Man with his local contacts, and probably a little eavesdropping on police radios.

Under her supervision – she knew where people left fingerprints better than they did – they wiped the inside of the Renault with petrol-soaked rags and then left it; the shotgun and submachine gun were at the bottom of the Aldam Dock but they hadn't had time to dump the last of the grenades from the Renault's boot. They risked taking those on the journey south.

Maxim drove – insisted on driving – since he was still too tense to sit and be driven.

"Mina's safe with some of our people," Agnes said. "Once we've established a little agreement with East Berlin it'll be okay for her to go back to Ramsley."

"How are you explaining away tonight?"

"Oh, you were a group of East German dissidents, emigrés, trying to stir up trouble and disrupt trade. We'd heard rumours and we're sorry we didn't warn the local Special Branch people, but we never thought it could happen in Goole. You know."

"Are they going to believe it? – the police?"

"Not one word in ten, I imagine, but nobody local got shot and they'll settle for a fuss between two sets of foreigners that was only technically on their patch. They won't lose their no-claims bonus for that. And whatever the captain and crew and the Colonel say, it won't be the truth either, we can count on *that*. Are they going to identify Caswell?"

"Have you got a cover story for him, too?"

"A mercenary, hired by the emigrés . . ."

"They won't identify him by any photograph. His finger-prints . . . he's still got those left, but I don't suppose they're on file anywhere."

She looked into the back where Blagg, with his wound and the blessed talent of youth for unwinding fast, was already asleep.

"What should we do about her? – Caswell's wife?" Agnes asked.

"I'm going to talk to her now. As soon as I get there."

"What are you going to say?"

"I don't know yet."

"Look – our people can do that."

"I was in charge."

"There won't be any problem with an increased pension or whatever."

"How bloody right you are."

She let the silence between them run on for a long time, then said: "Why don't you come home with me?"

He let the silence run, too. "I've got to talk to Mrs Caswell."

"Look, nothing has to happen, I just don't like to think of you going back to that crummy little flat of yours and . . . oh *hell*."

After a time, he said: "Loneliness isn't enough reason." Then he thought for a time, or perhaps just drove, and said: "Did I ever tell you about the first time I got posted to Germany? All the houses, the buildings at the small stations, they all seemed familiar. I'd never been there before. Then I realised: they were the big versions of the kits I'd had on my model railway when I was a boy – all the best kits are German – so now I think of them the other way round: the buildings you see from a train window are just oversized plastic fakes. . . ."

She didn't see why he was saying all that, but she understood the ridiculous logic of it and couldn't help laughing.